Praise for the no

"A grim and unbearably tense debut chiller with an unexpected and utterly fitting finale."

—*Kirkus Reviews*

"A compulsively readable thriller."

—*Booklist* (starred review)

"Written with panache, the book skillfully captures the nature of obsession and its consequences, and culminates in a climax Patricia Highsmith would have admired."

—*Daily Mail* (UK)

"Slick, smart and very timely, this confident debut will hook you in."

—*Sunday Mirror* (UK)

"Deliciously tense and twisty."

—*The Sunday Times Crime Club* (UK)

"Lloyd keeps the reader guessing until the very last page. Make sure you have an excuse for being sleepy at work the next day because *The Innocent Wife* is unputdownable."

—*Criminal Element*

"Amy Lloyd's debut thriller, *The Innocent Wife*, is a stunner. A smooth and confident new voice in the world of crime fiction, Lloyd leads the reader down a twisty path to a surprising yet satisfying conclusion. You won't be able to stop turning the pages!"

—**Karen Dionne, author**
of *The Marsh King's Daughter*

"If you're an addict of true crime documentaries, you will binge all night on *The Innocent Wife*. It's a terrific, believable thriller that answers a seemingly unanswerable question: What kind of woman falls in love with a stranger an ocean away? In this breathless, pounding ride, Amy Lloyd keeps us guessing about a convicted killer thrust into the world as innocent online hero and the woman who begins to reluctantly dig into his murky past."

—Julia Heaberlin, author of *Black-Eyed Susans*

"I devoured Amy Lloyd's novel *The Innocent Wife* in one sitting, ignoring everyone I knew until it was done! A unique setting, deeply flawed characters, a crackling mystery, and an unexpected ending make this one of 2018's must-reads!"

—Hollie Overton, author of *Baby Doll*

"This is an original, assured and compelling tale of obsession. Amy Lloyd is a startling new talent, destined to become a big name."

—Peter James, international bestselling author

"Loved *The Innocent Wife*! Dark, twisted and compelling. Kept me guessing and totally gripped!"

—C.J. Tudor, author of *The Chalk Man*

"I read *The Innocent Wife* in one sitting—a deliciously wry and dark exploration of fascinating subject matter that will keep you guessing until the last page. Amy Lloyd is a fresh and original new voice in thriller writing who deserves to go straight to the top."

—Sarah Pinborough, author of *Behind Her Eyes*

the
innocent
wife

Also by Amy Lloyd

One More Lie

the innocent wife

AMY LLOYD

HANOVER
SQUARE
PRESS

HANOVER
SQUARE
PRESS™

Recycling programs
for this product may
not exist in your area.

ISBN-13: 978-1-335-14074-6

The Innocent Wife

First published in 2017 by Century, part of the Penguin Random House group of companies.

First Hanover Square Press trade paperback edition published in 2019. This edition published in 2020.

HanoverSqPress.com
BookClubbish.com

Printed in U.S.A.

To Rhys, thank you for helping me become a better writer and a better person.

the innocent wife

prologue

The girl was found seventy-six hours after she was reported missing. The fingertips had been removed with cable-cutter pliers, a calculated attempt to hide DNA evidence, the flesh of her attacker gathering beneath the whites of her nails as they dragged over his skin. Her body had been moved shortly after death; wherever she was killed had been private enough for a prolonged and violent attack, followed by the mutilation of her corpse. Holly Michaels was dumped in the dark water of the bayou, in the northernmost part of Red River County, Florida, ten miles from her home.

In the photos of the crime scene she was lying facedown. This made it slightly easier to stomach the first time Sam studied them, alone, in the unlit living room of her terrace house in Bristol. At first the photos seemed indecent, not so much because of the gore, the blood matted into fine blond hair, but the sight of Holly naked from the waist down; Sam wanted to lay a blanket across her, to protect her modesty.

Over time she stopped flinching at the sight of her. The more she browsed the forums and saw it again and again, it became less about the body, the waxy pale skin and dark patches of blood, and more about the details around her. Now her eyes focused on the edges of the picture, the patch of ground circled with a red line. Sam squinted. It was a footprint. But, the forum members discussed, there were no casts of footprints taken or mentioned anywhere in the files surrounding the case. The questions started: Was this footprint purposely omitted during the investigation? Overlooked? Or are we looking at evidence of some clubfooted Red River police officer who potentially disturbed the crime scene? They debated late into the night, Sam unsure what to believe except for one thing: that whatever had happened, it left the *real* killer free.

Her obsession started eighteen years after the first documentary.

"Seriously, I know it's not your type of thing but you'll love it, it's unbelievable, it'll make you so angry," her boyfriend Mark had said, his face lit up by the glow of the monitor.

Sam was sitting next to him in his bed, in the house he still shared with his parents. As the story unfolded on screen everything else started to fade away. At the heart of it the boy, too young for the suit he wore in court, blue eyes blinking confused at the camera, alone and afraid. It hurt her to look at him, beautiful in an ugly room, harsh light and severe edges, his own face so soft with sadness.

Dennis Danson, barely eighteen years old, alone on Death Row.

After the film ended she wanted more, she wanted answers.

"I told you," Mark said. "I told you it would make you furious."

Soon Dennis occupied her waking thoughts and lingered on the edges of her dreams, always too far away to speak to or hold, his fingers slipping from hers.

So she joined online groups, a dedicated fandom that pored over every photograph, witness statement, court transcript, coroner report and alibi. They debated minute details until Sam felt exhausted but unable to stop, digging for a truth that could right all the wrongs that had led to this point.

There were subgroups who passionately defended their theories. They suspected Holly's stepfather, or the sex offenders who lived in trailer parks on the outskirts of town. They drew comparisons with other unsolved murders across America, which conjured an image of a transient evil, a trucker fueled by dark fantasies, a man who lived by night and killed alone. Then there were the conspiracy theorists, those who thought the whole Red River police force was covering for a ring of local pedophiles who had some kind of hold on them.

Sam believed it was simpler than that. A week before the murder a short man had been reported outside the middle school. He'd been stopping the children as they walked past, asking them for the time. He said he'd lost his watch and asked if they would help him look for it, with the promise of a reward. A mother who was picking up her boys approached him, telling the police later that he had made her suspicious, that he had been acting cagey, his eyes darting as he spoke. He was unknown in the relatively small community and had fled the scene before the police arrived. The man's presence had left the parents feeling uncomfortable and teachers patrolled the school gates each morning and afternoon as an added precaution. With very little to go on, the police filed the incident and put it to the back of their minds. No crime had been committed and the man didn't return to the school. A week later, Holly was reported missing.

On the message boards they referred to him as the Short Man. The police interviewed the mothers again and a composite sketch of the Short Man was published in the paper and posted around the town. But the search turned up no suspects and no leads. Eventually the police dropped the line of investigation entirely and, seemingly under pressure to make an arrest, focused on other rumors.

Still, the forums followed up the Short Man theory, comparing mug shots of recently arrested sex offenders to the police sketch. Sam read the threads obsessively and marveled at the investigative skills of the fellow posters, the way their minds could identify the clues that the police had once missed and create stories that seemed so much like the truth that had been missing.

There were other forums, about other cases, with other victims. There were other documentaries and podcasts and TV shows but *Framing the Truth: The Murder of Holly Michaels* was the one that spoke to so many people, that grabbed them and wouldn't let go. Sam read everything she could on the internet, signed petitions to get new evidence admitted in court (the footprint, a statement from a family member about the stepfather's alibi) and found the message boards she now browsed obsessively. They were all driven by the desire for the truth, to free the man at the center of the case, a victim of a gross miscarriage of justice.

The fans connected with Dennis on a deep level. In part because, after his arrest, over the years, they watched him change from a troubled eighteen-year-old boy to the man he became in prison. There was something almost holy about him, the way he looked in bright white overalls. Serene like a monk, his hands and feet bound together with I-shaped chains as if in some kind of penance. Though he never accepted the sentence and consistently protested his innocence, he was calm. "I don't want to think of it in terms of fighting," he said at the end of the documentary, "fighting exhausts you, fighting breaks you. I'm handling it. I'll get there." When his image faded from the screen Sam felt a pull in her guts. Overwhelmed by helplessness, she felt the crush of all the unfairness in the world, and wept.

Sam felt that the people on the message boards were the only ones who understood. They'd all experienced the same sense of impotence the first time they watched *Framing the Truth*, years ago, and welcomed her to the community. Some were sarcastic: "Uh, where have you *been*? Welcome to 1993." But overall she felt at home there, and contributed as herself, shared her thoughts and feelings not only about Dennis but about her personal life, on the General Discussion board. They were the people she turned to when Mark left, when she returned home to find the house stripped of his things, no note, only his toothbrush resting with her own, entwined like the necks of swans in the cup on the sink. The others on the message board soothed her, messaged her with their Skype details if she needed to talk, assured her she didn't deserve it. They were all she had.

Most of the group were American but there were British members who sometimes arranged meet-ups and events. Still, it was the Americans who drove the discussions and organized protests. Twice, Dennis had been given a date of execution and the members had gathered outside the Red River County courthouse and the Altoona Prison, protesting and talking with the media to raise awareness of the cause. They slept in tents, handed out information leaflets and collected signatures for petitions until another group formed across the street with signs that read "MURDERER" and "WHERE ARE THE BODIES." The groups shouted back and forth and barriers were placed on the curb on each side of the street to separate them. Police officers stood in the middle staring straight ahead with neutral, indifferent expressions.

When Dennis was granted a stay of execution the national media published photographs of the group crying and holding each other. Sam read through the blog posts and the threads about the protests and posted to the Brits in their private forum about how she would love to be able to do something that amazing but it was hard living so far away.

"They didn't really do anything," one member replied, "it's just the way the system works. People are on Death Row for forty years and never get executed. So did they actually do anything to help? Debatable."

It seemed to Sam that the British members were less serious than the Americans, that for them it was a hobby. On one meet-up they'd all visited the London Dungeon, bloody waxworks posed in eternal agony with rusted medieval torture devices strapped to their necks, a chorus of screams played on a loop over the speakers. As the group shrieked and laughed she'd felt a disconnect, as if they were more interested in the morbidity of the case than the human elements. To them, she thought, Dennis wasn't even a real person. It didn't break their hearts as it broke hers. There was a British cynicism, a poisonous lack of emotional investment, that made Sam want to distance herself from them. She felt better surrounded by people who ached the way she did and needed to *do* something.

The American members were the closest friends she'd had in years. She stayed awake to chat to them, her laptop perched on bent knees in her bed. A lot of them wrote to Dennis and scanned in the responses. Sam still felt an awkwardness about the familiarity with which they spoke to him. It took her months to write a letter and weeks more until she actually sent it.

29th January
Dear Dennis,
My name's Samantha, I'm a 31-year-old schoolteacher from England and I know you're innocent. It feels weird to write to you, I've never done this before, written a letter to someone I haven't met. I know people must write to you all the time and say the same things, like, "Your story really moved me," and, "I can't stop thinking about it," but your story really did move me and I really can't stop thinking about it. There are so many people out here, Dennis, all working hard to prove you're innocent. I wish I could help but I just don't know what I can do. If there's anything you need please tell me, even if it's something small; I'll do my best.

It feels strange to know so much about you and you to know nothing about me, so I'll tell you a bit just so we can even things up a little. I live alone; my grandmother died three years ago and left me her house, so my mother hates me even more than she already did (if that's possible). Like you I'm a bit of a black sheep in my family. I hope that doesn't sound bad, I mean people don't understand us because we're different to them, not because we actually did anything wrong. My grandmother always understood me, she was more like a mother to me, really, and I haven't healed from losing her yet. Maybe this is why your story hit me so hard. I'm newly single (it wasn't a good breakup) and I hate my job. Some days I wake up early and I can't even move, I just lie there wishing it could stay that inky-light time of day forever. I'm probably saying too much but it feels good to actually be saying it to someone.

I'll understand if you don't write back, you must have so many letters, but I just wanted you to know there are lots of us thinking about you. We're all really excited about the new documentary: it sounds stupid to say but as soon as I heard about it I just felt this new sense of hope, almost a certainty that this time you could get your retrial. Are you excited? (Sorry if this is a stupid question.)

I hope I hear from you, you always write such thoughtful letters to people (they post them online, people really love to know you're doing well, in spite of everything) and I would love to write to you again, if you wanted me to.

Yours sincerely,
Samantha

She didn't mention it to anyone in case he never replied, and then didn't post about it when he eventually did because she wasn't sure if this letter just felt different because it was written for her, or if

it really wasn't like the letters he'd sent to everyone else.

4.14
Dear Samantha,
Sorry for the delay in writing you. You're
right, I get a lot of letters and it takes me
some time to read through what is sent to me.
But even though I have a lot of time I do not
reply to them all. Something about your let-
ter stood out to me. I'm sorry to hear you are
lonely. I'm lonely too.

Carrie tells me about the support online,
it's a great comfort to me. It's difficult to un-
derstand sometimes. When I was in school we
had one computer and we would type in the
coordinates on a screen and it would make
this robot move around the classroom. It was
really slow. I think it was supposed to be a
tortoise. One day we came back from recess
and it was broken. The teacher didn't even
ask who it was. She just said my name straight
away. I didn't do it but everyone thought I did.

There. That's something you didn't know
about me. I haven't written that to anybody.
It is strange that people know so much about
me. I think they know more about me than I
do.

Thank you for your offer but there's noth-
ing I need financially. Carrie—I keep men-
tioning her but I'm not sure you know who I'm
talking about, she coproduced and directed

the documentary and she remains a great friend—visits and arranges for my commissary. I'm fortunate to have her. A lot of inmates don't have anybody. To answer your question, I am excited about the new series but I have had my hopes up before only to be disappointed. So I'm trying to remain levelheaded.

I would love for you to write again. I like the way you write. It's very sweet. I get some strange letters. I'm sure you can imagine. I'd like to know more about you, please write, if you want to. Please recommend me books. That is always helpful. You don't need to send them, I will be able to get them.

I hope to hear from you again soon, Samantha. Your letter brightened an otherwise dark day.
Best,
Dennis

She read it again. He'd told her something he'd never told anyone before. It felt like having a piece of him. She took the letter with her everywhere. Each time she felt lonely she read it again. As the letters continued she felt lonely less and less. It was like falling in love, she thought, more like falling in love than she'd ever felt before. There was no pretending to be too busy to reply, or struggling to appear aloof, or agonizing over the number of kisses at the end of a text message. It felt natural, right.

9th October
Dear Dennis,
Now I feel excited every time I hear the letter box or get home to see an envelope on the doormat. Is that pathetic?? I just love reading your letters so much. I know you're just being nice, though. That photo of me is not great but it was the most recent one I could find that wasn't completely awful. Lots of people love taking photos of themselves (they're called "selfies," ugh) but I just absolutely hate it. I didn't used to. It's not that I thought I was beautiful or anything but my ex definitely made me paranoid about photos. There were things I didn't even know to hate about myself until he pointed them out.

I'm doing it again, moaning! I'll stop. They've delayed filming again? You must be so frustrated. I want them to get on with it. The sooner, the better. I know you're cautious but I don't have to be, I can just fully believe for the both of us.

The nights are getting longer. This is when it used to be hardest, being alone, but now I don't feel so lonely anymore, knowing you're there, waiting for your letters. It's so good to have someone I can be honest with. When I'm teaching I have to fake this strength all the time or the kids just go feral, it's exhausting. I don't really get along with the other teachers. They're all married with kids, they look at me like there's something wrong with me because

*I'm not like them. I couldn't tell them about writing to you, they wouldn't understand that either. I saw one of them reading that book about your case the other day—*When the River Runs Red, *by Eileen Turner—and I almost said to them, "I know Dennis Danson! We write to each other like every week!" but I knew it would end up being gossip. Besides, there's something nice about people not knowing.*

Love,
Samantha

10.25
Samantha,
Your ex sounds like an idiot. You are beautiful. If I were your boyfriend I wouldn't be stupid enough to let you go. I've put your picture on the wall. You have such a beautiful smile, when I look at you I can't help smiling back.

I've read When the River Runs Red. *Eileen still writes me. It was weird to read about myself like that. I haven't seen* Framing the Truth *but from what Carrie tells me it's comprehensive, whereas Eileen's book is more sensational. Sometimes I didn't recognize myself. It made me sound weird.*

Yes, it's frustrating about the new series, but Carrie tells me it's for the best. There are legal hurdles to jump before filming starts and I've had meetings with my new lawyers that give me some hope that a retrial will take place in the next twelve months. *Everything moves so slowly. Each day here is like a week. I didn't get my outside recreation today because of rain and my head is hurting again. I've read your letters many times and when I read them I am less lonely, as if you are here.*

I admit I'm starting to like you as more than a friend, Samantha. I can't help it. I look forward to your letters, too. Every week I search for yours in the bundle which is delivered to me and when I find it my heart beats faster. I'm almost sure I shouldn't tell you this. I worry that I'm only going to be a burden to you, Samantha. That the commitment of writing to me each week is too much. That our friendship makes you more solitary or secretive. But I'm too selfish to stop. You make everything more bearable. I can't promise you anything. You deserve better. I'm worried you will figure this out soon and forget me.
Love,
Dennis

13th January
Dennis,
Don't talk like that. Ever. I love you. You're all I want. It doesn't matter to me that we're far apart right now. I'm happy. But I've been thinking and I want to visit, if you'll have me. I still have a lot of the money my grandmother left me and there's not much keeping me here.

I was saving the money for something special and I can't think of anything that would mean more to me. It's time for me to stop wasting my whole life wishing for things and actually do them.

I know you'll say no but I don't accept that. I know what's best for me. I've made up my mind. I could leave as early as next month. Just say the word.
All my love,
Your Samantha

1.24
Samantha,
The idea of seeing you here has lit me up, too. I can't stop moving. Pacing. In the yard I ran circles and the ground threw dust up my legs. The guards laughed and they all said you must be something special. No one ever sees me like this.

I hope you don't mind but I gave Carrie your name and address. She will be filming in and around Red River starting in April and I would like it if you could meet. At least I know she can look after you, even if I can't.

Of course I will love you when I see you. I worry you won't love me. I've changed. Gone slack. But I'm working on it, for you. I'm older. I think people forget this. Some men still write to the eighteen-year-old I was. Love letters. I'm sure you can imagine. And I don't want you to be shocked when you see me in chains. They make us wear them when we leave our cells. They say it's for safety but, well, it's humiliating.

I won't give you the word. Come when you're ready. Come when Carrie is here. But come. I need you, too. I love you.
All my love, always,
Your Dennis

Subject: Dennis!!

Sam!
This is Carrie, Dennis's friend. He gave me your address but I figured it was easier to track you down online. Nice nudes! I'm just kidding, I didn't find anything weird. Anyway, Dennis talks about you A LOT. I'm kind of sick of hearing about you! Nah, honestly, I haven't seen him like this in years. With you and the new series he's like a new man right now.

He tells me you're coming out here to visit and he wants ME to be your guide! I'd be super honored to entertain you while you're around. I'll be filming most days but I thought you could come along, if you're into it. We'll be going around Red River shooting some interviews, following some leads we have, witnesses, that kind of thing. Heard you're a big fan of the doc (thanks!) so maybe you'd like to get involved.

Let me know. Any friend of Dennis is a friend of mine. If you need any advice on where to stay/eat/avoid like the fucking plague then I'm your guy.
See ya soon!
Carrie

She booked the flights before she could change her mind. When she left, no one even seemed to notice she was gone.

altoona

she held them. She checked the mirror again. She thought, *Maybe I'm one of those people who think they're ugly but really they're beautiful and they can't see it.* She flipped the visor back up and said to herself, *Body dysmorphia. You wish.* Then shook her head quickly to get rid of the negativity.

She parked the car and walked toward the guarded entrance. She paused, thought about turning back. Over the past twenty-four hours she'd changed her mind a million times. None of it had seemed real until she'd walked into the wall of heat outside the airport doors. This was a mistake, she told herself, an expensive and terrible mistake. Their letters had been a kind of shared madness, just two people wishing so hard for something better that they manufactured it themselves.

Inside she handed over her visitor's pass and identification, watched her handbag roll through an X-ray machine as she walked alongside it through a metal detector. They were briefly reunited on the other side before a man took it away and gave her a numbered ticket in return, as if she were checking her coat at the theater. One female guard patted her down; another stuck a numbered sticker to her chest. People gently pushed her in the right directions, saying no more than one or two words, until she arrived in a long mint-green room, stiflingly hot, a small rattling fan in a corner. There were green plastic chairs bolted to the floor; Sam sat in the first available one. In front of her was a thick plastic window with holes around the level of her lips, a small shelf like a desk, and privacy screens

to each side. None of the visitors—almost exclusively female—spoke or looked at one another. Sam
peered through the plastic window; the opposite
side of the room was empty, apart from one guard
standing against the back wall staring at his shoes.

There was a door on the far right with a light
above it, framed in a cage. For a second she wondered why and then it hit her, the reality of the place
she was in, the violence. Men so dangerous they
had to cage the lights, screw down the chairs, bul-
letproof the glass.

When a buzzer sounded the light came on, red,
and the guard's head snapped up; he caught Sam's
eye and she smiled; he did not smile back. A memory, when she was a teenager, at a Take That con-
cert. She'd leaned toward her friend and they'd
clutched hands; *We're breathing the same air as
Robbie!* The air fizzed with Dennis's presence,
somewhere out of sight.

Inmates shuffled in, their ankles and wrists in
the cuffs Dennis had described in his letter. Fingers
crept over Sam's spine; her stomach felt as though it
was floating away from her. She thought about running, looking back at the heavy metal door through
which she'd come in: locked. She realized she was
trapped, that the only way out of this was to get
through it. It'd be over soon, she reassured herself
as the men filed in.

And then there he was. Different from the others, softer somehow. He'd put on weight, she noted,
which made her feel better for a second before he
turned his head and she saw his profile, all con-

tours and cheekbones. He was wearing a pair of fake-gold-framed glasses, the lenses tinted brown so she couldn't make out his eyes with the way light reflected from them. When he saw her, he smiled and she waved in a way she regretted, loose-wristed and undignified.

She tucked her hands between her knees. His ankles were chained and he took only small steps, like ones taken in the dark. At the window he stopped, shrugged.

"Humiliating," he said.

"Sorry?"

"For what?"

"I didn't hear what you said," Sam said, pushing her hair away from her face.

"I said this is humiliating," he repeated, sitting, the chains clanking against the table in front of him. "Chains, like a junkyard dog."

"Oh. No, don't. I can't believe this is actually…"

"I know."

They sat, quiet.

"Weird, isn't it?" Sam tried.

"What?"

"This."

"Yeah."

She looked at him and it was as if he was a stranger. Sam felt cold and exposed, wanted to turn and leave. But the sensation passed, leaving her head ringing as if she'd been slapped. He smiled; she covered her mouth as she smiled back and cleared her throat.

"I'm sorry, I don't date much," he said.

Sam laughed appreciatively. "Actually, me neither."

"When did you land?"

"Yesterday," she said, thinking of the first mouthful of Florida air as she left the airport, the moment it all became too real.

"Good flight?"

"It was OK. They feed you all the time, to stop you getting bored."

"Like here."

It was gone. All the warmth of the letters. Sam blamed herself.

"When are you meeting Carrie?" he asked.

"Tomorrow," Sam said, thinking of how insistent Carrie had been that she join the crew while they filmed the new series. She didn't want to feel she was in the way but when Carrie had probed and asked her how else she would spend her free time here, Sam hadn't been able to answer.

"You'll love her."

Sam felt a twist of jealousy and knew it was all still there, that she still loved him. "She seems so great." She pulled her lips into a smile that didn't reveal her teeth, which were too small, or her gums, too big.

"She really is. You know, I don't really get many visitors. Carrie tries, but she lives so far away and…" Dennis let the unfinished sentence hang between them and they sat in silence for a moment before Sam felt words tumbling out of her mouth.

"It's my fault, I'm shy and my mind has gone completely blank and I don't know what to talk about because everything seems so insignificant, you know? I just feel like a complete idiot. It's so hot in here and I'm jet-lagged and it's not you, it's all me, I'm sorry."

Dennis looked at her, face slack, surprised. "You're not an idiot," he said. "And, you know. I love you, you know."

It was as if something broke inside her.

"I love you. Too."

"You have something," he said, pointing to his right cheek, "there." She pulled a strand of hair away from her face and relaxed.

"Thank you."

It got a little easier then. He spoke excitedly of the extra visits he'd received lately, of new lawyers with bespoke suits and tailored strategies. Of the new series, *A Boy from Red River*, and Netflix, which he understood only abstractly. Of new director Jackson Anderson, fresh off the back of a trilogy of blockbusters, who spoke with complete certainty of Dennis's release, as if it was an inevitability. He told her about Carrie, how he knew she wanted the best for the film but how he could tell, after all these years, that she hated playing second fiddle to a man. She'd always been the one in charge, no question. Dennis laughed.

"She's pissed but also she knows Jackson can take this further than before. It's a money thing, she knows that. She'll still be doing most of the legwork."

Jackson had brought an increased level of publicity to the new series. Celebrities tweeted their support, their fans downloading the first film, interest snowballing. Suddenly the message boards had been overrun by new names. Angelina Jolie wore a T-shirt with Dennis's mug shot on it, and underneath: #FreeDennisDanson. He was trending on Twitter. He wouldn't have known any of it but for the influx of new letters, more than he'd ever received, too many to read.

"I'm starting to think this is it," he said to Sam, "this could be it."

"Me too," she said. "The whole world knows now. Everyone is on your side." She wondered: How could one judge fight off the whole world? There'd have to be a new trial.

There was a buzz; the people around her leaned in to say goodbyes. Some pushed their lips against the dirty window, breathed to their loved one on the other side. Guards turned their heads.

"I have to go," he said.

"I know."

"Next week?"

"Of course. Den, I love you."

"I love you too, Samantha."

As he left she blinked away tears, feeling a burst of pleasure from his voice, and the pain of seeing him go. She pulled her dress straight. As she allowed the row of people to filter past her so she could join the back of the exit line, a woman behind her spoke, close enough to her ear that she felt breath tickle her neck. "You like child killers, huh?"

"I'm sorry?" Sam turned, smiling, sure she'd misheard.

"Got a thing for guys who kill little girls. I saw who you were talking to."

The woman had curly red hair that looked crispy with hairspray and a T-shirt that hung off one shoulder exposing her bra strap. Sam looked around for the guard but the guards at either end of the room were occupied.

"I got family from Red River and they all know what he did, they know *who he is*, they know more than some movie can tell you." The woman spoke so softly no one paid them any attention at all.

"I'm not arguing with you, OK? I just want to leave." There was a shake to Sam's voice that she couldn't control.

"He tell you where the bodies are? That's all we want to know. Let those girls rest in peace, let the *families* rest."

They were the only two in the room now.

"Do you get off on it? Is that it?"

"Let's go, time's up." The officer placed a hand on the small of Sam's back and pushed her gently.

"Bitch," the woman said finally. The guard moved his hand away from Sam and took hold of the woman's wrist, a smirk on his face as he walked them both out.

2

Extract from *When the River Runs Red*
by Eileen Turner

The Danson family lived on the outskirts of
the county, where the last remnants of civilization gave way to the backwoods, miles of
land unsuitable for development. It was the
type of land that got sucked into itself after
storms, swamps that led to mangrove coast-
lines, tangled roots in water so black you
couldn't see anything under the surface. The
family lived two miles from town, down a dirt
road that became inaccessible after periods of
heavy rain, and as a boy Dennis had walked
over a mile each day to reach the school bus,
often muddy and soaked through by the time
he arrived.

Even by the standards of Red River, Dennis was considered poor, and his neglect was
recognized early on by his teachers. Though
intelligent, he was often tired in class and
his clothes were dirty, or his schoolbooks
went missing. Child protective services were

called and the house inspected. It was described by the social workers as "unfit for human habitation"[1] and Dennis was sent to live with a foster family while his mother and father were given time to clean and renovate the property. His father, Lionel Danson, was advised to begin a twelve-step program for his drinking, while his mother, Kim, was medicated for depression. Dennis returned six months later under the supervision of a social worker, who would visit twice weekly for inspection. The visits lasted a few months before tailing off. The caseworker assigned to the Dansons later admitted he believed the family were coping and decided phone calls would be sufficient to check on their progress, as it was time-consuming to drive all the way out there each week.[2]

It wasn't long before the house returned to its former squalor and his father returned to his usual drinking patterns. By then the upheaval seemed to have caused a shift in Dennis's behavior; formerly quiet and shy, he started to act out in class, was prone to sudden outbursts of noise and violence, to standing up abruptly and flipping the desk or screaming in the middle of a test as if he found the silence and stillness of the room unbearable. Teachers

---

1   Taken from caseworker notes, 1981.

2   Statement from caseworker during investigation into practices, 1991.

who had once wanted to protect him, who'd found his blond-haired, blue-eyed shyness appealing, now pushed him away, suspending him, sending him to stand in the hallway or outside the principal's office, while they focused on the children that could be helped.

It was an isolating existence. Through elementary and into middle school, Dennis arrived alone, spent days segregated from his classmates, and went home by himself. As he entered high school he became more intriguing to his peers, less of an outcast and more of a misunderstood loner. He was popular with girls, though he didn't date much, and started as a running back on the football team. The Red River High School football team were decent players but underfunded and lacked any real dedication. The coach testified for the defense at Dennis's trial, describing him as "kind of a lone wolf" but "a good kid"[3] who just needed a little discipline in his life. Coach Bush was an important witness, a respected man within the community who could confirm Dennis was with him at the school between four and five the day Holly went missing. The last time she had been seen was riding her bike away from her house at roughly four thirty. It meant Dennis couldn't have taken her, or, at least, the timeline should have cast his guilt into reasonable doubt. But

---

3 Taken from court transcripts, May 1993.

when asked to provide the roll call for that practice the coach was unable to do so, though he had registers for all other practices dating back a year, and the prosecution called another player who couldn't recall Dennis being at the practice that day either.

Several boys remembered him being there but others thought he left early. He usually did, they said, as he wasn't one to hang out after the practices or games. He was popular but formed no close friendships with the other players. Instead, he spent most of his time with other misfits in the school, notably Howard Harries, son of Officer Eric Harries, and Lindsay Durst. This was something his team and his classmates couldn't understand, why he still felt so attached to these perceived "losers." But this, the defense's psychologist argued, was a classic symptom of abuse. "[Dennis] feared being exposed and vulnerable to his peers [...] that they might see what his home life was like."[4] Dennis couldn't escape the feeling he was a loser, even if, outwardly, he wasn't perceived as such.

Life at home was becoming increasingly difficult. Twice Dennis found his mother unconscious after an attempted overdose. His father was a violent drunk. When he was away from the house Dennis could relax. But when he returned he would beat Dennis for

---

4   Court transcripts.

the smallest of infractions. Once, Dennis recalls, he had been eating his food in the TV
room, sitting cross-legged on the floor, when
his father appeared behind him and punched
him in the back of the skull. Dennis spat the
mouthful of food onto the floor and as he
turned to ask what was going on his father
hit him again in the mouth, kicked him in the
stomach, unhooked his belt and whipped him
three times. "You were chewing too loud," he
said eventually, breathless and sliding the belt
back through its loops.[5]

To earn money, Dennis took a job at a re-
tirement home cleaning rooms and washing
clothes. Over time the residents started to
enjoy his company. He was funny and quick,
they said, never spoke down to anyone, always listened. He helped organize the enter-
tainment and events, served food and talked
with some of the people who didn't have as
many visitors. Some of the residents showed
him their keepsakes. He saw photos and med-
als and furs. They showed him jewelry. As he
cleaned rooms he saw shoeboxes under the
beds, belonging to the residents who didn't
trust banks. At first he took only a few hundred bucks here and there, enough to squir-
rel away for a plane ticket, a month's rent in
New York or Los Angeles, food. Next it was

5   *Framing the Truth*. Florida: Carrie Atwood, Patrick
Garrity, 1993. VHS.

jewelry, which he took to a pawnshop for a disappointing amount of cash. Then a resident's daughter visited and wanted to borrow her mother's antique brooch for a wedding. The brooch was tracked to the pawnbrokers in town and they told the police straightaway: Dennis Danson sold it to them.

"I wasn't thinking. I needed to be gone. At the time I figured, you know, there weren't really any victims. That stuff was just sitting there, waiting for them to die and their shitty families to come and sell it off." Dennis sighed. "I guess if I knew that everything I ever did in my life would one day be analyzed like this, like everything would be used as evidence to decide if I was a monster or not, I would have lived differently."

3

"So?" Carrie asked Sam, eyes on the road ahead of her. "How was your first date?"

Sam laughed; she'd barely stopped smiling since their visit yesterday. She'd slept well for the first night in days and when Carrie came to pick her up at the motel for the drive to Red River she was waiting outside, eager to talk about it all.

"It was good—it went well." Sam tried not to ask if Dennis had said anything, her instinct to appear aloof still strong, even after traveling across the globe just to meet him.

"Is that it? I'm not going to tell you what he said until you give me a little more than that."

"Fine. At first it was awkward and I think that's my fault, really, I just got a little…overwhelmed, I suppose. But he was so sweet."

"Right?"

"Completely." Sam got along easily with Carrie. She was short, with thick brown hair that stopped just above her chin and stuck up wildly when she ran a hand through it. "And, you know, he's handsome and stuff, obviously."

"Obviously."

"I was so gutted when I had to leave. It was like we'd only just started to get to know each other outside of the letters." Sam didn't mention the woman, the confrontation. There was a silence.

"And?" Carrie teased.

"Stop it! Oh my God." Sam burned. What she felt for Dennis felt so different from the last time she'd started something new, from that secret fumble at the staff Christmas party, from Mark telling her quietly, "I'm not looking for anything serious. No strings?" And she'd said yes, of course, because what else could she say? His hands already inside her clothes, months of longing and shy glances culminating in this. Sliding his fingers inside her, painful, too soon, her body stiff and cold with the effort not to cry. *Are you OK?* And she said yes because you had to be. OK with being fucked but not wanted. OK with being a consolation prize. OK with being OK.

"Well, he thinks you're totally hot, obviously," Carrie said.

"He said that?"

"His exact words were, 'Samantha's totally hot.'"

"Seriously?"

"And he loves your accent. He was bummed out it had to end so soon too but he's really excited about seeing you next week. It's so cute I can't even handle it. My little Dennis, finally dating."

Sam committed his words to memory, tried to hear how he would say it, only half listening while Carrie told her about her first visit with Dennis, how scary walking into the jail for the first time had been. She talked about the death threats and hate mail she received, how they hadn't been able to work up any funding for the first documentary so she and her coproducer Patrick had to work nights just to get it made.

"You put me to shame," Sam said.

"It was essentially totally selfish. It was a story that needed to be told and so we made the film. Like, I always cared about Dennis, right from when Patrick first told me about the case. Of course everyone thinks I'm *in love* with him." She rolled her eyes. "A woman wouldn't make a documentary about a guy otherwise, right? The fact that I'm gay doesn't seem to matter. I get it all the time. It was just the case, it seemed so unfair, this kid who obviously didn't do it. I couldn't get it out of my head."

Sam thought of how close they were, how Dennis spoke about her. "It's so overwhelming, though. I can't even believe I'm here and all I'm doing is visiting. It's like a really weird holiday," she said.

"It's huge what you're doing! Before you, Dennis was really starting to give up. It's amazing you came out here. Don't put yourself down, you're a strong woman."

Sam flushed.

"Ugh, I hate that though. *Strong woman*. What does that even mean? Like, a strong man is a guy who can drag an eighteen-wheeler along by his testicles but a strong woman is like…" Carrie clicked her fingers, searching for what she meant.

"A mum who petitions for a new road sign after her son gets knocked down by a speeding car."

"Right!"

"Maybe that's less stupid."

"Well, yeah, when you say it out loud. But you know what I mean. It's some bullshit thing people always say. I mean you're brave, is what I mean."

Sam opened her lips to protest but remembered how Mark had said she never accepted a compliment and it drove him crazy. Item number thirteen on the list of reasons he couldn't love her. She turned to Carrie. "Thank you."

The houses in Red River weren't uniform like the ones Sam had seen as the plane came in to land, with pools like surgical dishes and terra-cotta roofs. It was as if they were all built one at a time by people who ended up there by accident. The streets were wide and the houses spread apart; there were discarded sofas and chained-up dogs that barked as they drove past. There was a town hall, modest and white, and a central street with a convenience store, a hardware store and a diner. Most places were closed, with wood panels bolted over the windows.

They drove on to a prettier area, where the streets were shaded by large trees and the houses were painted different pastel shades, with love seats on the porches and big shining SUVs outside. They pulled up next to a pastel yellow house, smaller than the others, the paint starting to peel around the white window frames. The mailbox read "Harries, 142." According to Carrie, Officer Eric Harries had declined every request for an interview during the making of the first documentary in 1993. On this occasion he had contacted Patrick when it was announced Jackson Anderson was producing a new documentary series about the case.

"The lure of celebrity," Carrie said, rolling her eyes. "Of course, he's set us some serious restrictions." Carrie explained that if they even contacted Howard, his son, for an interview, he would see to it that their footage would never be released. "He wasn't exactly dedicated or talented enough to rise up the ranks but he still holds a lot of sway in this town," Carrie said. "Honor among thieves. No one understands that better than cops."

The interview was crucial, as Officer Harries was the first cop to interview Dennis after Holly's body was found. When asked why he called on Dennis he had testified, "Call it a hunch. Cop's intuition."

"The nerve of the guy," Carrie said while they looked at the house from the car. "I've got serious questions about his story."

They stepped outside and Carrie unloaded equipment from the back of the car onto the sidewalk. She had a camera, which she loaded onto her shoulder; she put her eye against the viewfinder and scanned the street, Sam instinctively ducking as if its gaze were a bullet. Carrie held the camera by a handle on top and cradled it from beneath, sweeping it around in a semicircle. She attached a pair of headphones, which she hung around her neck, and took a step back, cocking a hip to one side.

"So how do I look? Jack wants us to be on camera now, like we're part of the story ourselves. I don't know, I feel like I'm on fucking *Catfish*."

Inside, the rest of the crew had already set up and were adjusting lights, rolling a blind up and down, while Officer Harries sat in an armchair, pinching to release the top button of his shirt, the collar tight around his loose neck. Sam noticed that he looked at Carrie as she entered but looked away again quickly. A gangly man emerged from the kitchen, ducking slightly under the doorway, and introduced himself as Patrick, Carrie's partner. Together they had researched and filmed the first documentary, acquiring a small team as the story grew. Patrick seemed, to Sam, a little shy, his handshake limp and palm moist. He talked without looking into her eyes, asked a few questions—"How was your flight?"—but he didn't seem to engage with her answers. "Good, good," he said. "Excuse me." When Sam turned around to talk to Carrie she was gone and so she stood awkwardly at the side of the room and waited for someone else to approach her.

There were five people Sam didn't recognize, all busy setting up. A man swooped a boom mic over her head, apologized. She watched them, shifting her weight from one foot to the other and starting to grow flustered with self-consciousness, feeling as if she didn't belong. It was suddenly preposterous that she was here.

"You can take a seat, you know," Harries said from his spot.

"No, thank you," Sam said.

"You look a little flushed. Do you need a drink?"

He made to stand up until Sam waved him down. She needed a drink but not from him. "Well, if you need anything…"

With disgust, she noted the nose that swelled red with years of drink, open pores and the nick of a razor crusted with blackening blood on his cheek next to his moustache. His forehead was already shining with sweat, his belt buckle sinking into a gut that shone white through the gaps in his shirt.

Officer Harries cleared his throat. "That an English accent I hear? How do you like the weather? Hot enough for you?" Sam smiled politely, closed lips. "You move here or did you travel just for this?"

"Just visiting."

"What did they bring you here for then? You must be pretty good at whatever you do if they flew you out here."

"Well, actually"—Sam dared herself, feeling the tingle of confrontation—"I'm a friend of Dennis, actually. More like a girlfriend."

Harries's smile dissipated and he sat taller in his chair. "They don't got killers in England you can date?"

Sam turned and walked away, back out into the wall of heat outside. Suddenly it seemed as though everyone in the house was thinking the same thing. It made her sick, like she was spinning. She had to close her eyes and count her breaths and remember who she was, what she was doing, why.

She was standing in the shade, trying to bring herself back, when Carrie passed and handed her a bottle of water, dripping from the melting ice of the cooler in her trunk. Sam held it against the back of her neck and explained to Carrie what had happened.

"This guy is the actual...fucking...*worst*..." Carrie said. "Don't worry, we'll tear him a new asshole. He said we couldn't speak *to* Howard, he didn't say we couldn't speak *about* him." She coaxed Sam back inside. Sam stayed at the back of the room, as far away from Harries as possible, watching him sip from a cloudy glass tumbler and wipe his wet lips with the back of his hand.

Half an hour later Carrie took a seat opposite Harries, an iPad balanced on her knees along with some notes, which Harries asked to see before they started. Sam watched his eyes move over the pages, smiling to himself, a cluck every now and then.

"Happy?" Carrie asked him as he handed back the papers.

He nodded. Carrie gestured that she was ready; Patrick called for silence and counted down. Carrie started.

"Can you tell us about your personal relationship with Dennis, Officer Harries? About his friendship with your son, Howard?"

"I didn't have any kind of personal relationship with Dennis. But he was around a lot, started when he was...seven, I suppose. Howie was always a caring boy and he saw Dennis as a kid in need so he would play with him in the yard. Kid was always in here eating all our food. I used to say to him, 'Don't your folks ever feed you?' Well, I guess they didn't because he was always hungry, dirty, always stealing things. Though Howie would never say it was him, I knew it was him. Ten dollars here, a packet of cookies there. Nothing big. You ignore these things, at first."

"You never asked Dennis about it? Or visited his home to see if he was being properly cared for?"

"We all knew what was going on at that house; it wasn't a secret. Not much you can do. I go round there and give his daddy a warning and what happens? They probably stop him coming round— Howie won't forgive me. Those boys, they were inseparable. I had my concerns right from the start but—"

"What were your concerns?"

"Howie was so impressionable. He was always trailing behind other kids his age. Never invited to the parties or to play ball games in the summer. So I was suspicious when some kid like Dennis starts hanging around. He seemed whip-smart to me. He shook my hand like he was a grown man the first time I met him. Then Howie started cussing, and I knew he got that from him. Broken toys, buried in the garbage. Howie snapping his wrist after some stupid stunt, jumping off a bridge into the river. I knew who made him do this stuff, I saw him changing. But how can you take away your boy's only friend? So I overlooked some things, I made exceptions. I had a quiet word with Dennis, told him, 'Now, I don't want a bad influence round my son, you need to adjust your attitude or you can't come round here day in day out, you hear me?'"

"Did it work?"

"Week later my vehicle was vandalized, a key scratch right down one side. I asked him but he denied it. Always suspected him though. That was my mistake, letting too many things slide, watching my Howard get dragged into delinquency."

Carrie sat forward, frowned. "Some people see it the other way round. Teachers say Dennis was better behaved before he met Howard; some locals say Howard was always a problem child, ever since his mother left he was, quote, *out of control*, end quote."

Harries grunted. "Well, whoever said that has an ax to grind. Howie reacted badly after his mother left—who wouldn't? He was a little loud and prone to tantrums, but he was slow with language, he just got frustrated is all."

"By high school Howard was dealing drugs. Was that just caused by frustration too?"

"That was Dennis's doing."

"Did Howard tell you that?"

"No, he didn't need to: it was obvious. Where would Howie even get… Look, Howie wasn't the brightest kid. He was covering for someone. He was a pleaser; he just wanted friends. There's no way he was capable of orchestrating something like that himself."

"But he swore it wasn't Dennis, even at the threat of expulsion."

"Like I said, he wanted to cover for his friend."

"So did you resent Dennis?"

"No."

"Not even after your son was expelled and sent to juvie for nine months?"

"Not even then."

"Because some people say you had it in for Dennis after this. That it was you who knocked on his door after Holly's body was found, though there was no reason to link him with this crime at all."

Harries took a breath. He was still calm, still composed. "We had to investigate everyone in the area who had a record for sexual misconduct."

"Right, the public exposure charge *you* pushed for. What everyone recognized as a football prank and you insisted was sexual deviancy."

"I didn't insist on anything. Dennis exposed himself in front of teenage girls."

"He was thrown naked from a moving car, after the football game, and had to run back to the gym. The same prank had been pulled every season."

"I wouldn't know about that as I only know what's reported. Some of those girls were very upset. We had to do our jobs."

Sam clenched her fists, cracked a knuckle. The boom mic guy turned and shot her a look. To Sam, right then, Harries looked every part the villain. There was a shape to his lips, a not-quite smile, that suggested he didn't believe a word he said and that he wanted them to know it. He rested his hands on his thighs, tapping the tips of his fingers while he spoke.

"What about the real flasher?" Carrie asked, looking through her notes, then back at Harries. "A man was reported for exposing himself to a group of girls at a cheerleading camp on the Saturday before the murder. The girls were interviewed and described the man as 'short, dark-haired and a little pale,' and a police artist drew this…" Carrie held out an iPad. The drawing looked undeniably similar to that of the Short Man, seen outside Holly's school the week earlier. "Yet, months later, you spoke again to these girls and you showed them pictures of Dennis. You asked them if he was the man they'd seen. You interviewed them again, even after they'd said no, and you pushed and you pushed until one of them said *maybe* it could have been him."

"We felt we had compelling evidence that Dennis was our guy."

"But this picture couldn't look *less* like Dennis!"

"You don't get accurate descriptions from people who are in shock. And when you're dealing with children…"

"What made you think Dennis could have murdered Holly Michaels?"

"We had a witness who heard him outright confess, we had fibers from a carpet that matched the one in his house—"

"Those fibers, according to our forensic specialist, are present in roughly seven out of every ten households in America. That's hardly *compelling*."

"When you combine it with the witness statement—"

"A fake witness, a woman who has since confessed she made the whole story up."

"Why would she do that?" Harries's voice rose. "It's the pressure you put on her, the liberal media who hounded her year after year until she told you she lied just to get you to leave her alone." It was the first time he seemed rattled. He crossed and then uncrossed his legs. Sat taller.

"She called us. Guilt-ridden, miserable. Said she tried to contact the police, the court, that she tried to undo what she'd said."

Harries sighed, his eyes closed. "All I can say is that at the time she was a reliable witness, her story checked out. Dennis had a criminal background. My fellow officers had previously suspected him of being involved in the disappearance of Lauren Rhodes."

"He was never questioned though."

"No, not officially, that's correct."

"Why was he a person of interest in the Lauren Rhodes case?"

"They were acquainted with each other, went on a couple of dates before she disappeared."

"Several months before she disappeared."

"Any ex-boyfriend is always a person of interest in these cases."

"What made him different from the other ex-boyfriends?"

"The night after Lauren was reported missing the whole town came together to search for her. Everyone was there. Dennis, he showed up and he was smiling, joking around. He didn't even bring a flashlight. It was pitch-black. No flashlight."

"And this made you suspicious?" Carrie cocked her head again. Harries took a look around the room and continued, his expression cemented.

"It was my colleagues who were suspicious. They said it was like he wasn't really there to look for her. More like he was there to watch us look for her. Like he was gloating."

"But you didn't think this?"

"Hard for me to say. I wasn't present and didn't witness this behavior myself. I was with the Rhodes family. We followed all leads and we came up short. Possible runaway. I don't know, it's the unsolved ones that haunt you."

It was quiet for a moment. Sam felt they'd been manipulated, that he was buying himself time.

Carrie snapped them out of it. "Let's get back to Holly Michaels. The hair."

"The hair?"

"The hair found on Holly's body, described in the forensics log as 'short, dark brown/black, most likely from the head,' not belonging to the victim; not, it seems, a hair from Dennis's body."

"Yeah, that was obviously one of the first things we sent for further testing. Unfortunately, as you well know, it was lost in transit."

"The single most important piece of evidence just went missing?" Carrie raised her eyebrows, shaking her head.

"I'm not defending my department; that was one hell of a screwup. Could have saved us months if we'd had a match on that. A few people got a disciplinary, careers were knocked off track, we had to regroup and focus on what we had left."

"Dennis is fair. Blond. The hair they found didn't sound like a match for him, would you agree?"

"We would have had to test it to say for certain. But following the rest of the evidence and the successful prosecution of Dennis I'd say it was pretty likely that if we had that evidence today we'd find it was a match."

Carrie's voice was firm and in control, it carried across the room and the power shifted with it; Harries was clearly less confident. "But there was no DNA evidence from Dennis at all. Nothing. The blood on the girl's shirt was neither her own nor Dennis's."

"We discussed the possibility of an accomplice."

"There was none of his DNA at all, nothing to suggest there were two murderers and nothing to suggest Dennis was ever present at the scene of the murder."

"The evidence—"

"There was no evidence. Your department misplaced the hair. You led witnesses until they said what you needed them to. You put together a crazy story, and framed a teenage boy because you personally resented him for his friendship with your son."

"Listen to me, young lady, perhaps I did resent him but"—Officer Harries looked into the camera—"I would never let that cloud my judgment as an officer of the law."

4

Extract from *When the River Runs Red*
by Eileen Turner

Drugs were an industry in Red River. The school halls were rife with illicit deals and exchanges; you could buy anything from a couple of joints to prescription painkillers on your way to gym class. James Lucas remembers the drug "epidemic" during his time as school principal: "We'd search lockers routinely. First we'd make an announcement over the speakers and request every student stay in the classroom they were in until we announced the search was over. Every locker would be opened and searched, no exceptions."[6] It wasn't unusual to uncover a stash of narcotics during one of these searches but on one occasion the culprit was a surprise. Howard, son of respected police officer Eric Harries, was concealing a small fortune's worth of controlled substances. In particular, Princi-

---

6 Interview, telephone, June 1996.

pal Lucas recalls, a couple of hundred baby-blue pills. "Perhaps some kind of imitation Valium," he speculates.

Officer Harries has always denied his son's responsibility[7] and declined to be interviewed for this book but Howard made a statement to Principal Lucas in which he took full responsibility and admitted to selling the pills to fellow students. Harries tried to settle the matter privately but due to the street value of the find the case was escalated, resulting in permanent expulsion and a six-month stretch in a juvenile detention center for Howard. Following this, Howard was homeschooled and, sources say, Officer Harries developed a deep mistrust of Howard's only friend, Dennis Danson, who he felt was responsible for his son's arrest.

The blue pills became notorious in and around the school. It was widely speculated that it was the pills that led to the disappearance of the first girl, Donna Knox. She was last seen at a party attended by most of her classmates. Friends say she had a few drinks, her usual, Jack Daniel's and Diet Coke, but didn't drink excessively. A witness recalls her taking two pills around nine o'clock, "light blue, round, I didn't know exactly what they were,"[8] and by nine forty-five Donna was re-

---

7   Anonymous sources close to the subject, June 1996.

8   Statement taken in Red River High School, anonymous, March 1990.

portedly intoxicated; unusually so, according to her friends. Her behavior was bizarre. She became belligerent and refused all offers to drive her home. Friends let her storm off into the night, expecting her to return half an hour later, remorseful and embarrassed.

But she never returned. Her boyfriend and her best friend left the party an hour later, drove slowly along the route she'd take home, but didn't see her. They parked outside her house and looked up to her unlit bedroom window, assuming she must be asleep. They called the next morning and spoke to her anxious mother, who told them she'd never returned home the night before. Not wanting to rat out their friend, they told Mrs. Knox that Donna had left the party early and had stayed with a friend. They reassured her that Donna would call her as soon as she woke up, that she was probably still in bed.

It was over a day before Mrs. Knox reported her missing. "I didn't know I should be afraid, I was so angry I didn't even think to be afraid."[9] Two days after she disappeared her sweater was found, two miles off the path she'd taken home, just a short distance from the bank of the river.

The search focused on the water; forensic divers found no evidence of a body, but heavy

---

9   Interview with Mrs. Knox, Channel One News, April 1990.

rainfall in March can cause strong undercurrents and there was a chance the remains had been dragged to sea. Police didn't suspect foul play. All evidence seemed to suggest Donna had been too drunk to navigate the roads in the dark, took a wrong turn and wandered into the tangled and dense woodland. Perhaps she stepped into the water willingly, discarding her sweater and jumping in for a swim, sucked into the powerful pull of the high river. Or perhaps she fell, her sweater caught on the low-hanging branches. Either way, police were not pursuing anybody in relation to her disappearance.

The blue pills have been discussed many times, particularly by the extensive piece "The Girls of Red River" published in *The Red River Tribune* in 1992 shortly before the arrest of Dennis Danson. The piece asks, "Why was this line of investigation not pursued? Little to no interest was shown in this piece of evidence at the time, even with ongoing concerns about the level of drug use at the school." And many agree it is a curious omission, one that ensured Howard Harries was not interviewed in relation to the girl's disappearance.

Next Lauren Rhodes disappeared. Then Jenelle Tyler, Kelly Fuller, Sarah West. Vanished, no bodies, no blood. As if they'd never even existed.

Finally they found Holly Michaels. They

5

Sam was starting to recognize certain things Dennis said or did with his face when he spoke, the little inflections she never expected him to have, like the way he blew hair out of his eyes as he talked, taking small pauses and continuing as if he'd never stopped. The way he said her whole name, "I've missed you too, Samantha," and shrugged his shoulders when he was pretending something wasn't a big deal even though she could tell it was.

"They said Johnny Depp is involved." Shrug. "I guess he wanted to visit in person soon or something."

They pressed their fingers against the holes in the plastic divide, skin turning white, stroking the fraction of flesh that appeared. Even that was electric. Sam left feeling drunk, and had the air-conditioning on full blast as she drove back to her hotel. Not being with Dennis was agony, being there but not being touched was somehow worse. They talked about the lawyers, the research, the billboards Sam drove past on her way to the prison that offered a twenty-thousand-dollar reward for new information. So far the line hadn't yielded anything but the mutterings of the functioning insane, fantasists and a few psychics peddling unconvincing stories. But there was a resurgence of hope.

"I just want to be with you," Dennis said, both of them leaning closer, their breath against the window.

"Soon." Sam's eyes searched for his behind the lenses. A guard asked them both to lean back.

"You know more than I do," Dennis said. "What's the atmosphere like? Out there?"

"About you? It's always so positive. I mean, on the internet. I would say ninety-five per cent positive, apart from Red River…"

"It doesn't matter about them. Everywhere else?"

"Positive. We all want you out, Dennis. We can definitely win this."

Sam hadn't planned to stay more than a couple of weeks but before she knew it the Easter holidays were over and she found she wasn't ready to leave. She called the school and told them she wouldn't be coming back yet, she had personal issues that she needed to resolve. When they responded with kindness and sensitivity Sam only felt more miserable; she swaddled herself in her guilt.

The days when Carrie and the crew weren't around were lonely. Sam holed up in her hotel room, watching Netflix and eating fast food she bought at the drive-ins, cold by the time she got back, laid out in cardboard boxes and paper bags on the bedspread. But when Carrie arrived to pick her up for interviews Sam left her room reluctantly.

The day they were due to shoot in Red River again she complained of a headache but Carrie pointed a thumb to the passenger seat.

"Stop whining and just get in. I promised Dennis I'd look after you. Look at you, you've been here two months already and you look like raw chicken. Do you ever get out when I'm not here?"

Sam looked at herself in the side mirror. "Well…"

"Get out there! Ride an airboat in the Everglades, drive down to SeaWorld! I'm just kidding, have you seen *Blackfish*?"

But Sam wasn't there for SeaWorld or airboats. She was there for Dennis. Everything else just felt like killing time. She recognized it then, the isolation, the tendency to focus entirely on the relationship and let everything else come second. If she were in therapy they'd call it a pattern, she thought. With pity, they'd tell her it was an addiction. She thought of Dennis in his six-by-nine-foot cell, eating from a tray on his knees, the television a constant noise in the background. It seemed so much like her hotel room.

They stopped for iced coffee, Carrie slowly dragging Sam out of herself and into the world until she even found herself laughing. Instead of heading into town they skirted the edges of Red River, heavily wooded and secluded. They passed just one house, a dilapidated building, its skeleton black from fire damage.

On they drove, the SUV skidding in the mud the worse the road got. They parked in what seemed to be the middle of nowhere, next to the white van she recognized from the interview with Officer Harries and another vehicle that could have been abandoned. They had to make their way on foot over fallen branches and the ground was soft underfoot from yesterday's rain. Sam's ballet flats were sucked from her feet and mud spat up the back of her calves.

"Shit, I should have warned you, my bad," Carrie said, retrieving a shoe and sliding it back onto Sam's pointed foot. "Jackson wanted some material that shows the *real* Red River. The…character of the place, so to speak." They heard the noise of the crew through the trees and saw the side of a trailer covered with creeping plants and windows so dirty you couldn't see inside.

Behind the trailer the earth fell away into a sinkhole so deep Sam could only see a blackness that seemed to pull her in. The remains of a house were teetering on the edge, splintered wood and wires dangling like spilled guts. The owner, Ed, stood stiff and uncomfortable while someone clipped a microphone onto his shirt. Sam had to take a few steps back from the hole, the pull of it like a deep breath, as though she might step forward and throw herself in. It made her bones ache.

"Well, it happened like this," Ed started on command. "One night my wife told me she was going to bed early, I kissed her goodnight, she went to the bedroom, which would have been right around here." He gestured to the edge of the hole, the beams still hanging over the abyss. "I'd had a few that night so when it seemed like the house was rockin' a little I thought it was the beer. It was soft, not like an earthquake but like just before you pass out, like the whole world is gently swayin' beneath you. Then there was this noise, unearthly, like a growlin'. Like old pipes, kind of. And then it was all at once. The whole left side of the house was just gone, sucked down in seconds. I didn't even hear my wife scream or nothing. I went out there and I could see rubble. I tried to find her but the ground was still sucking everything in, like it was hungry. Water was bubbling up around me, little pools of filthy water burbling, like a fart in a bathtub. I didn't know what to do. Phone was out— we're pretty off the grid here.

"I had to drive to get help. We never found her, she was just…gone, sucked into the soil while she slept. I wonder to myself: Did she drown? Was it like drownin'? Or did her nose and mouth fill with mud? Can you imagine that? Entombed alive in wet, stinkin' mud. Couldn't even bury her. She's got a plaque, in the ground, at the chapel, but she ain't there, she's here.

"I couldn't leave her like that. They tried to get me to leave, the county marked this place uninhabitable so I got a trailer and put it over there instead. The hole gets bigger—I've got photos." Ed held up some pictures that showed how the hole was expanding over time, the house getting smaller and smaller by comparison. "Whenever we have a good storm, that's when it gets bigger. All that water. When it dries out again the pressure changes and"—he made a suction noise—"I can hear the house cracking and creaking some nights.

"Way I see it, worst that can happen is I get sucked in too, and that ain't so bad. They say it's dangerous but it's no more dangerous than anywhere else here. The whole state's built on bad rock."

Sam tried to make herself light on her feet. Everything tingled as Ed led a nervous cameraman to the edge of the sinkhole, and bent over it precariously. "Come on now, it won't bite."

"Does staying here help you grieve?" Carrie's partner Patrick asked.

"Yeah, I suppose it does. I miss my wife. I talk to her every day."

"Does she ever answer you back?"

"Yeah, sure, right now she's saying, 'Why'd you let this bunch of assholes come here to disrespect you in your own home?'" He clucked and rolled his eyes. "What kinda question is that? Huh? I know you're looking for the odd folk, to make our town look like a freak show."

"I'm sorry," Carrie jumped in, "I think Pat meant it, like, metaphorically. You're right, we are looking to show how colorful and diverse the population of Red River is but our motives are honest. We're not trying to make it look like a freak show."

"Mm-hmm." Ed raised an eyebrow. "I'm not an idiot. I saw the film. In fact, Dennis used to come around here and do some work for us."

Carrie seemed surprised. "Really? Can you tell us about that?"

"He came over here, did some yard work for us, we paid him of course. One evening I was taking him a glass of water, set to tell him to quit for the night, he was totally absorbed by something. I called him twice but he didn't look up. When I reached him he was bent over a metal bucket, face lit up with fire. He had a snake in there, *writhing*, burning and twisting inside the bucket. He poked it now and then with a stick. I poured the water into the bucket and asked him what the hell he thought he was doing.

"He looked like someone you just woke up from a nap. He said he was getting rid of it for me, said it would die slower now. I told him to go home. Handed him twenty bucks. He didn't come back.

"Tell you the truth I didn't feel too comfortable around him, especially after that. Don't know if he really killed that girl, don't know about that, but there was just something not right about him."

Sam sat in the car wishing she'd stayed back at the hotel. Mosquitoes bit at her limbs, some trapped in rolling sweat while she waited for Carrie. The whole place made her uncomfortable and she kept thinking of the snake and what it could mean.

"It's a snake," Carrie said when Sam asked her. "It's not like he was putting kittens in a fucking microwave. Boys are gross. My brother put his goldfish in the freezer and he's a full-blown vegan now. It probably wasn't even as bad as he says."

She and Patrick had a hushed argument after the interview with Ed. Sam listened while she sat in the passenger seat, door open, dangling her legs into the air.

"We can't use any of that," Patrick said. "Burning snakes? How does that sound?"

"It's fine. We got some great stuff about the sinkhole. That's all Jackson wanted. The guy's clearly a storyteller, who knows how much of that is even true?"

They argued in muted tones until eventually Carrie appeared back at the wheel, tense and maybe even upset.

They drove back to the center of Red River, this time in silence, Carrie's thoughts clearly somewhere else. Sam didn't know what to say to her, so she said nothing. The houses that rolled past the windows started to look shabbier as they went by until they reached a street with barred windows and more furniture in the yards than there could be inside the houses, overflowing trash cans and a cacophony of dog barks.

Sam knew Lindsay Durst from *Framing the Truth*, though she'd never been on screen for more than a few minutes. She had been a key witness for the defense; she was with Dennis on the evening Holly was murdered, had met him after football practice, driven around with him for a while, and stayed out until after midnight before dropping him near his home. But on cross-examination the prosecution had portrayed her as a liar, someone who would say anything to help a boy she was obsessed with. She was always driving him around, people said, waiting for him after school, ditching classes to take him someplace. "And he wasn't even that nice to her..." a girl had said in *Framing the Truth*, outside the court, wind blowing her hair into her lip gloss as she looked away from the camera self-consciously. "It was actually kind of desperate, you know?"

Now Lindsay stood outside her house, wearing a Free Dennis Danson T-shirt tied into a knot at the back, exposing a patch of tanned skin at the base of her spine. Sam noticed a rip under the left buttock of her jeans, how she hooked her thumbs through her belt loops and jutted a hip to the side as she spoke. It was, Lindsay told them, the same house she'd always lived in. She walked them around to the back and showed them where Dennis had carved his name into a fence post. Patrick and Carrie took some exterior shots, had her stand looking seriously, which made her laugh. "I'm sorry, I can't do it! Oh my God, let me try again..." she kept saying. Sam wondered why the guys on the crew all seemed to find it so cute.

Behind the houses was a lake: still, black water. Trees hung lazy in the heat and dangled their limbs into the pool. Lindsay walked to the edge of a dock that looked rotten and slippery with green slime. "We used to go down to the water right here, a whole bunch of us, and hang out. People used to dare each other, 'Go swim to that post and back!' because there's alligators in there. Some guys would walk to the edge of the dock but they never did it.

"I was always one of the boys, you know? Never

got along with girls, too bitchy, so this was what we did. Only one day Dennis just stood right up and said, 'I'll do it.' We're like, 'Yeah, sure,' but he took off his shirt and kicked off his shoes, got down to his boxers and just ran, jumped.

"Well, I was *screaming*, right? I'm like, 'Get back here!' But he swam all the way to the post and when he got there he just waved. He swam back and the boys went to the end there to pull him out. I've never seen anything like it—he was crazy sometimes. He was always doing the stuff no one else would do. That's how he got into trouble: dares, streaking and all that.

"We were *real* close. Still talk—I visit when I can get up there. I miss him. I know he didn't kill that girl, cops just have it out for people like him and me."

Sam realized that until then she'd thought she was the only woman who visited Dennis, aside from Carrie. He'd never mentioned Lindsay. They'd shared letters where they peeled themselves bare, and the whole time he had someone else, someone he never mentioned, a secret woman.

"Look, look right there," Lindsay said, pointing to the water. "Right on the far side, you see?" Everybody edged forward, cameras trained to the spot where she pointed. Sam peered reluctantly and saw nothing until what she thought was debris sank slowly back under the blackness. Everybody whooped. "It's lousy with alligators in there, see? Dennis always had a lot of balls."

For a time everyone was preoccupied with the

water, every ripple causing a rush of excitement. Eventually attention turned back to Lindsay.

"Can you tell us about the trial?" Carrie asked.

"What you wanna know?"

"Well, why didn't they believe your testimony? That Dennis was with you that day?"

"Oh, that." She shook her hair. "They tried to make out like I was some *fangirl* who only wanted a boyfriend. They had people from school saying I was, like, obsessed with him! Which *wasn't* true. We were never involved. I mean, we *did stuff* but it was more like friends with benefits, you know?"

Sam stayed by the water while Carrie and Patrick packed. The whole thing was ruined, she thought. Until then it had been perfect. Almost. Until Lindsay. But the poison was seeping in, just as it always did. The paranoia and the pain. She and Mark would argue for hours until she stormed off, expecting him to follow, but he never did. Because she didn't matter. Maybe she still didn't.

A white bird tipped its beak into the water and Sam stared, waiting for jaws to snatch it from the bank, both wanting and not wanting to see it. But the bird flew away and she brushed herself off, relieved, disappointed. She'd been an idiot to think she was special.

"I can tell she bothered you," Carrie said later as they drove back to the motel.

"I didn't know he had anyone else visiting," Sam said.

"Maybe she's exaggerating. She seems kind of off to me."

"Off?"

"'One of the boys'? That's just code for crazy. Never trust a woman who doesn't like women. I'm telling you."

6

Extract from *When the River Runs Red*
by Eileen Turner

One afternoon in the late summer of 1992
Officer Harries knocked on the Dansons'
front door. From the couch, Dennis's mother
shouted for Dennis to answer it. Normally, he
said later, he would not have been home. In
fact, he'd spent less and less time at the house
that summer. He was sofa-surfing, staying
with friends until their parents had enough,
and started tidying around him in silence as
he blinked awake and peeled off the borrowed
sheets. He'd stopped home that day only to
throw his clothes in the machine and grab a
few things to take back to Lindsay's.[10]

The police had first approached Dennis at
the search party for Lauren. Dennis recalls,
"They were asking questions like they were
trying to say something, but I couldn't figure out what it was." So when he saw the po-

---

10 Interview, Altoona Prison, 1996.

lice officer behind the torn screen door he immediately tensed. When Dennis recognized Officer Harries he suspected it would be something petty, such as the break-in at the general store that he'd heard about. "Officer Harries always tried to pin stuff on me," Dennis tells me during one interview. "He always thought I led Howard *astray*. Like I was responsible for every bad thing he ever did."

Dennis opened the door to Officer Harries. "Yeah?" he said.

"Who is it?" his mom had yelled from the house.

"It's Officer Harries," Dennis shouted.

"A cop?"

"Just here to ask your son some questions, ma'am." Harries claims that at this point he offered for a parent or guardian to be present for whatever he asked Dennis next,[11] though he insisted that this was only an informal meeting.[12] *Framing the Truth* would question the motives here: why would a police officer travel all the way out there just to ask a seventeen-year-old some informal questions about a murder that occurred five months ago? "Cop's intuition," Harries said. Another officer would report Harries seemed more concerned with

---

11 Conversations loosely recorded in Harries's notes, 1992.

12 *Red River Tribune*, 1993.

interviewing Dennis, for whom he had a personal and "intense" mistrust, rather than pursuing other leads early on in the case.[13]

"What do you want?" Dennis appeared short-tempered and stood blocking the doorway so Harries couldn't see the mess behind him, ashamed of the conditions in which his family lived.

"Want to let me in?"

"Not particularly. I've got places to be, what do you want?"

"Where were you on April tenth?" At this, Harries noted, Dennis smiled. He repeated himself.

"April tenth? How would I remember that? Am I supposed to remember that?"

"So you're saying you can't remember?"

"I don't know…what day was that?"

"Friday. April tenth."

"A Friday? School?"

"After school. Late afternoon, evening."

"Maybe practice? I don't know, I really don't."

"Can anyone help you remember where you were? You have any witnesses?"

"I just said, I don't remember. So how would I know who I was with?" Later, Dennis admitted to losing his patience. Harries had a way of smirking when he asked him

---

13 Anonymous source, 1996.

things. "I knew," he admitted. "I knew I was walking right into their trap but I didn't know how to avoid it."[14]

That was it for a couple of weeks, long enough for Dennis to think it might be behind him, and for the sensation of eyes on his back to fade, when Officer Harries arrived at school, and knocked on the door during detention. He and the teacher exchanged a whispered conversation while the rows of children watched silently. But Dennis just knew. He was standing before they'd even called his name.[15] Harries led him out of the school by the wrist. Dennis was confused, unsure of his rights, or if he was being arrested.

At the station he didn't ask for a lawyer, because he believed he'd done nothing wrong. Even after six hours of questioning he didn't ask for one and he didn't think to call his parents. As he answered their questions ("I don't know... Can't remember... Not sure..."), he scrolled through the months in his mind. He thought of the things this might be about. Was it the fire he started at the back of the hardware store? Or when he broke into the gymnasium? But this seemed too serious for anything like that. There were two detectives in the room with him. For the first five hours

14 Interview, Altoona Prison, 1996.

15 Interview with eye witness, Jeff Bailey, 1996.

they made notes, but at eight thirty p.m. they took out a tape recorder.

Transcript from the interrogation of Dennis Danson
Time: 20:51

Officer #1: Come on. Tell us how you killed Holly Michaels.
Dennis (laughing): Who?
Officer #1: Holly Michaels. You know who she is.
Officer #2: Everyone in town knows who she is. You're telling us you're the only one who doesn't know?
Dennis: I'm not good with names.

The detectives felt that Dennis was "goading" them and that his laughter only proved he "got off" on doing so.[16] Dennis, though, remembers his laughter as discomfort, a reaction to the ludicrous situation in which he found himself.

Officer #1: Holly Michaels. Eleven years old, murdered, national news.

The officers slid him a picture of Holly, taken at school, her hair in a high ponytail tied with a scrunchie. Dennis remembers looking into the girl's eyes, hand hovering above the photograph.

---

16 *Framing the Truth*. Florida: Carrie Atwood, Patrick Garrity, 1993. VHS.

Dennis (whispering): She was so young.

This, Harries recalls, as he watched from the next room, was the moment they knew they had him.[17]

---

17 Interview with Harries in *Red River Tribune*, 1992.

7

Sam knew she was being cold. She'd planned to be. Back in the prison, behind the plastic divide, she looked lazily around the room, avoiding looking at Dennis. She allowed herself to yawn when the urge came, responding with one-word answers just slightly too quietly, so he had to ask her again and she could sigh and roll her eyes and repeat it louder. For twenty minutes she'd waited for him to ask her what was wrong. *Nothing*, she would say, in a way that let him know there definitely was something wrong. She would repeat this until the moment felt right and then she would tell him, *We spoke to Lindsay yesterday.*

It was a well-rehearsed performance, at once second nature and so completely at odds with what felt natural. It made her hate herself. This she admitted to Mark, late in the night, after it had led to another argument that outran her, that she'd lost control of until it burned her out completely. Afterward she told him that she didn't understand why she did it. She felt like she was rotten inside and crawling with worms. But she couldn't stop it. Not even now, as she looked into Dennis's beautiful face, a light stubble along his jaw. As he talked she willed herself to hate him even as she lost herself for a second in the thought of his chin against her cheek, rough, his breath on her ear.

She sighed.

"And Jackson wanted to use some things I've written in the movie, which is pretty cool. He's visiting next week so that means we won't be able to see each other... Why did you roll your eyes?"

"It's not like you want me to be here anyway."

"Next week?"

"Ever." Her heart was beating faster. She looked away while she begged him internally, *Please, please convince me that you love me.*

"I don't understand what's going on..."

"Do any other women visit?"

"Like Carrie?"

"No, not *like Carrie*. Other women." There were tears ready but she blinked them back. She looked at him to see if he was being purposely stupid. If he wasn't, she thought, he was doing a pretty convincing job.

"Then no. Why?"

"You're lying!" It came louder than she'd wanted. A few heads turned their way.

"What is this? Samantha..." He leaned forward and Sam moved back.

"Lindsay." Sam waited. His face was expressionless, unreadable. He said nothing. "We saw her yesterday. She was boasting about it."

"Lindsay? Lindsay isn't other women."

"What is she then?"

"I don't know, she's just… I've known her pretty much forever."

"Why did you lie, then?" The pinch of confusion on his face made her feel like a madwoman.

"I didn't lie. I just never thought to mention it. She hasn't been here in seven months. Why are you so mad about this?"

They sat rigid, unspeaking. Sam unwilling to back down and Dennis confused, possibly wondering what he'd got himself into, she thought, disgusted with herself. But it was happening now, the worms inside her were squirming, and she couldn't stop them.

"I just don't know how to trust you," she said, standing to leave.

"No, Samantha, that's not fair." He was standing too, a hand against the divide.

"Neither is lying to me."

"Come on… There's only you."

"I have to go." She turned her back on him. By now all eyes were on them, and a guard was moving toward Dennis.

"Don't go!"

She looked at Dennis as he banged the divide with the heel of his hand. She couldn't tell if he was upset or angry. The guard had his hands on Dennis's shoulders, trying to force him back into his seat. Dennis's chains sounded like smashed glass.

"Marry me!" he shouted as Sam burst into tears. "I love you! Marry me!"

* * *

"Can I tweet it? Holy shit, we need to get you a ring! Will you wear a wedding dress?" Carrie pulled Sam in and hugged her again.

"Yes! How do we do the ring thing? I don't know about wedding dresses, I thought I'd just buy something colorful?"

Sam and Carrie got into the car and shut the doors. The radio switched on as Carrie turned the key but she turned it off. Sam had told her everything: how she'd said yes, how the guard had loosened his grip on Dennis's shoulders and patted him, congratulated them quietly but sincerely. How she hadn't seen Dennis smile like that since she met him.

"Maybe we should get the ring first and *then* we'll tweet it, with a picture."

"Do I buy the ring?"

"Fuck off, we'll work it out, you will not be buying your own engagement ring. How did he propose? Tell me about it again."

Sam glowed. She edited the part about the argument, unwilling to peel away the costume of sanity she wore around Carrie, feeling they were getting closer and worried if she revealed herself in her true form she might drive her away. On the way to the Danson house, to interview Dennis's father, they passed the sights that were becoming familiar: the field of solar panels reclining in the heat, the stretch of water along the side of the road in which they'd seen a tail slink quickly underneath, so quickly they weren't really sure if they'd seen it at all. They drove through town and onward, off the main road and onto a dirt road, thrown about in their seats and wheels slipping on loose gravel. The trees whipped the windows as they passed and stones plinked against the underside of the SUV.

Sam's stomach started to weaken. She'd seen the Danson house in *Framing the Truth* but hadn't been prepared for how isolated it truly was. The only thing that kept the trees from growing over the road completely was the path forged by cars. Now that Dennis's father, Lionel, was disabled, the only cars that came through were those of the nurses who cared for him by day.

Everything seemed to be creeping toward them, enveloping them, suffocating, then they were released into a clearing, grass worn from car tires, the one-story house so familiar to Sam from the pictures she saw on the internet that she could place Dennis, age nine, standing in the patch of dead grass by the garage, unsmiling, blond fringe combed forward over his eyes, squinting in the sun. Except now, across the front of the garage, the word "MURDERER" had been sprayed in red paint. Signs of more graffiti were all over the house, sloppily painted over in the same off-white the rest of the house used to be, now graying with neglect.

They parked outside, the first to arrive, and waited for the rest of the crew. "You ready to meet your new father-in-law?" Carrie asked, which made Sam more nervous than she'd expected.

The house, Sam thought, had an Amityville

type of presence, its image weighted with horror, as though it knew what you were thinking. Lionel haunted the place and refused to move on although he was unable to look after himself, relying on more care than he could afford, Medicare barely contributing at all. Instead Lionel made money selling stories here and there, as well as running a cheap website capitalizing on the "Christian spirit of giving" that allowed people to donate to help pay for his care. Occasionally he would sell family items on eBay, old T-shirts of Dennis's or half-finished schoolbooks. He was not ashamed to profit from his family's notoriety. Lionel argued that there were plenty of sites donating money to his murdering son while he was left to rot out in the sticks.

Sam and Carrie were reluctant to go inside and so spent more time than necessary fiddling with equipment from the SUV and taking exterior shots on a handheld camera. Eventually a woman called from the front porch. She was a nurse in light blue scrubs. She asked them if they'd like anything to drink and if they wanted to wait inside. The sheepish expression they shared with her made her laugh, so she walked over with her arms crossed and told them, "I know he's bad but he isn't *that* bad."

Inside the air was thankfully cool. An air-conditioner rattled in a corner, though there was a medicinal stink of sickness and antiseptic cream. Lionel was in a wheelchair pointed toward the television. A bag of yellow fluid hung behind his shoulder, and it was unclear whether the fluid was leaving or entering his body. He didn't turn when they entered but stared fixedly at the television.

The nurse came back with two glasses of iced water, flipped off the television and said, "Lionel, come on now, you knew we had company today. Least you can do is offer them a chair or something." She turned him around. Sam tried not to stare at the leg that stopped halfway down, or the swollen foot covered in a bandage, or the missing big toe.

"Carrie," he said, not extending a hand.

"Mr. Danson," Carrie said. "How have you been?"

He gestured, sweeping a hand like a girl presenting a prize car on a game show. "Just great, thank you. Diabetes, in case you were wondering." His voice was rough with smoke.

"Well, I'm sorry."

"Probably get more sympathy from you if I was in prison though, right?"

"Come on, this again?" Carrie smiled. He reached into his pocket for a packet of cigarettes.

"You're new," he said, putting a cigarette between his lips. His eyes rolled upward, shark-like, looking at Sam.

"Yes. Hello! I'm Sam."

"You're the girl," he said, exhaling. "Yeah, I know things. You're the one who's visiting. English girl, they told me. I thought, 'What kind of woman would want my Dennis after all this?' They said you seemed normal." He laughed. "Normal?

Well, it's not like I can tell if you're any different. You gonna say anything?"

"It's, um, nice to meet you," Sam said.

"And I'm Myra," the nurse said, taking each of their hands in turn and shaking firmly, "but he's too rude to tell you that. I've heard of your film but I've never watched it."

"That's why I like her," Lionel said.

"I didn't know Lionel was a celebrity when I started working here." She winked. "It explains why he's so much of a diva."

Lionel seemed to soften when Myra teased him and Sam was more thankful to her than she could express. Even Carrie seemed subdued in his presence. Sam thought how intimidating he must have been when he was younger, what a brutal force he would have been in this tiny house. Hate burned in her throat but she sipped water and talked with Myra while Carrie moved chairs to make room for the lighting. The rest of the crew arrived and alleviated the pressure with their fussing and shouting.

Sam stepped back into the hallway and looked around, noting the layer of grime that seemed to cover everything, the dead flies trapped behind the screen on the kitchen window. Inside you could feel the misery, as if everything were soaked in it. She checked to see no one was looking and made her way down the hall, glancing into Lionel's room: medical equipment left stagnant; the bed surrounded with bars so he couldn't roll out. She moved on to the room at the end, knowing what it was. The door was shut so she checked over her shoulder again before turning the knob, opening it slowly. The room was tiny, a single bed squeezed in and piled with boxes of miscellaneous junk. It smelled damp. She imagined Dennis cramped in this room, door closed, listening to the sound of his father's boots in the hall outside and praying they wouldn't reach his door. She opened a drawer and looked at the clothes. Not many; mismatched socks.

She took a notebook from the shelf and flicked through until she came to the final page with any writing on it, about halfway through: an unfinished essay about the Second World War, the corners of the page filled with skulls and misshapen swastikas. It looked like the notebooks she marked as a teacher, from boys who masked their fear with meanness, boys who were twitchy and suspicious as snakes. They were the boys who came to school with holes in their sweaters and frayed ties, who scratched at their heads and pretended not to care when chairs screeched away from them, or when someone said, *Miss, he stinks!* Any pity she might have felt at the first sight of Lionel vanished, replaced by a sickening hate, and the taste of acid at the back of her throat.

"Tell us about your involvement with the police?" Carrie started the interview and was looking at the iPad, one leg swung over the other, relaxed. "You spoke to them twelve hours after Dennis's arrest for the murder of Holly Michaels. Can you tell us what you said?"

"They were asking me where Dennis was that

night and I told them I didn't know. I told them honestly: he was never home anymore and that it didn't surprise me he was up to no good. Of course then I didn't know exactly what kind of trouble."

"Were you concerned they didn't call you while he was being interviewed? He was, at the time, a minor. Still a few months from being eighteen. By law he should have had a parent or guardian present but they kept him for twelve hours before they even called you."

"Like I said, the boy was never around. So I didn't know he was at the station until they called me. From what they told me they weren't keeping him there. It was all informal and he was free to go any time, but he never asked."

Of course Lionel didn't know, Sam thought. He was just a drunk, selfish and cruel.

"You don't think he was intimidated?"

"Nothing scared that boy."

"You scared him, didn't you?"

"That's what he says." Lionel shrugged. "Never seemed scared to me. Didn't scare him enough to keep him out of trouble."

"How did you try to discipline him?"

"Same thing my dad did to me. I'd ground him, give him a clip around the head if he needed it. His mother, she was too soft to do anything. Right away, soon as he could walk away from her, he was walking into trouble. Broke her heart. I tried my best."

"So did the cops interview his mom at all?"

"Kim wasn't much for talking to people. She

was pretty out of it by the end. She kept crying, telling them he was a good boy, always defending him. When she found out what he did she couldn't handle it."

"Why did you believe he killed Holly?"

"The cops were so sure. Wasn't like they had any reason to lie about it. I don't believe in these conspiracy theories."

"You let the cops in here, right? More than once. Without a warrant."

"That's right. I didn't have anything to hide. Now, Dennis…"

Sam drove her nails into her palms. It was his self-righteousness that really got to her. When she watched the documentary he had been such a villain that she'd wondered how much the film had been edited to portray him as such. Surely no father could be so callous, so snide? Here she saw it happening, how real it was, and she'd question his mental faculties if it wasn't for the slimy way he smiled every now and then, obviously enjoying it.

Carrie paused. "Why are you so willing to believe what the police say and not what your own son says?"

"They're the law. I believe they're good people."

"And Dennis?"

"Hm." Lionel stopped and looked toward the window. When he breathed his chest rattled with catarrh. "I never knew Dennis. Don't think anyone could."

"Do you think you could have tried harder? Do you have any regrets?"

There was a pause. Lionel licked his dry lips and closed his eyes for a second.

"Think maybe I coulda saved those girls, if there was something I could've done different."

"Girls?"

"Well, that's what they say. That he killed all those missing girls. I don't know about that, but somehow it feels like I'm responsible. I pray for them, pray for forgiveness for my part in it."

"You seem so sure they're dead. Why is that?" Carrie asked.

"It's been over twenty years and not a peep from any of them. I've personally never met a woman alive capable of keeping that quiet."

Carrie smiled and shook her head. "But seriously," she said, leaning in, "this is important. Why is it that this town is so sure those girls are dead? The investigations were all so sloppy, like they didn't even try to find them. Don't you ever wonder why, say, Kelly's stepdad was never formally questioned?"

"It's a small town. We know each other round here. He was a good man, a good father to those kids."

"He also had a history of violence toward women. His ex-wife filed for a restraining order during their divorce."

"Bitterness. She was a bitter woman. His money was good enough for her though, right?"

"What about Fintler Park?"

"What?"

"The trailer park home to about two hundred ex-cons. Most of them sex offenders. You know, guys who have to live one thousand feet from schools and playgrounds and stuff? Informally known as Fiddler Park. Well, after Jenelle disappeared the cops went door to door and asked guys where they were or if they might have seen anything suspicious. A couple of guys said, now you mention it, there was this new guy, kept himself to himself, packed up and left about one, two days after that night.

"One guy even took it upon himself to go down to the station and make an official statement. We have a copy of that statement; the guy seemed to be genuinely concerned.

"You'd think they'd follow this up, right? Maybe look at the records for recent releases, contact some parole officers, check the whereabouts of anybody suspicious, that kind of thing."

"I'm not sure what they'd do. I'm not a cop and I don't watch those shows, either. But I assume that the choices the officers made were more educated than you or I can guess at."

"Well, you'd *think* that. But instead it's just a lead they chose to ignore. It went no further. And there are literally dozens of examples of this stuff: witnesses who saw Lauren getting into a blue truck, family expressing concerns over a neighbor who paid too much attention to their teenage daughter, violent stepfathers. None of it was followed up. It's like half the town knows something we don't. Like they don't want us to know what it is. It's as if the town decided Dennis was trouble and that was enough, they didn't want to look any further. Maybe they were afraid of what they might see if they did?"

Carrie looked him in the eye. Sam held her breath and felt the crew around her doing the same. Lionel looked right back, unblinking. He parted his lips to speak but changed his mind. Carrie had him, Sam thought. And for all Carrie complained about being in front of the camera she seemed to enjoy the drama. Lionel bent forward and held his face in his hands. He parted his fingers and looked up at Carrie. Sam's skin began to prickle with goose bumps.

"And we would've gotten away with it too, if it weren't for you pesky kids."

Lionel laughed, his head flung back, the wheelchair creaking beneath him. The room collectively sighed, someone behind even emitting a low groan. Carrie didn't smile, didn't take her eyes off Lionel.

"You think there's some conspiracy?" Lionel continued. "That all these people could keep something like this a secret for all these years? Let me save you some time; often, the most obvious answer is the right one, the one that's right in front of you all along."

"It seems like you and I have different definitions of what's 'obvious' here."

"Why doesn't that surprise me?"

"We aren't talking about a conspiracy; we're talking about incompetence. We're not talking about hundreds of people, but a few people who didn't do their jobs, who had things they needed to hide and who had a vendetta against a troubled teenage boy—"

"This series is supposed to be a sequel, isn't it? Because all I'm hearing is the same old shit from your last movie. Looks to me like you're making yourselves a reboot."

Sam admired Carrie's cool in the face of Lionel. She thought he might be the worst human being she had ever encountered.

"We're just trying to establish the facts, Mr. Danson. Or people's *versions* of the facts, as it seems."

Lionel sighed and looked out of the window for a moment before turning back to her.

"There's no versions. No stories. There's just what people around here know to be true. It's something people from out of town will never understand because they weren't there, they didn't know the families like we did. And they didn't know Dennis. Not as he was then, before you people made him what he is. Before he learned to look like the prey and not the predator."

8

Extract from *When the River Runs Red*
by Eileen Turner

The trial took place between April and July
of 1993. By then, Dennis was eighteen and
would be tried as an adult. This, Dennis
knew, meant the judge could sentence him
to the death penalty at his discretion. Com-
bined with aggravating factors—such as the
victim being under twelve years old[18]—and
the emotional nature of the case this meant
that in the event of a guilty verdict the death
penalty would be a likely option. However,
as they entered the courtroom on day one of
The State vs Dennis Robert Danson, a guilty
verdict didn't seem likely at all.

The prosecution's case would rely entirely
on witness statements that fell apart easily
under further questioning. A key witness for
the prosecution was a local woman named
Bonnie Matthews who claimed Dennis had

---

18 Florida Legislature, 1993.

confessed to her, at her house, on the night of Friday, May 29, 1992. It was a night when Dennis was at an away game against the Jacksonville High School football team. As the defense questioned her she backtracked, admitting that she might have the wrong date, even though she'd been so sure of it in her initial statement.

Transcript: Statement from Bonnie Matthews to Red River County Sheriff's Department

Officer: Can you tell me why you're certain the date was May 29th?
Bonnie: It was the day after my birthday. I remember because there were still balloons—my friends put up balloons for my party—I remember because of the balloons.[19]

In addition, the defense asked why Bonnie, age thirty-six, was hosting a seventeen-year-old boy at her house on a Friday evening and why it had taken her over four months to bring this confession to the attention of the police. Within twelve minutes of questioning her account of the supposed confession, it was dismantled so thoroughly that the defense—and Dennis—felt there could be no way for the prosecution to overcome it.

Similarly, when a cellmate of Dennis's,

---

19 Transcribed from recording of statement made in October 1992.

Jason Gunner, was called to the stand, the details of his story were quickly torn apart. Jason claimed Dennis confessed that he had killed Holly Michaels by way of manual strangulation, which was confirmed as the cause of death during the postmortem. However, Jason further described how Dennis had confessed to mutilating the body, carving a pentagram into the flesh to "make a deal with the devil so he didn't get caught."[20]

This salacious statement did not hold up under questioning, nor did it correlate with the facts of the case—there was no pentagram or any "carving" on Holly's body.

Dennis was aware of the spectacle of the trial. Each day he entered the court with his head lowered, passing through a crowd of baying reporters all shouting his name, his attorney shielding him from the flashes of their cameras. Once inside the court the spectacle faded and in the quiet, the long stretches where the lawyers spoke quietly with the judge at the front of the room, the recesses, the endless rituals and procedures, Dennis felt a profound boredom. When he wasn't listening to people tell stories about him that weren't true, or cringing while his life was put on display and picked apart, he could only think of how desperately he wanted to get out

---

20 Taken from court transcripts, April 1993.

of there. "I wasn't thinking right," he says now, "I even used to think jail was better than the court because at least there I could read, I could talk to the guys or even do chores. Anything had to be better than court."[21]

Dennis's attorney—Charles Clarkson—assured him it would be over soon. Dennis wondered what would happen to him when it was over. On day one he had looked over his shoulder to the faces of those in the gallery, his parents not among them. It had been months since he'd spoken to his mother or father, who had all but disowned him as they believed him to be guilty. When this was over, where would he go?

The defense called upon forensic experts, each of whom concluded they could not with any confidence place Dennis at the scene of the crime. As the trial came to its end Clarkson assured Dennis that this was a done deal, he would be out in a matter of weeks. But public perception of Dennis didn't change, even in the face of such strong evidence of his innocence. Perhaps this should have been a warning for the defense, that in this case an argument of reason and fact would not be enough. They were competing with pure emotion, and there was no reasoning with feelings.

---

21 Interview, Altoona Prison, 1996.

Red River Tribune
June 12th, 1993
It has been revealed that just last year Danson's attorney was responsible for the release of known sex offender Lyle Munday. Mere weeks after his release Munday went on to rape and kill an eleven-year-old girl. The attorney, Charles Clarkson, stated he was not regretful about his part in this tragedy, saying at the time, "It's a tragedy that Lyle went on to take a life, I think of it every day. But he was found not guilty by a jury for a crime he didn't commit. We can't imprison people for crimes they have not committed, we can't speculate that someone may commit a crime in the future and lock them up, this isn't how the law works."

In the eyes of the public, Charles Clarkson was a defender of child killers. The people of Red River feared what might happen if the jury were to find Dennis not guilty. Would their own children be in danger?

The defense stayed their course. They asked the jury, could you find Dennis Danson guilty beyond any reasonable doubt? Not whether they liked Dennis, not whether they found him untrustworthy or cold or suspicious. Simply, looking at the evidence presented to them, could they say with absolute certainty that he killed Holly Michaels? "I couldn't," Charles Clarkson said. "I urge you to think this through, carefully, without any personal bias. The evidence is not there. Dennis *could not* have killed Holly Michaels."[22]

The jury deliberated for just six hours. "Guilty," the foreman said. Some started clapping in the gallery. Dennis felt "blindsided"[23] by the verdict and returned to jail unable to fully comprehend the outcome. Then, the next day, he was taken to the warden's office. His mother had been found in the garage, her skin duck-egg blue. The car had been running all night. By the time they found her there was nothing they could do. The warden said he was sorry, his voice low, eyes softened in solemnity, and Dennis was taken back to his cell.

The funeral took place without him, his father not willing to sign the papers that would allow him to attend under police supervision. There was no privacy to mourn. Instead, Dennis felt himself go numb. Even at his sentencing he stood only half present, not even sure he cared what would happen anymore. He'd learned to tune out the monotonous voices in the court; they became like white noise to him. So when a group started to cheer in the back of the room he snapped to life and looked at his lawyer, his eyes wide with hope. But his lawyer took his shoulder and squeezed, shook

22 Court transcripts, closing statement, July 1993.

23 *Framing the Truth*. Florida: Carrie Atwood, Patrick Garrity, 1993. VHS.

his head, *no.* The judge called for order but a man shouted, "Tell us where they are! Only God can judge you now!"[24]

---

24 *Framing the Truth*, Atwood, Garrity.

9

The money Sam's grandmother had left her was running low. She'd underestimated how expensive it would be and now she needed to be careful or she wouldn't be able to afford the flight home. She said it out loud, "Home," and felt nothing. The house in Bristol was empty and she thought of renting it out, but even that would require a trip back and she wasn't sure that it was something she could handle. There was no reason for her to go back except the money. And what would she do when she got back there? She'd left her job, her home, her family. Everything that mattered to her was here now.

She checked the mirror. The dress for the bachelorette party Carrie was throwing her looked good but her face was still puffy from crying on the phone to her mother that afternoon. "What are you doing?" her mother had asked, strains of hysteria in her voice. "What are you thinking?"

Sam kept trying to tell her about the miscarriage of justice, the gentle man Dennis was, the group of friends she was with who were so happy for her.

"It's a fantasy. You can't possibly know anything about this man," her mother said.

"His name is Dennis," Sam said.

"It doesn't matter whether he's innocent or not."

"Of course it matters!"

"He is in prison. They will execute him." It hurt, the way her mother said it.

"No! They won't! Mum, you have to understand how big this is. This petition has hundreds of thousands of signatures—"

"Oh, what good will a petition do. Samantha, be realistic. I know you aren't as stupid as this."

"Even if he's never released, even if… I will still love him. I still want to be his wife."

"Why? I don't understand. Why?"

"I love him."

"What are we supposed to tell people?"

"Tell them the truth. Everyone else in the world understands what's going on here."

"I'm just…ashamed. I feel so deeply ashamed. If your grandmother were alive to see this—"

Sam hung up, lay in bed and wept until her phone finally buzzed with a message from Carrie, reminding her she'd be there at six. Sam got up and ran the shower too hot, forcing herself to stay under, the spray hitting her back, until it hurt enough to forget. Once ready she sat on the edge of her bed and tried not to sweat her makeup off before she'd actually gone outside.

"You look hot!" Carrie told her when she arrived. They went to a nearby chain restaurant where balloons tied to bar stools quivered in the air. Road signs, guitars and antlers decorated the walls. The crew clapped as they arrived and each came over to shake her hand or hug her, say their congratulations. Sam took a seat in their booth, sliding next to Patrick, squeezed in further by Carrie. Her cocktail arrived with a sparkler and as it burned down the crew hushed into an organized quiet. Carrie presented her with a ring box. "This is from all of us. It's not big or anything but you know..."

The engagement ring was white gold, a small diamond, delicate and simple. Sam couldn't look at anyone for fear of crying again but Carrie hugged her. "Dennis is like my little brother! And you make him so happy. It's the least we can do, really."

"I can't—"

"Oh shut up, you totally fucking can," Carrie said, and that was it.

Sam slipped the engagement ring onto her ring finger and posed for a photo at Carrie's insistence, then more photos with Carrie at Carrie's insistence, who posted them on the series's official Twitter page. As she sat down Carrie put a veil and a plastic tiara on her head. The grips tugged her hair and dug into her skull, the warmth of the alcohol and the sugary fruit punch were giving her a buzz and she felt present, alive.

They'd had an argument a few days ago, Carrie and Sam, a small one. Sam was talking about Lindsay. Perhaps she *had* been talking too much but Carrie had groaned, loud, interrupting her.

"Oh my *God*, girl, you need to stop. Seriously. It must be so stressful inside your head."

"Actually, yeah, it is," Sam said. "If you wanted

me to stop you could've just said. You didn't need to be so…about it."

"I've tried to change the subject about a thousand times. It keeps coming back to Lindsay. Like, who cares? Dennis doesn't even care. He forgot she even visited until you brought it up. He has *no one* most of the year. You want to stop her visiting just because it makes you feel shitty? Dennis won't say it but I will: it's pretty fucking selfish, Sam, and borderline crazy. Dennis loves you, I love you, so please, for the love of God, let it go."

"I get it, but—"

"No, uh-uh, just let it go."

"It's not that easy."

"It really is."

"Fine."

"Thank you."

It left her embarrassed, tingling from shock, unsure whether Carrie and Dennis shared secret conversations about her. What else had they said?

They ordered food; platters of nachos and wings to share, huge racks of ribs and burgers.

"By this time tomorrow, I will be Mrs. Dennis Danson!" Sam said, draining her cocktail. The crew cheered. She had the wedding dress—brightly colored, modest, a flattering wrap around her waist and the three-quarter-length sleeves the prison dress code demanded—and the legal team helped with the paperwork. It wasn't the wedding she might have dreamed of, she admitted, but then she'd never cared much for weddings. The group around her were easy with their joy, which helped quell the rise of doubt that swelled in her every now and then. Dread like rising floodwater, cold and insidious.

The music was loud and everyone in the restaurant was shouting to be heard over the music, a child threw a tantrum and a group of waiters gathered to sing a birthday song to an embarrassed-looking teenage girl, her mouth twisted in a half smile. Patrick was telling everyone about a documentary he'd filmed in Iraq when Jackson Anderson appeared and stood at the end of the table. Surprised, everybody stopped to greet him. He leaned in and gave Sam an awkward hug. "I heard about your engagement, congratulations!" She thanked him and scooted over to offer him a seat but he stayed standing, his hands in his pockets. "I just thought I'd drop by and introduce myself before we film tomorrow."

"Tomorrow?" Sam slid her tiara off her head and put it on the seat.

"We're filming the wedding. We spoke to Dennis about it, and we agreed it was best for the story we're telling, to show the other side of Dennis, because without your relationship he just comes across as…kind of one-dimensional. You know?"

All of a sudden Sam felt sick, her stomach swirling with booze and fried food and fear. Instantly the dress she planned to wear seemed dowdy, her skin cratered and blotchy, waist thick and lumpy.

Behind him two smiling waiters held a chocolate cake lit up with sparklers and a candle in the shape of a bride and groom. Sam blew out the candle as Jackson swung a chair around, adjusting the cap on his head.

Sam had seen Jackson before, when he was interviewed on BBC News in a beige room with drawn curtains. His adaptation of a young adult dystopian trilogy had grossed hundreds of millions. Yet it was obvious he wanted to be taken more seriously: the way he carried himself, answering questions about the films with pretentious statements. She hadn't liked him then and she didn't like him now as he straddled the chair, his cap low even indoors. "He thinks he's Ron fucking Howard," Carrie had said once.

"So anyway, we'll be filming—since you need witnesses anyway—and then we'll leave you be for the rest of the visit. I think you get an hour? That's pretty good, right?"

"I don't know. Isn't it, um, kind of personal?" Sam looked to the others for support but they were all gazing elsewhere, twirling cocktail umbrellas and twanging tiny plastic swords, sticky from maraschino cherries.

"You are…OK with that…right?" Jackson asked.

"Yeah, I'm just surprised," Sam said. "I thought I'd have to sign something."

"No need, it's all sorted out, so I'll see you all tomorrow, bright and early. Carrie, *loving* the cuts you sent. Keep it up." He swung the chair back to the empty table next door and left. The group let out a synchronized breath.

"It's like all our dads just showed up trying to

be cool in front of our friends," Carrie said and the group laughed in relief. But as they cut the cake, Sam's buzz was subsiding to tiredness and she wondered how to excuse herself, wanting to be alone.

The next morning Sam lay waiting for her alarm to go off. Her dress hung on the back of the door, the tags dangling at its side. She'd stayed out too late and drunk more than she'd meant to. Throughout the night she'd run to the bathroom and emptied her stomach until it was just the water she forced down her throat that came back up, fibrous and warm. The grease from the food still seemed to be clinging to her skin.

She brushed her teeth too hard and spat blood, scraped her hair into a ponytail and wound it into a tight bun, stabbing hairpins deep and hurting her scalp. Her skin was gray and her eyes looked watery and tired. The dress that had felt so good the week before seemed frumpy and clingy, but she ripped the tag off, threw it in the bin and decided she would look at herself today only if absolutely necessary. On her way out she bought a bottle of Dr Pepper from the machine, so bubbly it burned her tongue, and waited for Carrie in the shade of an awning in the parking lot.

When they arrived in the visiting room they were greeted by the crew, headed by Jackson, along with a court official who was there to perform the ceremony.

"Here comes the bride!" Carrie said.

"Nervous?" Patrick looked as pale as she did.

"Excited?" Jackson said, peering through a camera.

"I'm OK, I'm fine. Where's Dennis? Is he…"

"Five minutes," said one guard. "My daughter *loves* your movies, she's gonna be so jealous when she hears about this!"

"Well, leave your details with Carrie there and we'll get something sent out to your daughter," Jackson told him.

Carrie nodded and waved, turned to Sam and mouthed, *Dick*, flicking her eyes in Jackson's direction.

Sam felt a familiar sensation, like something pulling away from her body, as if she wanted to run. Instead she breathed deep, fixed herself to the ground. Cold feet, she told herself; everyone gets cold feet.

They heard Dennis before they saw him: the chains, the squeak of a heavy metal door like some kind of B-movie monster. He was in his whites and he'd had his head close-shaved, which made her want to reach out and touch the short hair that glittered under the light. But they would be separated, as always, by the plastic. No exceptions, not even on their wedding day.

As they both sat down at the divide Sam looked at his arms, new contours that hadn't been there before, the way his stomach seemed to stay flat even as he leaned in. "Have you lost weight?" she asked, pulling her dress down over the roll on her own stomach.

"Yes," he said, pleased she'd noticed, "I've been working out, since you got here. I didn't realize how bad it had gotten."

"You look…great. You do."

"Thanks." He glanced down and twisted his arm to look at the muscle. "You look different too. Are you tired?"

"Um… Yeah, we had a bachelorette thing last night. I kind of drank a bit." Sam looked away from him, face on fire.

"O-kay." Jackson clapped his hands and rubbed them. "We ready?"

"Hey," Dennis said, "sorry. You look beautiful."

She raised her head and saw him pressing his finger to the plastic; she smiled and did the same.

As neither was religious, they had decided on a civil ceremony. A justice of the peace, a man in a beige suit with a blue tie, read from a plastic ring binder, the spine of which creaked as he turned pages and shifted on his feet. The room felt unbearably stuffy and sweat collected in Sam's cleavage. As the official spoke, she and Dennis looked at one another. She said her vows, listened while he said his, looked into his face and wondered what he was thinking, whether he felt as weird as she did, repeating those words that didn't suit her lips, that hung wooden in the air. She wished they'd written their own vows, so she could tell him she would be there whether he was ever released or not, that she would fight for him until all was lost, that she loved him so much it hurt her bones.

They could not kiss. Prison rules dictated they

must stay on opposite sides of the divide, no exceptions. The crew hugged Sam and gave Dennis their congratulations before excusing themselves.

What might have been, Sam wondered: their first dance and feeding each other cake, a wedding night tangled in white sheets. Instead they talked, and he asked her to promise she wouldn't leave. "I thought I could handle it," he said, "but I can't, I need you to stay."

"I haven't got enough money. I'll need to go back to England, work for a while, save up."

"Please," he said, "I spoke to Jackson about this and he said he could get you some work here. Just stay a couple of months. I live for these visits…"

"What about my visa? I don't think I can work…"

"We're married now; you can become a citizen. Stop looking for reasons you can't stay. You're my wife now, I need you."

10

A few weeks later and Sam was living in a cheap apartment on the outskirts of Gainesville paid for by Jackson Anderson. He occasionally threw her menial tasks to make her feel as though she wasn't freeloading, things like reading and replying to emails from fans of *Framing the Truth* or looking through the social media comments and sharing anything related to the upcoming series with their followers. But this took up only a small part of her day, the rest of which she spent watching TV or wandering the aisles of Walmart unable to decide what to eat later, forgetting what she'd come there for in the first place and buying the junk that made her teeth feel furry and her stomach ache.

Carrie moved back to LA after they'd finished filming. She called regularly and stayed on the phone for an hour at a time. The silence was like a vise after they hung up. Sam became obsessed with watching people from back home on Facebook, who seemed to be posting exclusively to her, showing off, new babies and new jobs, mud runs and restaurants. She hadn't looked at Mark's page since he left her, and now she looked at it just to hurt herself, scrolling through it for any suggestion of her, but it was as if she'd never existed.

The message boards weren't kind about her marriage to Dennis. They called her a groupie, and were more concerned with the progress, or lack of progress, in the case. They wanted a different judge, one who wasn't biased, and organized a petition for someone new to work on the appeal. Sam wondered how she'd ever admired these people. Didn't they think that Dennis's lawyers would already have done this?

Once a week she visited Dennis, brushing her hair and smiling, with less and less to talk about.

Then the cycle broke, her phone ringing in the middle of the afternoon. "I've got news," Carrie said. "Are you sitting down?"

Carrie explained: the tips line had received a call from a man who wanted to remain anonymous. He told them he'd been in prison for child sex offenses for ten years and saw the billboards months after being released. When he was first arrested, he said, he shared a cell with a man called Wayne who had told him how there were girls he'd killed the cops never knew about. He'd said they'd even found one of them and he thought for sure he was going down for it but the police never came. The shock made him stop killing for years after that. At first, the caller said, he thought Wayne was lying about it because who's dumb enough to admit being a fucking serial killer to some guy he just met? But it stuck with him because of the eerie level of detail and the pride Wayne took in the story.

What color hair does Wayne have? the agent on the tips line asked. The caller told them it was salt-and-pepper but in patches it was a thick, wiry black. Wayne had also boasted about how he hacked off a lock of the girl's hair as a keepsake but burned it on the side of a road weeks later for fear of the cops finding it. The girl had scratched him up pretty good, he'd had to cut the fingers off, and it made Wayne sick to his stomach at the time, the caller said, though he had laughed when he recounted it, and made the sound of splintering bones with his teeth. Wayne told the caller he never felt satisfied and every time he got a girl it always escalated. It's how he got caught, eventually; he'd hung around at the crime scene too long, and it all got messy. The caller didn't like the guy, was glad to be moved away from him. He wasn't a snitch, he said, but it was hard for a sex offender like him to get employment and the reward money looked good.

The detail about Holly Michaels's hair had never been released to the public, how a knife had left a nick in the back of her skull where he caught her while cutting off a lock. It sent Dennis's team into overdrive, and they started putting together new applications for the testing of evidence and calling authorities. Eventually they tracked down a Wayne Nestor, who had been transferred from the prison the caller mentioned to another in Kansas. He'd been arrested for the violent murder and rape of several young girls. So his MO was in line with Holly's murder, as was the fact that at the time he'd been residing in Ocala driving a truck that took a route right by Ocklawaha, the cheerleader camp where the sighting of the flasher had originally been reported.

Carrie waited long enough to make sure it was worth getting excited about and made everyone promise she could be the first to call Sam.

"So? What do you think?" she said now.

"What happens next?" Sam was chewing her thumb. In the mirror she saw herself: pale and dark-eyed, a cluster of acne on her chin.

"We get Holly's shirt retested. If Wayne's DNA is on there it'll flag up on the CODIS, the criminal database, and, well, Dennis could be released within days of that happening. I mean, it's fucking *him*, right?"

Sam stopped pacing, held the back of a chair and tried to focus. The room around her was littered with discarded clothes, dirty glasses and plates, empty food cartons.

"Days?" she said.

"Yeah, bitch, days. Exonerated. There was never a shred of Den's DNA on Holly, so if we can put a name to the blood on her shirt they'll have no choice but to release him. And this caller has given us strong grounds to get that shirt retested."

"How likely is it they'll let us test the shirt?" Sam no longer knew what she wanted. Was it this?

"I'd say it's pretty likely. They've turned us down before but with an actual, probable suspect to test it against? The lawyers are fairly confident right now. Patrick and I are coming back with the crew to Florida on Wednesday so we don't miss anything. I'm so psyched right now. How are you feeling?"

If the appeal fell through and the authorities refused to retest the shirt, there'd be nothing left to hope for. "Has anyone told Dennis yet?"

"No. There's been so much fact-verification to do in case this guy was just some loser or fantasist. No one wanted to get his hopes up."

"I don't really know what to do." Sam sat, her legs weak beneath her.

Whatever was next, she had to be ready for it.

11

Sam got the news just three days later. Wayne Nestor had admitted to the prison pastor that he'd killed Holly Michaels. Seeking redemption, he confessed to everything, repeating it all to a video camera with his lawyer at his side, and asking for nothing but God's forgiveness. The courts retested the T-shirt and got a positive match. Finally, Dennis was to be released. After so many disappointments and false starts, life was suddenly on fast-forward.

The night before Dennis's release, Sam had a drink to calm her nerves, then several more, until her phone was waking her up and Carrie was saying she'd be with her in twenty minutes. Sam asked if it could be more like an hour and Carrie laughed, as if the idea Sam could wait even another second was unbelievable.

She washed in the sink, sprayed herself all over with deodorant until the small, windowless bathroom was cloudy with it. She applied fresh makeup over yesterday's makeup, pulled a dress from the laundry basket, wrinkled and musty, and shouted when Carrie arrived in just fifteen minutes. She threw things at random into an overnight bag, not knowing where she would be staying, not believing Dennis would be with her.

Carrie beeped the horn again and she screamed, "Fuck! Fuck! Calm the fuck down! I'm coming!"

There was a coffee waiting for her in the cup holder in the car, giant, just cool enough to sip. Carrie was talking about her girlfriend, Dylan, who complained about the demands the case was putting on her. "I don't think she really believes he's getting out, you know? It's tough. I've been doing this for twenty-one years now but we've only been together for three. Dylan doesn't get it sometimes. It's so good to have you, you *get* it."

Sam kept agreeing as she watched the car dealerships and discount stores zip by. They seemed to be hurtling toward the court. Carrie's voice was manic and hard to follow, the radio noise was getting louder, her chest was tight, and her ribs clutched at her lungs like fists.

"Stop, we need to stop, I can't breathe," she said.

"Now?" Carrie looked around, and Sam realized she couldn't change lanes to get to the shoulder.

She rolled down the window but the air was more suffocating than inside. She undid her seat belt, letting it snap back, the sensor pinging and screeching, urging her to buckle back up. But she was pulling her dress away from her chest, nails dragging over skin cold and clammy. "Stop, stop the car."

Someone leaned on their horn as Carrie pulled over sharply. Sam opened the door before they'd stopped, tumbling out onto the rough ground beside the highway.

"What's wrong? What's happening?" Carrie ran around the front of the car and squatted. She held Sam's hair off the back of her neck and told her to slow down and breathe deeply.

"I don't know if I can do this," Sam admitted after she'd calmed slightly.

"With Dennis?" Carrie stared at her, eyes wide with anxiety. Sam felt awful knowing what pressure she was putting on Carrie but she couldn't help it.

"It's happened so fast."

"It has, I know. Look, you don't have to do this. I can take you home, or you can come and wait somewhere else, take it one step at a time. You can come to the party later? Or...just say what you need and we'll do it." Carrie's voice was sincere and she rested a palm on Sam's back as her breathing slowed.

"I have to be there. I'm his wife."

"Bullshit, he'll understand. It's a lot for him, too, you know? I'll explain it to him."

"No...it's not that I don't want to... It's just— I'm scared." The truth was that Sam had grown used to their relationship as it was, separated by a thick Plexiglas wall. Without that wall, Sam worried, there was nothing to stop them from hurting each other, as she and Mark had done. Or all the other things people did to each other: walking away, lying, switching off their phones, little cruelties she and Dennis had so far been shielded from.

"Of course you are. So am I! This is fucking crazy."

"You're scared?"

"Yeah!" Carrie laughed nervously. "I've known him twenty years and I've worked all that time for *this* moment. It was my whole life and now suddenly…holy shit! I should already be there, you know that? I was supposed to be filming this but I just couldn't handle it. I decided I wanted to go with you because, I figure, you feel about as crazy as I do right now. I know it's difficult to process; I'm feeling it too. It's normal to feel like this." She looked anxiously at her watch. "It's up to you. We can do whatever you want to do."

"I'll come," Sam said. Her breathing was even. The fear was still a knot inside her but she imagined other things, the good things, how Dennis would lean toward her and kiss her, the heat of his mouth, pressing against him so tightly she'd feel the beat of his heart on her own. Just to touch him, finally, and be touched—wasn't this what she'd always wanted?

"You sure?"

"Yes."

Carrie held out her hands to help Sam stand. Together they got back into the car and carried on toward the court.

"Are you sure you're OK?" Carrie asked.

"Yes, I'll be fine."

"I know." Carrie smiled at her. "You've got to be *strong*, hook that eighteen-wheeler up to your balls and pull."

* * *

There were crowds around the courthouse, separated by striped barriers. On one side a hundred or so people with Dennis Danson T-shirts, signs that read "Justice at last!" and "EXONERATED" and "End the death penalty!" On the other a small group of vocal protestors: "Still guilty!" and "WHERE ARE THEY DENNIS?" and "LET US GRIEVE!"

Closer to the doors stood reporters, some speaking live to cameras, some waiting around looking bored and restless, paparazzi poised and boisterous. Sam shielded her face as they walked through the press, strangers calling her name. When they entered the courtroom, it was fairly full, and the rest of the crew were at the front right, filming, with Jackson Anderson seated behind Dennis's lawyer. Carrie suggested asking people to move so they could sit closer but Sam wanted to stay further back. "You go," she said, but Carrie took a seat next to her and held her hand in both of hers.

"Who are all these people?" Sam asked.

"Who the fuck knows. Fans, I guess."

To Sam it felt like an invasion. The atmosphere was rowdy, and conflicted with her long-held fantasy of this event in which there'd be only the crew and herself, a somber atmosphere and a softly spoken judge. Dennis would be freed from his cuffs and he would turn to her and approach her tentatively. He would hesitate before kissing her— he would be shy, of course—and the kiss would be gentle, his hand on her cheek, fingers in her hair. Dennis would be reluctant to take his attention away from Sam but he would, eventually, to thank everyone, to shake hands and hug and answer questions. Then he would excuse them, take her by the hand to their car, and they would be alone, unable to keep their hands off each other, driven to whatever hotel the team had booked for them. They'd spend days locked away together, entwined and slick with sweat. They'd start making love when they were still half-asleep, grinding lazily against one another, the covers tangled around their ankles.

A cheer snapped her out of her daydream. The crowd shifted and she saw Dennis, his back to her, in an oversized beige short-sleeved shirt, a brown tie slipping out of the collar. He spoke to his lawyer next to him, who was grinning and kept shaking him by the shoulder. Sam almost called out to him, wanting him to turn around and see her, but he stayed facing straight ahead. Near the front she saw the back of a woman's head, hair long and straight. *Is that Lindsay?* she asked herself, a rush of cold up her neck. She almost asked Carrie but stopped herself, thinking of the fight and the feeling of sickness it left her with for days.

The court was called to order, the judge entered and everyone stood, the murmuring fading to a few whispers and the squeak of shoes on the polished floor. There were formalities, the words brushing past Sam, her eyes on her husband's back, watching his shoulder blades move under his shirt. Carrie squeezed her hand and she started to listen, trying to focus over the sound of blood in her temples.

"As someone who has worked in the justice system for over forty years, I've seen the best of our system and, unfortunately, the worst. It is not infallible, and this does not excuse the huge miscarriages of justice the likes of which we see here today. For a man to lose twenty-one years of his life, a young man, is a loss for which there is no compensation.

"That more children lost their lives due to the failings in this case is another tragedy. As a country we should mourn the incalculable loss that has stemmed from this evil.

"It is not my place to tell you how to live your life now, Dennis, but I hope that you can find peace through everything and live well, be happy, do good and spread kindness where you have been denied it yourself.

"So it is with both sadness for your loss and joy for your redemption that I hereby exonerate you of all charges…"

There was a roar of applause, and people swarmed forward. The woman in front was swallowed by the crowd, and Sam saw her duck as someone pushed past her. Dennis and his lawyer stood and Sam saw Dennis bow his head a little toward the judge. With everyone standing Sam lost sight of Dennis for a moment, but Carrie pulled her along by the arm, wading through people to get her to him. When they saw him again he was having his cuffs unlocked by an officer who shook his hand vigorously before he turned around and was embraced by his attorney. Everyone wanted to shake his hand. Dennis grinned as he was pushed forward by the men around him but when he approached the swing door he looked back over his shoulder as if someone were about to stop him.

It was hard for Sam to tell if he had seen her, the way his glasses reflected the light and shielded his eyes, but when he turned toward Sam his smile seemed to waver. She and Carrie continued toward him. Heads turned and she heard someone murmur, "Wife."

He held his hands out to her, palms up, and she touched them. Their fingers laced together and he pulled her a little closer.

She tilted her head to kiss him and he flinched. "Sorry," he said and quickly pushed his lips against hers. She realized she had her eyes open and squeezed them shut; their teeth clacked together and his breath was stale. When she pushed her tongue into his mouth he jumped, startled. Sam disconnected, and they both looked away, wiping their lips.

As they left he held her hand, fingers laced together, his knuckles digging into hers. They were hit by a wall of noise beyond the heavy doors, reporters shouting questions all at once. Dennis's lawyer read a prepared statement. "Justice…innocence…" she heard. "Freedom…support…fight…"

Police escorted them to a silver car with blacked-out windows that Jackson had arranged to take them to the hotel. They opened the door and Sam climbed in, eager to get away from the journalists who cascaded forward, shouting to be heard. But

new york

12

It was a two-hour drive to Orlando. Sam rested her head on Dennis's shoulder and listened to his voice through his chest, deep and echoey, her head bouncing up and down when he laughed. The radio played songs he'd never heard before and occasionally a news bulletin about his release would play and they'd all laugh: Dennis, Sam, Jackson; even the driver, every time. Jackson was talking about filming something later, something for the end of the series to complete the story, and Dennis was complaining that his clothes were itching.

The hotel at which they were staying was surrounded by palm trees. There was a fountain outside the foyer that Dennis stuck his hands under as though he were a child again, water pouring cold over his skin. Every few steps he tripped over himself. "I think it's these shoes," he said. "I haven't walked around in real shoes for a long time."

The staff met them outside and led them through to the conference room, which was decorated with a banner that read "CONGRATULATIONS." Cakes, chicken wings, tortilla chips, oysters on crushed ice, hummus and celery and carrot sticks were piled onto tables draped in white cloth. People Sam recognized from magazines came toward them and she watched them hug Dennis and hoped he'd introduce her, but he didn't. Some of the crew arrived behind them. There was more clapping, and Patrick hugged Dennis roughly, patting his back hard. The staff were bringing out more food, hot food: fries and burgers and pizza.

"We didn't know what you'd like so we decided to order everything," Jackson said. "Help yourself."

Dennis piled a plate high with fresh fruit and vegetables, telling everyone that they were the things you craved most in prison, that you dreamed of the high-vitamin stuff, of fruit that dribbled down your chin, of the crunch of cold carrot sticks: these would make your mouth water when you lay in bed after a day of dry chicken nuggets or hot chili con carne that sank like a stone in your stomach.

Sam stood on the sidelines holding a plate of food she didn't eat, watching the double doors for Carrie. They'd been rushed out and into the car so quickly Sam hadn't had the chance to look for her, and now she felt terrible for every moment of Dennis's first day of freedom that she was missing. As people passed they chirped, "You must be so happy!" and Sam smiled, trying to ignore the lurching guilt she felt in Carrie's absence, as if Sam were never meant to be here and had stolen her place.

Waiters offered Dennis wine, beer, champagne, but he asked for sparkling water, which made him hiccup as he drank. Jackson handed him several bags. "Clothes," he said. "We figured you'd need a new wardrobe."

Dennis disappeared for a while and came back in blue jeans, an open-necked checked shirt with a white T-shirt underneath. The light was dim but he kept his shaded glasses on. Jackson told him, "We'll need to get you some new glasses, some Warby Parkers or something."

"Some what?"

"Designer glasses, you know?"

"Sure, sure, OK." He was rubbing his arms again and someone went to ask the staff to turn the air-conditioning down.

Some people recognized Sam and talked to her, told her again how happy she must be, and she nodded and watched her husband move around the room. Some of the women there were beautiful, more so than she'd thought they would be in real life. She'd hoped that actresses were only as beautiful as the makeup and lighting that shrouded them, but up close she could see it was for real.

"Hey!" A hand pinched her shoulder. It was Carrie, holding Sam's overnight bag.

"Oh my God, Carrie! I'm so sorry! I lost you…"

"Don't be stupid. This is crazy, huh? Where is he?" Carrie put the bag down at Sam's feet.

"He's right there."

"Oh shit! Look at him! In *jeans*!" She called to him, "Dennis!"

He turned, put his glass down on the table and walked toward her with arms open.

Carrie shook her head and covered her face but

kept walking to him, into his arms, letting him hold her at first and then holding him back, her face pressed into his clean white shirt. He lifted her and she laughed, leaned back, her arms around his neck. Sam looked on, sick; it was how it should have been for them, in the courtroom. Dennis was speaking into Carrie's ear, his cheek pressed against hers. A few people sighed, *Aww*. Draining her glass, Sam smiled, tight-lipped. They looked, she thought, entirely connected in a way she'd wanted to feel. It was almost like a betrayal.

Eventually they disconnected, he kissed her on the top of her head and she smoothed her hair in what Sam assumed, rolling her eyes, was faux-bashfulness. They continued to talk as if she wasn't even there. She looked at the overnight bag and started to kick it across the carpet, toward the table. When it was concealed behind the white tablecloth she started to walk over to them, refilling her wine glass as she passed a bottle. It took some concentration to walk in a steady line but she felt confident in the clarity of her thoughts, the certainty of her emotions. She stood near them and waited for one to notice her and invite her into their circle.

"This is such a trip, Den. I can't… *Look* at you! Oh my God." Carrie was touching him, frequently: a pat on his arm, another quick hug, adjusting his collar after it was left askew by another quick hug.

"Thank you, really."

"No, don't, because I will literally cry."

Sam watched them embrace again and stepped forward, closer.

"Sam! Can you believe this?" Carrie said, turning to her at last. "He looks great!"

"I know," Sam said.

"So what's next for you guys? You going to take her on a date or what?"

Sam smiled and looked at Dennis, but his face was serious, concerned.

"I don't really have any money. I have…three dollars. They gave me my wallet back, look." From his pocket he pulled a navy Velcro wallet. Inside were three dollars and a library card.

"You don't need money, dude," said Carrie, laughing. "These people will take care of that shit. Have you been up to the room yet?"

They shook their heads.

"It's like Christmas up there," Carrie said. "Listen, if you guys want to get started together somewhere else you can stay with Dylan and me in LA for a while. You'll be getting a lot of offers for TV, so it's something to think about, maybe?"

Dennis and Sam made noncommittal noises and shared an awkward glance, not knowing what they would be doing in the next hour, let alone the coming months. Then Sam's mind started racing again, thinking about how, soon, they would be alone together, and she couldn't hear what Carrie was saying or what Dennis replied with while she watched him, stared at the way his fingers curled around a glass, the way his other hand moved to the back of his neck, how he stood and gestured in ways she'd never seen before.

Other guests were circling and craning their

necks to see if Dennis was available. Soon he was occupied with others and Sam looked pointedly away from Carrie, spiky with irritation.

"Is everything OK?" Carrie asked in a voice that sagged with the knowledge she was not.

"Not really," Sam said, vague, a sigh.

"OK, you're acting like a dick with me. What's going on?"

Sam immediately felt sick with herself, and apologized. "It's just...you're all over each other and it's like he doesn't even want me around. Doesn't he like me? What if he doesn't anymore? Now he can have anyone."

"Stop! You're freaking out over nothing. You're like his first girlfriend and you're his wife, that's a pretty big deal. He's only *all over* me because he doesn't really think about it; it's nothing, you know? It's been like five hours, give it some time."

Sam knew Carrie was right but even so, she couldn't stop the creeps, the worms that wriggled. She wanted to ask Carrie, *Why would he like me? Even I don't like me.* But she couldn't.

So she walked around with him, just to stay near him. Jackson introduced him to various people, Sam following, silent and seething each time no one introduced or acknowledged her. She drank more, held on to Dennis's arm, wanted him to herself, but people just kept approaching. Dennis went to the bathroom and left her standing at the end of the buffet table. She saw Katy Perry and tried to take a photo covertly but the phone slipped from her hand. She squatted to pick it up and check it was still functional. There were hundreds of notifications and missed calls. She closed one eye to focus but the words seemed to sway.

"What are you doing?" Dennis helped her up, holding her elbow.

"I have so many messages!"

"You're drunk."

"I know, I know. It's just this is so *weird*. Don't you think this is weird?"

Dennis glanced around him. "You're embarrassing yourself. Perhaps you should go to the room."

"Will you come with me? We've hardly even talked…"

"It would be rude if I left."

"But I want to spend time with you!"

"You should really go to bed," he said, walking away. "We'll talk later."

13

Sam opened the door to their room and stopped, amazed, looking at what people had sent for Dennis. Inside were piles of gifts: a stack of white Apple boxes with a note that said, "Enjoy the rest of your life! Johnny Depp." There were baskets packed with grooming products and wrapped in sparkling cellophane and foil streamers, crisp shirts and suits hanging in zipped covers, and flowers everywhere with gift cards for designer stores tucked in like love notes.

Sam ran her hands over everything, dying to open the sealed envelopes, turning the box for an iPad over in her hands. Instead she lay on the bed and looked at the room-service menu. Inside, another note, "Tab's taken care of—Jackson."

She had a shower and ordered a Coke and a mineral water, then called back and ordered a pizza. Her mother had been calling; her Facebook was, for once, alive with notifications from people who had seen her on *Buzzfeed*: "Hey! OMG, I can't believe it! Haha, haven't spoken in ages, let's catch up, are you coming home soon??" Not ready to deal with anything she switched off the phone and buried it in the bottom of her bag.

The room spun a little, so she took deep breaths and put a damp cloth over her face. After a while she sat up and half watched a double bill of *Real Housewives of New Jersey* on TV, ate her pizza and let sobriety creep up on her until she felt worried again over how poorly everything was going. Finally, having kicked the pizza box off the end of the bed, she fell asleep, the damp cloth on the pillow beside her head. It was two in the morning when Dennis knocked on the door.

"I can't get this thing to work," Dennis said, waving the key card. "Why is there pizza on the floor?"

"Sorry about that." Sam smoothed down her hair but it felt matted, like straw to the touch. "Look, look at all the gifts!"

Dennis got into bed, kicking his shoes underneath it as he did so. "The pillow's wet."

"I had a headache and…are you OK?"

"I'm tired. You've really made a mess in here."

"I'm really sorry." Sam got in next to him, put her head on his shoulder and he put his arm behind her neck. He turned the TV off and the room fell silent. He sighed. They lay together in the quiet; she rested her head on his chest and listened for his heart but all she heard was the gurgling and growl of his stomach. She tried something, a hand over his torso, hard, rising and falling with his breaths, wanting to feel close to him. To make it real.

"I'm sorry, babe, I'm tired." He moved away.

"This has all been a lot to take in. I'd like to just get some sleep."

Sam blushed. "I understand," she said and got up to brush her teeth.

When she came back his clothes were folded neatly on the chair at the dressing table and a bare shoulder poked over the sheets. As she pulled the covers back he rolled toward her; she saw light hairs on his chest.

"Listen, don't take this the wrong way but do you think we could just…for tonight, maybe could we have our own rooms?"

"But why?" Sam pulled her bathrobe tight and crossed her arms over her stomach.

"I haven't slept in a good bed in more than twenty years. Actually, maybe not ever. And this is all really fast, you know? I just—"

"Do you want me to sleep on the sofa?" Sam wanted to turn the lights off so she could cry, quietly. So he didn't have to look at her.

"Are you sure?"

"It's fine! Honestly."

"Well, if you're sure you'll be comfortable… And could you turn down the AC while you're up? Here." He threw her one of the heavy down pillows, the one with the damp patch.

In the wardrobe Sam found a fleece comforter and made her bed on the sofa, lying curled, neck bent. She ached to be nearer to Dennis, and watched his form in the dark, but she thought of how the bed must feel to his aching bones and knew this was right, even if it hurt like hell.

"It's so quiet," he whispered.

"Yeah." The silence soothed her and eventually she too fell into a light sleep.

Rustling woke her up at just past nine in the morning. In the corner Dennis was searching through a bag of clothes.

"Good morning," he said without looking up. "I need something to wear to the gym. Do you think they sell anything here? I'd really like to work out."

"Call the front desk. They'll know."

"Right." He went to the phone. "You want breakfast?"

"Do they have eggs Benedict?"

"I'll order. You should shower, you don't look so hot right now... Hi, can I get—"

As he turned his attention to the phone Sam gathered her wash bag and makeup and ran to the bathroom. Inside she studied the lock. Did married people lock the door when they showered? She decided they did not and left it unlocked, but as she put one leg into the bath she changed her mind and quietly, slowly, turned the lock until it clunked into place.

After her shower she dressed in the bathroom, shy with the sensation of only the door between her and Dennis.

Back in the room Dennis was piling his gifts into different categories: electronics went on the dressing table, clothes into drawers and wardrobes, cards on the bedside table. The food arrived with newspapers and coffee. They ate in silence, the knife and fork awkward in Dennis's hands, the shrill scrape of cutlery on plates. When he finished eating he went back to the cards, opening and reading each one before putting them back in their envelopes on the dressing table.

"Don't you want to put those out?" Sam asked.

"Clutter," he said. "Look, a check for ten thousand dollars." He laughed.

"That's...so generous."

"I don't even have a bank account." He folded the check and put it in his little blue wallet.

There was a knock on the door and a concierge dropped off a bag of gym clothes. "I'll see you in an hour," Dennis said, and left.

All the times Sam had pictured their first night together—knotted limbs, lazy half-asleep sex while he kissed her collarbone and told her how much he loved her—she'd never once considered it would be like this. She pushed the trays of food outside the door and fell back onto the bed, her neck aching from the sofa. The pillow still smelled of him. She buried her face into the linen and inhaled. She could wait, she told herself, she'd have to.

14

Dennis was in a better mood after the gym. He walked into their room with red cheeks and glowing skin, ran a hand over his hair and a fine spray of sweat flicked into the air; he dropped his soggy shirt into an empty brown bag and disappeared into the shower, the lock clunking as soon as the door shut. Sam picked the T-shirt up and smelled it. It still had a chemical-tang of newness, the sweat didn't smell of anything, and she let it fall, disappointed. Before he came back she positioned herself with a book in what she hoped was a cute, unself-aware pose, her dress tugged up slightly too high. She tried not to look at him when he emerged from the bathroom, a towel tied around his waist.

His back was striped with scars, some raised and shining pearly white.

"What are those?" she asked, putting her book down and marking the page she wasn't reading.

"What are what?" He pulled on underwear beneath his towel, like a girl at the beach.

"The marks on your back." *Scar* felt like a dirty word.

He looked over his shoulder as if he was checking what she was talking about.

"Those"—he pulled the towel over his shoulders
to dry his neck—"are the scars my dad gave me. He
used a belt. He only beat me really bad one time.
Most of the others were pretty tame."

Sam imagined running her hands over the scars,
how Dennis might tremble slightly, and how she'd
hold him and he'd know he was safe. Instead, an
awkward silence loomed over them both while he
chose from the bags of designer shirts and covered
himself up. Eventually she turned the TV on just
to break the silence.

But when she did he pinched the bridge of his
nose and squinted. It was just like prison, he said,
that thing quacking away in the background 24/7
as though people were afraid to hear their own
thoughts. Sam switched off the TV and tapped
away on her laptop, looking enviously at the unopened MacBook Air on the dresser. Her computer
was scuffed and scratched. She was looking up
news about Dennis too, looking at the pictures of
them both outside the court: him, light dripping
over every angle in his face; her, hair chalky with
dry shampoo and the shadows creating shapes on
top of her own shapes that made her look like a
beanbag.

"Um, Dennis?" she asked.

"What?"

"In court yesterday, did you see Lindsay?"

"Lindsay?" He looked up at her and frowned.

"Yeah. In court."

"No, I didn't notice. Why? Was she there?"

"I thought I saw her but I wasn't sure."

"Oh. Would it matter if she was?"

"No! No, I just thought I recognized her."

"If she was there, wouldn't she have come up to me? Seems kind of weird that she wouldn't."

Sam agreed, though she was almost certain it had been Lindsay. She let it drop and continued scrolling through the pictures of them both. She felt stupid for asking. For a while she managed to stay in the articles but the temptation to scroll down to the bottom of the screen proved too great. Soon she was crying.

"What's wrong now?" Dennis asked, folding the paper, still on the same page about his release.

"The things people have been saying…" She turned the computer toward him. "Look at this."

"'Wow, he's hot, no offense but he could do better…' That's not that bad."

"Yes it is! Look at this one!"

"'W-T-F—'"

"It means 'What the fuck…'"

"'What the fuck is he doing with her?! He could murder my vagina!!' What does *murder my vagina* mean?"

"It means they want to fuck you and they think I'm too ugly for you!"

"And it bothers you?"

"Yes!"

"Maybe you shouldn't read this stuff, then."

Sam buried her laptop in the bottom of her bag along with her phone, feeling exposed, judged, just

as she had when she read the posts about her on the
message boards after they'd got married. It was as
if the moment she'd married Dennis she'd agreed
to be scrutinized mercilessly and always compared
to the man by her side. It was a deal in which she
could never be evaluated favorably, no matter what
people thought of Dennis. That burden felt suddenly heavy and she wondered why she had ever
thought this would be easy.

When the phone rang Dennis answered with
his full name and told the operator to put the person through, his voice high with a happiness Sam
wished she could make him feel. When he'd hung
up he told Sam to get ready: they were going to
meet Jackson and the manager he'd recommended
in the bar downstairs. While he checked himself
over she stood behind him. He took off his glasses
and Sam stared at him in the mirror, at the flecks
of gold and green in his blue eyes. She thought of
kissing his neck but did not.

Downstairs, in the empty hotel bar, Jackson
greeted them both, introducing them to a man
named Nick Ridgway, who was almost as tall as
Dennis but softer, his belly too big to button his
suit jacket.

"First off, congratulations!" he said, slapping
Dennis's arm. "Fantastic news, fantastic. A lot of
people out there have been rooting for you. I've
been reading about it all day. You're one popular
guy right now."

"Thank you," Dennis said.

"I've known Jackson for many years and I was

really flattered he'd recommend me to you, because I know how much he cares about you and your situation. I just wanted to have a chat with you today to see what kind of things you'd like to get out of a manager and what I think I could offer you."

Dennis explained he didn't have any specific plans, but that Carrie had said people might want to interview him. Nick laughed and told him he was being modest. He threw out a list of people who were lining up to talk to Dennis, and read some of the messages left at reception.

"They've been screening calls from everyone so you could have your privacy while you adjust to things! How's that going, by the way?"

"I'd like to go out sometime today..." Dennis said.

"Have you seen it out there? There's a crowd of fans and journalists! By all means go out but have a strategy and right now I wouldn't talk to anyone! Give nothing away for free. I've been looking at the reaction to your case, and we need to capitalize. We need to start working on building your brand."

"My brand?"

Jackson and Nick explained how Dennis needed to market himself in a certain way to maximize his return on this situation.

"In a settlement you'll get a million, couple of million, I guess. If you play this right, do the media, write the book, market yourselves as a couple, too, I really think you could get upward of ten million out of this. You know, if that's the way you want to go?" Nick leaned forward, his belt buckle digging into his belly.

Dennis agreed that it was, and they discussed what he might expect to happen over the upcoming days. Nick told them both to pose for pictures if people stopped them and to give them a simple but unrevealing quote: *We're very happy* or *We're enjoying this new time together.*

Dennis held Sam's hand, and she moved her thumb in circles inside his palm, feeling the room rock her gently. She stopped listening to what was happening around them, sleepy with pleasure. Then Dennis stood abruptly.

"Get that cell phone set up. You're going to need it!" Jackson told them as they left.

Back in the room they opened the iPhone.

"How do I turn it on?" Dennis asked, turning it over in his hands. Once it lit up, he prodded at the screen, holding his finger down too long, clumsy, highlighting things, closing pages. Finally he became frustrated and handed it to her. Together they created his first email address, *dennisdanson1975@icloud.com*, and took his library card, aged dollar bills and the check out of his old wallet and put them into a black leather Dolce & Gabbana one. Sam tapped her number into Dennis's phone and got her own back out of the bag. There had been more missed calls, and a few more emails. Work had called. She told him to call her so she had his number.

"How do I...?"

Sam smiled and guided him through it.

She showed him the internet, and explained Twitter, Google, blogs, YouTube, apps. She enjoyed how closely he leaned in to look at the screen and how he looked at her when she showed him something that impressed him.

Dennis tweeted for the first time. "Hi," he wrote, and eight thousand people retweeted it. Sam sighed. Her most successful tweet had had seven likes and three retweets and she'd thought it was cutting-edge satire. They read about themselves on *Huffington Post* and they took a selfie, Dennis sliding his glasses off and looking seriously into the lens. She took an eyelash off his cheek and tried to kiss him when he said, "Can you show me the loggers thing?"

"Bloggers!"

"Whatever." He stared at the screen and Sam tried to find a blog about him. It didn't take long to find someone who thought he was obnoxious. "What does this mean?" he asked.

"Right," Sam exhaled. "'Cis-gendered' means you're a man who was born a man. 'Hetero-normative' means you're, you know, straight. 'White-male privilege' means—why are you laughing?"

"It's funny!" He took back the phone and tried to scroll down. "How do I go to the bottom? To lower?"

She showed him again how to stroke the screen, that he didn't need to press down. She felt a band tighten around her skull. Suddenly it seemed as though she'd spent the whole morning teaching him how to ignore her.

"Wow," he said when he reached the end of the blog post, "this girl really hates me."

Sam stood and rubbed her eyes. "Before we meet Jackson and everyone for the interview, can we go to the pool or something? I feel like I need some fresh air."

15

At the pool, people recognized Dennis straight-away. Most looked for a beat too long, then turned and spoke in whispers that made Sam twitch. Dennis shook hands with people who came to say congratulations and posed for a couple of pictures. Some girls moved their towels off a pair of sun loungers for him and he pulled his shirt over his head and left it there. The sun dazzled Sam and she shaded her eyes watching the surface of the water glitter in the light. Dennis leaned down to feel the heat of the stone patio with his palm before walking into the pool.

In the movie, she thought, he'd dive. Instead, he was awkward in the water, each stroke producing a noisy splash as he powered boisterously from one end to the other. Against the side he stopped and breathed heavily, beads of water rolling over the contours of his muscles. Finally he took his glasses off and left them on the edge of the pool before diving under and emerging in the shallow end.

That evening, as they got ready for dinner and an on-camera interview with the crew, Sam saw Dennis's pale skin had turned a hectic red.

"Maybe we should have worn sunscreen," she said, rubbing lotion into his skin. She did it awkwardly, with the tips of her fingers, sensing the tension in his back as she did so. How long had it been since he was touched like this? She felt a degree of power, which surprised her. He sucked in his breath at the cold between his shoulder blades. "You're just not used to the sun anymore," she said.

"You think?" Dennis said, shrugging her off.

They left for dinner with his skin still greasy with cream. His mood was dark and he hissed in pain as Sam brushed his arm when she pressed the button for the elevator. But when Carrie, Jackson and Patrick greeted them in the lobby he lit up. "Look," he said. "My first sunburn in twenty years!" He rolled up his sleeve to show them and they winced in sympathy.

They'd booked a table in one of the hotel restaurants, in a room lit a soothing blue and with a pianist in the far corner. Although the others were sharing a bottle of wine, Dennis wanted only sparkling water. When Sam looked at the wine menu she felt him watching her and decided she would stick to Diet Coke.

"How are you enjoying yourself, Dennis?" Patrick asked.

"I'd really like to go out sometime. Around. I don't know."

"Must be pretty overwhelming," Carrie said and everyone murmured in agreement.

"We've been looking at the internet," Dennis said.

Carrie laughed. "You're going to have to be more specific, Dennis."

"At what people are saying. You know—comments."

"Oh man, don't look at the comments," Patrick said.

"Why?" Dennis asked.

"I have to admit, I've been looking," Carrie said, taking out her phone, flicking through with one thumb, still moving risotto from her plate to her lips. Sam forgot it could look so easy. "Have you seen Twitter? Most of it's OK but…" She started to read aloud: "'Where are the white filmmakers getting black men released from Death Row? Hashtag white justice.'" There was an uncomfortable laugh. "This shit is trending now. I lost, like, an hour of my life to this earlier. I mean, I guess they're right but what can we do?"

Dennis put down his fork, the blood from his steak soaking into broccoli. "I know. It's like it's a bad thing to be a white male right now."

There was a pause, exchanged looks, and the table exploded with laughter. Sam was first frozen in horrified embarrassment but eventually it got to her too, and she joined in.

"Oh my God, you sound like my grandpa." Carrie leaned across and held Dennis's wrist. "But, like, seriously: don't *ever* say that in public, OK?"

Dennis nodded, confused, a new redness to his cheeks on top of the sunburn.

Back in their room, the crew set up the camera and a light, positioned the chairs in front of the drawn curtains. Carrie powdered Dennis's face with some of Sam's makeup, and angled the light to try and make him look less pink. She and Patrick had decided to interview Sam and Dennis together first.

"What's it like to be together so suddenly?" Carrie asked.

"Surreal," Sam said, holding Dennis's hand, the arm of the chair digging into her elbow.

Dennis nodded. "Yeah, surreal."

"It's like…getting to know each other all over again."

"Right, yeah." He squeezed her hand.

"I didn't realize how much he's missed, being in prison. We've spent a lot of time today just looking at the internet, learning to use a computer and a touch-screen phone."

"I didn't even have an email address."

"You don't realize how much has changed until you have to explain it all."

"It's going to take a lot of getting used to. But Samantha, she's so great, she's patient. I'm so lucky."

When they were being observed they really existed, Sam thought. They were the couple she wanted to be. He was vulnerable and she was caring. She wondered if they were always like this and she was too caught up in herself to realize it.

Then it was Dennis's turn on his own. They moved the empty chair so that he would be in the center of the shot and Carrie smiled warmly before she started the interview.

"How does it feel to be a free man, Dennis?"

"Uh, it's…overwhelming, I'm overwhelmed by everything."

"Can you tell us about what it's like to adjust?"

"Right. It's difficult to adjust. I hadn't slept in a couple of nights because I was moved from Row so suddenly. I knew there was a chance I'd be released. I've been sleeping in the same place for twenty-one years, and I was used to the noise of it. Then I was here, in a different bed. It was so quiet in the hotel room last night I couldn't fall asleep for a while. I'm used to the noise. The bed was so comfortable I couldn't stop thinking about it. Last night we had a party and I was up late and that made me sleep until nine which is something I haven't done in a long, long time.

"I'm a little disoriented, I guess you could say. Part of me wants to go out, anywhere, to the mall or something. And part of me can't figure out what I would do when I get there. Some people have given me checks but I can't cash them, because I don't have a bank account. I can't drive, I never got my license. There are so many gifts in this room, everything I need, but I don't know how to use a lot of them."

Carrie asked him about what he'd missed most while being in prison; they talked about food and clothes and the gifts he'd been given. Then Carrie became serious. "Do you have any anger or hatred toward Wayne Nestor?"

"Is he the guy who actually killed the girl?"

"He killed Holly Michaels, yes."

"Not really, no."

"Why?"

"Anger isn't productive."

"Do you think it's good her real killer is finally brought to justice?"

"Yeah."

"Can you say that?"

"Say what?"

"That it's good her killer is finally brought to justice. For the camera."

"Oh, yeah. Sure. It's good the real killer is finally brought to justice."

"What are your plans? Do you think you'll turn your long incarceration into something positive?"

"My manager said we can probably capitalize on it."

"No, I mean… Will you be campaigning? Will you work with any groups?"

"For what?"

"A reform of the justice system, abolishing the death penalty."

"Oh. No, I mean, there's nothing wrong with capital punishment, just so long as the guy actually did it."

Carrie waved her hand. "Cut, cut. Dennis, I can't tell if you're being serious."

"I am serious," he said, frowning.

"After all that you've been through, you honestly think the death penalty is a good thing?"

"Not a *good* thing…" He thought about it. "It's necessary, isn't it? I'm not saying it's good."

"Oh, Dennis." Carrie sighed. "What are we gonna do with you?"

16

The crew left early the next day and it was finally just them, Sam and Dennis, learning what it was like to be together. They filled out forms to get Dennis a bank account, everything complicated by his missing life, the fact he had no previous addresses, no current address for that matter, no history. They cashed the checks he'd been given and they were desperate to go out but didn't know where to go, or what to do. So Sam booked a car to take them to the Florida Mall, where they wandered with their fingers knitted together, Dennis posing for photographs when people asked. Others turned and took pictures as they passed by, arms extended, Dennis looking confused until she explained they were taking selfies.

Magazines interviewed them as a couple and Sam kept a copy of every piece, tucked in her suitcase to stay flat. Dennis signed a six-figure advance with a publisher for two books, one autobiography and one compiling his writings in prison, including the letters between Sam and himself. Sam agreed, but cringed at the idea of people reading her letters. They'd picture her, mousy and pale, alone in her dingy house, pouring her heart out to a complete stranger, she thought despairingly.

She googled her name constantly and pored over the comments sections. Some people questioned why a man like Dennis would ever love a woman like her. They used words like fat, ugly, basic, groupie. Others asked why any normal woman would want a man like Dennis. They said she had what was coming to her. They said she deserved it.

It hurt. Each comment rubbed away another layer of her until she was raw.

But when she cried, Dennis held her, and when they were out he linked his fingers with hers and he kissed her, his lips cold from the iced water he sipped constantly. He didn't say it but she knew he wanted to show people he did love her. And she thought that was all she needed; it would make up for everything else.

Once he had his ID, Nick booked Dennis for interviews on the late-night TV circuit, and told them both to prepare to spend the Christmas season in New York. There was also talk of another movie, based on Eileen Turner's book, *When the River Runs Red*.

"Jared Leto's going to be you," Nick told Dennis.

"Who?" Sam showed him a picture on her phone. "He doesn't look anything like me."

"They'll dye his hair! He's going to totally inhabit the role. He's going method so he wants to spend some time with you, observe you, learn what makes you *you*."

"Method?"

Sam explained.

"Absolutely not," Dennis said. "Seriously? No."

One evening he stopped outside the window of a jewelry store and told her to pick a ring, any one. "I never got to buy you one," he said, his hand on her lower back. Sometimes she felt dizzy from how happy he could make her.

Other times he was difficult, dark moods that swept in suddenly and made him quiet and inaccessible. They were together almost all the time, except for when Dennis was in the gym, or on the rare occasions one of them went for a walk or a swim by themselves. The hotel room became more and more cluttered, their whole lives packed into one space. They bickered and sniped and then spent silent hours lying still, loosely entwined, unsure what they were supposed to do or how they were supposed to feel.

Each night Dennis got into bed and Sam lay on the sofa. She would lie awake wondering why he didn't want to make love to her, whether there was something wrong with her, or if there was something else.

Neither had any clothes suitable for winter in New York, so they shopped more, spending money as if it was nothing. They tried on thick winter coats, lined with goose down. "I've never bought a winter coat before," Dennis said, putting his hands into the deep pockets. They took everything to the counter without looking at the tags, and he handed over a MasterCard and carried on talking, "Do you think it'll snow?"

"Maybe." Sam thought of Christmas lights and gloved hands and hot chocolate. She longed for the sensation of cold air, where outside was cooler than inside, her breath fogging in front of her face.

They took the car back to their room and piled their new clothes on top of the old ones. Sam knew she would have to call her mum back to explain she wouldn't be coming home for Christmas, and apologize for not calling in weeks. But so much had happened, so fast. She ignored the calls from work, and hadn't replied to the email they sent to tell her not to bother coming back at all.

Sam hadn't wanted to speak to anyone from home because she knew exactly what they'd say. Now she couldn't avoid it any longer, so she excused herself and took the call on the balcony, sliding the glass door shut behind her.

Her mother answered right away. "Sam?"

"It's me."

"Why haven't you called me back? I've been so worried."

"I'm fine, I'm still in Florida."

"I know! I've seen the pictures. You've been in all the papers. Our phone hasn't stopped."

"Then why did you say you were worried?"

"Because I don't know how you are. Or whether you're OK with him."

"We're happy." Sam leaned on the white balcony wall, watching a lizard skitter on the patio below them.

"I can't understand it."

"I love him, Mum."

"He scares me."

"Why?"

"You can't spend decades in prison and be a normal person. You just can't."

"But he is normal." Sam moved back into the shade. "He's sweet and kind and shy."

"But he's a murderer."

"He isn't a murderer, Mum. That's the whole point. They exonerated him."

Sam heard her mother sigh. "I know it ended badly with Mark but—"

"Don't."

"It doesn't mean you don't deserve someone who—"

"Mum, please!" Sam realized she was shouting.

"You didn't mean it, sweetheart. We know you didn't. If you come back home we'll find you help."

It went on. Sam kept her back to the patio doors so Dennis couldn't see how upset she was. She wasn't ready to tell him about Mark yet but she knew she would have to eventually. What if Mark sold a story—was that possible, now? Or if someone else did, one of his friends, maybe? Or even his mother, who'd called her from the hospital, using Mark's phone, and told her he refused to press charges but that Sam was never to contact him again. One moment, a slip, was all it had been. It wasn't her. It was the games, how Mark had played with her. How he'd said he loved her, but he hadn't meant it. And then she'd just… She shook it away.

They'd come while she was at work, cleared all Mark's things and posted the key back through the letter box. She wished he'd come back and trashed her house, cut her dresses, smashed a window, anything to show he was angry, or upset—anything at all. But in the end all he felt when he thought of her was fear.

Mark always told her, right from the beginning, their relationship was *no strings*. It was her fault when he hurt her. She understood that now. She'd known the rules and she'd ignored them, and pushed too hard. This time it was different, she told herself. Dennis was all hers. They were married; he was unquestionably committed. She wouldn't lose her mind again, not even for a second, even if she had to fold the bed covers and put them away every day before housekeeping arrived to make sure no one knew they weren't sleeping in the same bed. Dennis needed time, she knew. Time and space after the confinement of the past twenty years. He was so beautiful she sometimes forgot she was not. When he held her and his fingers danced just under the edge of her T-shirt, she would hold her breath and hope for more, and when he curled them back into his palm and turned away she would have to understand. He wasn't ready. That was all.

17

They left for New York a few days later. The flight
made Dennis grouchy; his ears popped on landing
and left him temporarily deaf, separated from the
world in a cotton-wool shroud. "What? What?" he
kept asking Sam as they navigated airport security,
smiling agreeably at all the things he couldn't understand from staff and passersby, nodding, *Yeah*.

A car took them to the hotel, where a doorman
greeted them with an umbrella to shield them from
the freezing drizzle that didn't fall so much as float
all around them. Their bags were loaded onto a cart
and Sam and Dennis made small talk as they took
the elevator up to the fortieth floor. Their room was
all reds and golds, and at the center of it all was a
huge four-poster bed with carved mahogany fix-
tures. They looked out of the floor-to-ceiling windows in the sitting area at the gridlocked traffic
and the light caught in the drops that rolled down
the glass.

Sam took Dennis's arm and put it around her.
"I love it here."

"It's cold," he said, pulling away.

"You're a curmudgeon," she said, smiling.

"Curmudgeon. Samantha, I'm impressed."

"When you say Samantha, I feel like I'm in trouble."

"Maybe you are," he said, and Sam felt it again, a kick of desire. Maybe it was a move, she thought. Maybe this would be where it happened, but then he started unpacking the cases, hanging shirts in the wardrobe. She left her clothes in her suitcase, and slid it under the bed so he wouldn't complain.

He took out his laptop and placed it on the desk in the sitting area. Sam tensed, remembering the determined tap-tap-tap of his one-fingered typing. For hours, tap-tap-tap, their hotel room silent, no television so he could concentrate. Dennis wouldn't let her read his autobiography, shifting his body to shield the screen as she passed. Whenever he left she fought the urge to peek, to see the only thing he kept hidden from her. How bad could it be? *All work and no play makes Jack a dull boy*, she thought.

The room had a couple of armchairs, a dining table and a chaise longue. Sam took a pillow and lay down on the chaise longue, her legs hanging off the end, so that she had to screw up into a ball to fit entirely.

"Um, Den? I don't fit on here." She straightened out again to demonstrate, and he looked around the room, his expression darkening when he saw there was nothing else. "What shall I do?" Sam tried to sound light, not hopeful, just agreeable, willing to compromise.

"I guess I've had a lot of good nights' sleep now," he said.

"Really?" Her heart beat fast.

"Where else are you going to sleep?"

She went to him, kissed him and let him pick her up and drop her on the bed. She pulled him on top of her, holding him there so she could kiss him again. She wrapped her legs around his hips and pressed against him, his tongue hot in her mouth. A noise escaped her, a moan she wasn't expecting. He stopped.

"Are you OK?"

"Yeah." She tried to pull him back.

"Did I do something?"

"No."

"You sure?"

"Yes."

He started to pull away. She sat up, clutched his shirt, but he stood and stretched. "I'd better finish this." He gestured to the clothes spilling from the case. Sam lay back, feeling her heartbeat between her legs.

His phone buzzed on the bedside table. "Can you see who it is?"

"It says unavailable," Sam said, holding it out to him.

"What does that mean?"

"It's a private number."

He held it in his hand and watched it until the buzzing stopped, passing it back to her with a shrug. As he folded another T-shirt to put in the closet it buzzed again. "Answer it," he told her.

"Hello?"

"Who's this?" a man's voice asked.

"Samantha," Sam said. "Who's this?"

"Is Dennis there?" His tone was short, almost angry.

"Um, who is this?"

"Tell him it's an old friend. He'll know what it's about."

"An old friend?" Sam held the phone out. Dennis stared at the screen for a moment before putting it to his ear.

"Hello?" He held up a finger and disappeared into the bathroom. Sam waited a second or two before tiptoeing over to the door and pressing her ear against it. She heard nothing, and sat back on the bed disappointed and anxious for him to come out.

Dennis reappeared a few minutes later, wiping at the phone screen with his shirt and rummaging for his charger in the case.

"Well?" Sam said, "Who was it?"

"Nobody." He plugged the charger into the wall, the screen lighting up as he connected it. "Someone I used to know. How would they get this number?"

"I don't know. How did you know him?"

"School," he said. "Did you give anyone my number?"

"Of course not," she said. "Why would I?"

"I don't know how he got it, that's all."

"You think someone's stalking you?" Sam was concerned, but he snorted.

"Don't worry about it. It's just weird, that's all."

"You want to go somewhere? We can get food or go for a walk."

"I think I'm going to go to the gym for a while," he said.

"Oh," Sam said. "OK." She watched him change, fold his old clothes into a neat pile in the empty suitcase, and pull on a gray T-shirt.

As he was about to leave he turned back and unplugged his phone. "Music," he said, and left. She looked at his headphones still coiled on the dresser.

18

The next day Dennis visited an ophthalmologist about the detrimental effect long-term imprisonment on Death Row had had on his eyes. Twenty-one years of looking no further than a wall a few feet ahead had made his eyesight deteriorate, and the lack of sunlight had made him sensitive to brightness. The doctor prescribed eye exercises and new lenses in the hope that Dennis would regain some lost vision. Every day Sam sat patiently with Dennis, moving a pencil slowly toward and away from his eyes, listening to him breathe, feeling the space between them thick with tension. He'd go without glasses where he could, looking across Central Park with his face wrinkled in pain until he had to put them back on. He got new designer frames that softened his face and Sam couldn't help noticing the way the optician seemed to spend too long making sure they sat right on the bridge of his nose, her hands almost cupping his cheeks.

He was told he'd receive the maximum compensation for his wrongful conviction—two million dollars—but his lawyers promised they'd sue for more. There would be extra compensation for legal costs but as most of the money for his appeals had been raised by supporters, Nick suggested they make a donation to the Innocence Project.

"Yeah, it's up to you. I don't know what else we'd do with it," Dennis said.

Nearer Christmas Sam stopped at the front desk and asked them if they could have a Christmas tree. "It's his first since he...came back, you know? It would be nice to make it special."

"No problem," the receptionist said, and booked them in for dinner at the restaurant the next night so the tree could be decorated in their absence.

When they returned the tree was glowing in the corner, two stockings hung underneath the television. Dennis smiled despite himself. "Come on," Sam said, pulling at his T-shirt. "It's cute."

"It's *too* cute," he said, kissing her on the top of her head.

Carrie and her girlfriend, Dylan, visited for New Year's. They came back to their hotel room for drinks after dinner, already loosened by red wine and rich food. Dylan wore her hair short, and had a smarter, more businesslike dress sense than Carrie. They were different in many ways—Carrie more artistic, Dylan more academic; Carrie so brash and flippant, Dylan more considered and serious—but they worked together in a way Sam and Dennis did not. Sam noticed how they moved, limbs like water running over each other, whereas she and Dennis often collided with mistimed kisses and clumsy elbows.

"This is nice," Carrie said. "I could get used to

visiting you in places like this. *Much* better than Altoona. Right, Sam?"

"It's been amazing," Sam said, taking Dennis's hand.

"You guys thinking of making New York your permanent home?"

"No," Dennis said. "Too cold."

Sam said nothing. She loved it here, and she didn't want to leave. Dennis often stayed in the hotel room, or walked only as far as the waiting taxi as a concierge held the door open for them, but Sam walked for hours, closed her eyes and smelled the air, sat in the windows of cafés and watched the people. She'd started smoking again, secretly, hugging herself against the cold. Spraying herself with perfume before going back into the room. She knew Dennis hated smoking. He was always complaining about the smell, or coughing extravagantly as they passed through a group of smokers on the street. But more than that she just wanted to have her secrets. Just as he had his. *"An old friend,"* she whispered, the words leaving her mouth with the smoke, curling away into the air.

Later Carrie stood with Sam, looking over the view of the city from their window. "So, how's the honeymoon period going?"

"Oh, you know," Sam said, turning red. Carrie laughed, drunk, happy.

"Maybe it's best you guys are still living out of hotels. You probably aren't getting much else done right now, right?"

Sam thought of the nights she and Dennis spent

back to back, tailbones pressed together, of being woken by the sharp of his elbow in her rib cage.

"You're talking in your sleep again," he'd moan.

"What was I saying?" she'd ask, hot and clammy from dreams of him pressing her against walls and bending her over tables.

"Who cares?" He'd yawn and turn away from her, pulling the covers tighter around him.

"We're looking to settle down, soon," Dennis was saying to Carrie and Dylan. "We're tired of living out of hotels."

"Come to LA," Dylan suggested.

"You would love LA, Dennis. It's so you," Carrie said.

"Well, we'll be flying out in time for the series premiere," Dennis said. "Maybe we'll stay for a while."

Sam's stomach lurched. He knew she didn't want to stay in LA. She needed to get home to England for a while, get her house ready for sale. She wasn't ready to get back into the heat. She loved the days in winter that never quite got light, gray sky and orange lights from windows.

When Dylan and Carrie left the next day Sam and Dennis argued bitterly. He went outside for a run at eleven at night and didn't come back until one a.m., ice-cold when he slipped under the sheets, her skin jumping at his freezing hands.

"I'm sorry," he whispered, shaping himself to her back.

"Me too," she said. "It's fine if we stay in LA a while. I was just being selfish." He thanked her,

19

Over the next couple of weeks Dennis appeared on talk shows, giving practiced answers to the standard questions that everyone seemed to ask. *What has it been like since you left prison? Can you forgive the Red River police for what happened to you? Will you be helping others who are wrongly incarcerated?*

Dennis had sessions with a media coach on public speaking and communication. Controversial opinions—such as his indifferent stance on the death penalty—needed to be tamed or sidestepped entirely. The coach helped him formulate answers that wouldn't offend or divide people, that focused on forgiveness and understanding and moving on. She trained him how to share his attention between the host of the TV show and the audience, how to evade an awkward question and how to maximize the impact of his answers with well-timed pauses and sincere eye contact.

A nutritionist brought him smoothies the color of swamp water and all-natural protein bars that looked, to Sam, like something you'd hang on a bird feeder. Instead of coffee he sipped on cups of hot bone broth that smelled like the Bovril Sam's grandmother used to have on winter evenings. He kept trying to get her to eat unpronounceable things like acai berries and echinacea supplements but she drew the line after he gave her a coconut water that tasted, she thought, like sperm, though she couldn't tell him that.

People told him what to wear, how to pose for photographs, where he needed to be and at what time. There would be someone to drive him there and when he arrived someone to take him to a room where another person would pluck stray hairs and powder his forehead so that it didn't shine in the flawed way regular people's skin did.

"You're ready," Nick told Dennis over lunch on a Sunday.

"I don't know," Dennis said. "Live TV?"

"What's the difference between live TV and being interviewed in front of a studio audience? You did great on *Colbert*, they loved you. Trust me, you're ready."

Dennis and Sam arrived at the *Today's Talk* studio on Wednesday morning, just before the show started broadcasting at eleven a.m. Dennis wasn't due on until midday so he and Sam had some time to look around, the energy different from the late-night shows and prerecorded interviews they were used to, the pressure of going out live creating an atmosphere buzzing with excitement and dread. Nick called to wish Dennis good luck. "I'm sorry I couldn't make it," he said. "You'll be fine! Just relax and have fun." Then Dennis was being whisked away by a harried man in a headset and Sam was left alone.

She picked from a buffet table and made small talk with an *America's Got Talent* finalist. When Dennis was ready to go on she walked with him to the stage door and held his hand, which shook slightly with nerves she hadn't known he'd felt, and she kissed him as the lighted sign above the doorway switched to green when the show cut for commercial.

"Good luck," she said, and let go of his hand. He gave her a timid smile as a man in a headset walked him on to the stage. The set was a living room, all pastel colors, a fake window with a permanently blue-sky day painted behind it. The room was cut in half, facing a black space where the cameras and crew faced in. Sam thought of Ed and his sinkhole, the way his house hung half over the abyss.

Another crew member took her to a green room where she could watch the show as it went out. There were others there, the sister of a woman with a rare type of cancer, a man whose friend was on to talk about his best-man speech that went viral. Everyone smiled at Sam as she entered. There was an advert for baby shampoo on the TV and the water cooler burbled as Sam filled a plastic cup.

Then the show was back on and Sam felt the same flip in her stomach she felt every time she saw Dennis on TV. He sat stiffly on the sofa, his hands resting on his knees. Sam willed him to remember what the media coach had told him about posture, about relaxed shoulders and appearing open.

There were three hosts who sat together on a sofa to the side of Dennis: a man in a suit with Just for Men black hair, a woman in heavy makeup and a yellow dress, and a celebrity guest host who smiled too widely as they introduced Dennis with a brief rundown of his case and the new series on Netflix.

"First of all," the woman in the yellow dress asked, "you've been in prison for over twenty years. Did you even know what Netflix was?"

The celebrity laughed. Dennis smiled but it fell away too quickly as he started to speak.

"Not at first, no. People explained it to me—"

"Have you ever watched anything on Netflix?" the celebrity asked.

"Not yet, I'm not really a TV kind of—"

"For anyone who hasn't seen the first documentary, can you help them understand what happened in your case? It's one hell of a story, if you haven't seen it already." The man put his note cards down on the table and picked them up again while he spoke. But before Dennis could answer the other hosts started to chat about the lost evidence, the false witness statements. Dennis watched them silently. A camera cut to a close-up of his face just as he looked up and into the lens. Sam jumped slightly, as if she'd been caught staring at him.

"So what does this new series add to your story?" the man said, suddenly turning back to Dennis, who stuttered in surprise, unable to formulate the answer he'd practiced so many times.

"Evidence. New evidence. And what led to my being exonerated, of course."

"Because there were still a lot of questions left unanswered after *Framing the Truth*. Will people who have stuck by you since the first film finally get those answers?"

Dennis looked confused. "I mean, finally Holly Michaels's family can have some peace knowing that the man responsible for her murder is finally convicted."

"Of course. Holly's father has previously been quite critical of the media attention surrounding your case."

"It must have been difficult," Dennis said. "They're such a brave family—"

"What about the other families?" the woman in the yellow dress said. She looked at her cards and then smiled.

"Pardon?"

"The missing girls of Red River," the man said. "There was always the unanswered question after the first film—who had been responsible for the disappearance of all those girls? It was assumed that whoever killed Holly also killed the other girls but that theory was incorrect. Holly's killer—Wayne—he was pretty forthcoming in his confession to the murder and, as it transpired, two other murders that had remained unsolved. But he was adamant he didn't know anything about the missing girls in Red River. Does this series attempt to answer the question of where those missing girls are?"

There was a long silence. To Sam it felt like a lifetime. She hadn't seen silence like that on television before.

"No," Dennis said eventually. Everyone at the table stopped smiling, even the celebrity guest, who looked at her cards and frowned.

"Don't you think—"

"The series looks at the failings of the first trial and the ongoing effect of the first movie. It documents my journey to appeal the verdict and my eventual release. It is about the murder of Holly Michaels and the injustice that her family and I endured at the hands of a corrupt group of people."

Sam felt sick. It was everything he was supposed to say but the tone was all wrong, with none of the inflection he'd practiced. She wanted to be with him, she wanted to squeeze his hand and whisper into his ear, *Just stay calm, just defuse this*.

"But it's definitely still a question that a lot of people want answered. It's something that still follows you around, right? We had a couple of protestors outside the studio this morning. You're quite a controversial figure! It seems that there are some people who still believe that you are guilty."

"But I'm not." Dennis shifted in his seat. He leaned in. Sam wanted to pull him back. It wasn't the right time to lean in, it looked confrontational, like he might pounce. "I have been exonerated—"

"They think you are responsible for the missing girls," the woman interrupted.

"They're wrong," Dennis said. "And I'm not here to talk about all that. I don't have answers for those people."

"Of course not! *Of course* you don't have answers." The man tried to lighten the atmosphere that was developing, and the cohosts shared a quiet, uncomfortable laugh that didn't reflect anything that was happening between them. "But it must bother you, this question mark hanging over your head, no matter that you've been exonerated."

"Yes," Dennis said, "it does. Some people will never be convinced of my innocence, no matter how much evidence is presented to them."

"What would you like to say to those people?"

Dennis was out of his depth. Sam waited for him to say something but he didn't, the camera zoomed in on his motionless face.

"If you had the opportunity to put their doubts to rest once and for all, would you take it?" The hosts all watched him, waiting for a response.

Sam no longer knew where this was going either, but it was making her uncomfortable. The others in the room were transfixed; she wondered if they even knew she was his wife. A part of her hoped they didn't. They all seemed to look at him with suspicion. One woman shook her head as Dennis spoke.

"Yes. But I said already, some people will never be persuaded—"

"We could help you change those minds," the woman said, more to the camera, to the audience, than to Dennis. "Backstage we have a trained polygraph expert and one of the leading body-language specialists in America, as well as a man who worked for twenty years as a homicide detective for the NYPD. You could do an interview and put those questions to rest once and for all."

"I'm just here to talk about the series…" Dennis said. Sam saw his Adam's apple move as he swallowed, watched him reach for a glass of water and then change his mind.

"But the series doesn't tackle these questions, does it? So this is a great opportunity for you. The polygraph would take about half an hour—"

"They don't even use those anymore," Dennis said with a derisive laugh. "They are completely inefficient and often entirely inaccurate."

"Which is why we have a body-language expert and an experienced detective who—"

"It was detectives and experts who put me on Death Row for a murder I didn't commit! So thanks, but no thanks. Can we please talk about the series now?"

"Are you afraid of what the results might suggest?" the man said.

Sam knew they wouldn't let it go. She looked at the time in the corner of the screen and wondered how long until they cut to commercial again. Maybe Dennis could draw it out long enough that they would have to drop it and go to the next segment, she hoped.

"Look, I'm not taking any fucking tests—"

"We'd like to apologize for that language and to anybody who was offended—"

"I'm sorry, OK? I'm sorry for that, I didn't mean to offend anyone," Dennis said to the camera.

"It's getting very hostile in here," the celebrity said, voice laden with concern.

"I'm not hostile," Dennis snapped.

"It's not the response we were expecting," the woman said, widening her eyes.

"What were you expecting? That I'd be thrilled at the opportunity to be interviewed by an ex-cop and ambushed with a polygraph test?"

Stop, Sam thought, *please stop talking.*

"I am here to talk about the new series. The new series that is about my exoneration. That I am not guilty."

"Yes, but you said yourself there are still a lot of unanswered questions surrounding—"

"I didn't say that."

"Well, you said the new series didn't address the question of the missing girls—"

"Because I don't know anything about the missing girls!"

"Please don't raise your voice," the woman said.

"I'm done here," Dennis said, standing. He unclipped his microphone and pulled it back through his shirt. It made a whooshing noise as it brushed his skin. A woman next to Sam tutted and the man opposite laughed and shook his head. On screen Dennis continued to talk but the microphone was hanging from his hand and didn't pick up his voice. He was pointing. He unclipped the pack from his belt and walked away looking back toward the presenters, who spoke to the audience, apologizing for the disruption.

By then Sam sat with her face in her hands, her elbows on her knees, unable to look at the people around her. She stayed there while the music played over a clip of what was still to come on the show and no one in the room said a word.

Dennis pushed the door open and said her name. She looked up and the light hit her eyes all at once; little dots obscured his face.

"We're leaving," he said. "Now."

Sam felt them all stare as she picked up her handbag and reached to his outstretched hand. He took her fingers in his and pulled her with him, dodging the people who moved toward them in the corridor. When they got to his dressing room a member of security blocked the door.

"My phone," Dennis said. "I need to get my things."

Someone behind the man passed out Dennis's phone and his wallet.

"I had a jacket," Dennis said. They passed his coat to Sam and then Dennis was pulling her away again, through the lobby and out into the street. Dennis waved to a nearby cab and it rolled toward them slowly, not stopping entirely before Dennis had already opened the door and started to maneuver Sam in, his hand protecting the top of her head as she ducked under the door in a strange mixture of protection and control.

20

Back at the hotel, Dennis's phone lit up with notifications. There was a text from Carrie, "Oh Den, I'm so sorry xxxxx," and missed calls from Nick, all of which Dennis ignored, turning his phone off and tossing it inside a drawer.

Sam sat behind him on the bed and rubbed his shoulders until he shook her off him. She listened to him rail against the hosts and producers and tried to reassure him that he didn't look like the bad guy in that situation. But she had glanced at the reaction on her own phone while he was in the bathroom and she knew there'd been a shift. "K, seriously shady behavior from America's number-one creepy white guy here…" a *Jezebel* writer posted on Twitter, along with a YouTube video of the show that had already been watched tens of thousands of times.

When Dennis came back she flicked the phone to airplane mode and suggested he call Nick and see what to do next. It was unnecessary. Nick called the room from the hotel lobby and reluctantly Dennis agreed to meet him downstairs.

"Listen," Nick said as they sat down in the bar.

"I've dealt with worse, I promise you. It's important we write a statement, something that explains you were triggered by the interrogation, OK? Dennis, you've been through awful things, awful. You're bound to have some post-traumatic stress. These guys suddenly taking you into a room to be interviewed by a homicide detective? To strap you to a machine and ask you about school friends who disappeared twenty-four years ago? Unacceptable. No wonder you reacted like you did! And there are people out there who already see it this way."

"They do?" Dennis said, his eyes red and shining.

"Most people are saying it was completely uncalled for, totally sleazy. And not just for you, what about the families of those girls? Having all that trauma dredged up for some light-entertainment segment on a daytime show?

"Dennis, I never would have booked you on that show if I'd known—"

"I know. It's just such a fucking mess right now."

"We can turn this around. Make it a positive."

But even after releasing a statement the tide of negativity didn't turn. *Today's Talk* had returned to the segment later in the show, the body-language expert and the homicide detective had given their opinions on what Dennis's behavior during his interview had suggested. They had both agreed that he was hiding something, that his body language showed defensiveness and that he was evasive, never answering any of the questions directly, like a guilty politician. They were careful not to directly accuse him of any responsibility for the girls' disappearance but the implication was enough to spark frenzied online discussion, a new wave of petitions calling for Dennis to take the tests.

"Maybe we should just go to England for a while," Sam said after another day holed up in their hotel room. "Go somewhere you aren't quite as, you know, well-known?" She was already tired of hiding, restless and itching for a cigarette.

"I shouldn't have to worry about being 'well-known'! I haven't done anything *wrong*."

"I know, but maybe we could both do with a break from all this. So much has happened, we've hardly had any time to be together."

"We're together *all the time*," he said.

"I mean…it's all about the interviews and the photo shoots and writing your book. We could go away and just concentrate on us for a while."

"I don't do this because I *want* to. What else can I do? I didn't even graduate high school. It's not like you have a job."

"I'm not criticizing you," Sam said, ignoring his comment. She sat next to him on the edge of the bed. "I'm saying that now you've done so much of that maybe it's time for you and me to be alone and get to know each other without all this…noise and drama."

"We do know each other. You know *everything* about me," Dennis said. He sighed and fell back on the bed.

"I mean…intimately," she said, her face flushing. Dennis flung an arm over his face and groaned. "I'm sorry but…it's not like I don't think about it!" Sam tried to control the waver in her voice. "Sometimes I feel like you're not attracted to me."

Dennis sat up and held her while she cried. She felt ashamed for finally admitting it. And afraid that now there was no ignoring it, there was no way back. Perhaps he would say it was true, that he didn't feel attracted to her, and then he would leave her and she would have no one to blame but herself.

"It isn't that simple," he said as her tears soaked into his shirt. "A lot has happened to me. I'm not ready to talk about it. Not yet. It isn't you. I'm going to need time. Do you understand?"

For a second she was so relieved it wasn't about her she didn't think about what he might mean. She told him she understood and he kissed her temple gently. They lay down together, the bed still pristinely made from the morning's housekeeping. She rested her eyes while he played with her hair, coiling it around his finger, tighter and tighter, until it hurt.

The next morning when she awoke he was already up, tying the laces of his running shoes. It was only five thirty.

"Are you going out already?" Sam asked.

"My dad's in the hospital," he said without turning around. "Shot himself in the head. Blew out half his brains. His nurse found him, called nine one one. Now he's lying in hospital being kept alive by machines at my expense."

"Oh my God," Sam said, sitting up. "Den, I'm so—"

"It's fine. It's not like we were close."

"Even so, I'm sorry. Oh, Den."

"Least he could've done was aim right. You know?" Dennis made a sound somewhere between a laugh and a hiss. "Anyway. Now they're asking me to come down there—the son of a bitch had me listed as his next of kin. I need to sign papers if I want them to turn off the machines, can you believe that?"

"Is that what you want?" Sam asked.

"They say he's unlikely to regain consciousness and that even if he did he'd be reliant on the fucking machines for the rest of his life. So yeah, it's what I want."

"When did this…" Sam looked again at the time. "When did you speak to them?"

"About an hour ago when I finally switched on my phone," he said.

"Why didn't you wake me?"

"You looked peaceful," Dennis said. "You're a heavy sleeper."

Sam hugged him and told him she was there for him. Whatever he needed.

"I need to get out," he said, standing and pulling on a thick sweater. "I just want some space to clear my head."

He returned an hour later, his cheeks red from the cold. "I got you something," he said, grinning.

"You didn't have to," Sam said, confused by the

change in temperament, wondering if he was OK or if this was some kind of psychological break.

"Close your eyes and open your hands. Come on!"

Sam did as she was told. "Den, is everything OK?" She felt the weight of something in her palms, warm from his grip.

"Open them," he said.

She looked at the object, something luminous green and plastic. It looked like a lighter but bigger. "What is it?"

"It's an electronic cigarette!"

Sam laughed. "I don't—"

"I know you've been smoking, I smell it sometimes, and these are like cigarettes but instead of smoke it's vapor."

"I know what vaping is, Den."

"It's chocolate flavor! It smells better. Try it!"

Sam put it to her lips, feeling ridiculous, thinking of the caterpillar in *Alice in Wonderland*.

"Oh my God." She coughed. "It's disgusting."

Dennis's smile dropped. "But it smells so good."

"You try it," she said, handing it to him. He inhaled and his face twisted in disgust.

"It's stinging my mouth!"

"How about I just don't smoke?" Sam asked. Dennis tossed the e-cig into the wastepaper basket.

"The smell," Dennis said. Sam started to say she knew but he stopped her. "I guess it reminds me of my dad. I just hate it."

She understood then, and she didn't want to be the person who reminded him of that.

* * *

They went down as far as the hotel bar to meet again with Nick. There was no getting around the trip they would need to take to Red River.

"First we need to deal with my father," Dennis said. "Then we'll have to arrange some kind of funeral, I guess. And we can't just leave the house there like that. People will gut it if we don't get there first. Like vultures."

"How long will all this take?" Sam asked.

"A few days? A week?" Dennis said. "We don't want to miss the premiere."

Nick arrived, shaking the snow off his coat. "When it rains it pours, hey, guys? Dennis, I'm really sorry to hear about your father."

"It's fine," Dennis said, and he laid out the plans to visit Red River and be back in time for the series premiere.

Nick sucked in the air through his teeth. "Not sure it's going to be quite that simple, to be honest. I've been speaking to Jackson and we both agree it's best if you don't come to the premiere, what with everything that's happening right now. And with your father? Might be best if you lie low. You don't want to look like you don't care about his passing."

"But I don't," Dennis said. "And he isn't dead yet. That's what I'm saying, I need to go all the way there to sign the papers."

"But you see what I mean, about how people might think it's a little cold if you just continue as normal, even though the guy was a bit of a, you know…?"

"Asshole," Dennis said. "It's *my* premiere. I should be there."

"We have to think about what's best long-term. For you *and* the series. Listen." Nick leaned across the table and held Dennis's wrist. "Why don't you take some time off and let me worry about your public image for now?"

red river

21

Lionel was in a private room, with bandages wrapped around his head like the Invisible Man. There were tubes coming from his nostrils and neck, and a pump forcing his chest to inflate and deflate with a gentle wheeze and beep. The nurses closed the door behind them while Sam and Dennis stood hand in hand and stared at the body in front of them. Sam turned away, feeling suddenly queasy. She'd hated Lionel. But now she felt a sense of guilt, standing near him as he lay completely helpless, not even able to breathe for himself. What had driven him to this, she wondered. Why now? Was it Dennis's release? Could a father hate his son so much? She imagined the darkness of those last moments, Lionel alone holding the gun. She hoped Dennis was right when he said that Lionel had probably been drunk, that he didn't understand what he was doing.

"How long do we have to stay here?" Dennis asked. "I'm so bored. Hungry. We should eat before we drive to the house. Is there anywhere good nearby?"

"I'll find out," Sam said, though they hadn't

passed anywhere Dennis would eat on the drive from the airport. As they left behind each diner and drive-through Sam became hungrier, her stomach growling and cramping. They'd eaten breakfast on the plane, arrived midmorning and driven straight to the hospital, hoping they could sign the paperwork and be on their way in time for lunch.

"What do you want?" Sam asked, trying not to see Lionel in her peripheral vision.

"Find somewhere healthy."

Sam googled "restaurant, healthy." "There's a vegan café about—"

"No. Healthy *and* meat. I'm hungry, I need something real." Dennis walked to the machines and peered around the back, looking at all the different wires and workings. He poked the plastic IV bag dangling from the top of a pole and watched it wobble back and forth. "Shall we go now? I don't really see the point of this."

"Den… I know you didn't get along, but you want to look like you care, you know? Let's stay five minutes more."

"Fine."

He paced the room. Sam looked at the way the bed covers lay flat where Lionel's legs should be and shuddered. He must have lost his other leg, she thought, before he… Sam turned to the window and watched the people smoking in the parking lot. Now she wanted to leave, too.

After another few minutes they walked back out to the nurses' station and nodded sadly when asked if they were ready. A male nurse handed Dennis a clipboard with legal forms to sign. Dennis printed his name and signed with a slash of the pen, at which point a doctor shook his hand and led them both back to the room to switch off the machines. The beeping and wheezing stopped and plunged them into silence. The doctor shifted his stethoscope around his neck, put the ear tips into place and the diaphragm against Lionel's barrel chest, now still. The doctor looked at his watch, his head turned away from them. After a while he turned to them and nodded. Dennis shook his hand again, composed, and the doctor left them alone. After fifteen minutes, they left.

The nearest healthy restaurant was forty minutes away. Dennis ate a protein bar and clutched his stomach. The GPS directed them the wrong way, forcing them to loop back, and sent Dennis into a dark and cruel mood.

"You're hangry," Sam said.

"What?"

"Hangry. It's when you get angry when you're hungry."

"Hangry," Dennis repeated. Sam mused on the neologisms that had passed him by (hangry, mansplaining, clickbait, YOLO, fleek, manspreading, virtue signaling) and felt bad, again, for her occasional lack of patience. While he had been away the world had changed and there was a whole new language to accompany it.

By the time they reached the restaurant they were both hangry and Sam was relieved to get a

table straightaway. The restaurant was almost entirely open-plan, the kitchen clean and quiet behind
the counter, and every table had a wheatgrass cen-
terpiece, a pot with fresh leaves shooting straight
up. The menu was the kind of bland, clean-eating
food that pissed Sam off. She was starving, she
wanted grease: burgers and fries and onion rings.
Since Dennis had got a nutritionist they barely ate
together, Sam opting for salt-beef sandwiches and
oversized slices of pizza and everything else she
knew she shouldn't have.

Here, Dennis was in his element. He ordered
steak and poached eggs, plus several sides of mixed
greens, roasted sweet potato and a bowl of steamed
brown rice.

"And I'll have…the steak and the quinoa salad,"
Sam said hesitantly. Dennis snorted and exchanged
a smirk with the waiter, who coughed away a laugh
and took their menus. "What? What?"

"It's pronounced keen-wah," Dennis said, shaking his head. "Not kwin-o-ah! You're so funny!"
Sam's cheeks flamed as she waited for him to calm
down but he kept laughing, taking his glasses off
to wipe tears away.

"It's not that funny," Sam whispered. "It's not
that fucking funny! Stop it!" She was talking louder
now and customers were turning to look at them,
smiling uncertainly at a joke they wanted to be
a part of. "Weren't you on Death Row like five
minutes ago?" she shouted suddenly. "When did
you turn into such a snob?" Dennis's laughter died
instantly and the whole restaurant fell quiet. He

cleaned his glasses on his shirt and put them back on, turning away from her. The waiter returned with a jug of iced water and Sam's juice.

On the way out the young man who'd served them stopped them in the parking lot and held open a copy of *Men's Health*. Inside there were half a dozen pictures of Dennis, muscles hard, holding himself in planks and push-ups, frozen midair in a jump squat. The title read "Bodyweight Workouts You Can Do in a Death Row Cell... Or a Hotel Room" above a short interview. For a while Dennis didn't say anything and flicked through the pages, reading the pull quotes and smiling.

"When did this come out?" he asked, signing a full-page black-and-white photograph of himself.

"Only yesterday. I subscribe anyway so I get them right away." The man seemed nervous, Sam thought, as she watched Dennis flick through the pictures again in silence.

She lightly placed a hand on his bicep. "We should probably go."

"See you around," Dennis said, reluctantly handing the magazine back.

The road turned uneven beneath the wheels and they bounced in a pothole. Dennis told Sam that they needed to pick up some essentials from the store, so they drove to the main street and parked in front of the hardware store.

They looked up and down the street, saw the general store with a sign for the *Tribune* outside and headed in that direction. There was no one around, just an old German shepherd dog that lumbered up to them panting in the midafternoon heat, a red neckerchief tied around its collar. "It's a ghost town," Dennis said. He pushed open the door, the bell ringing as he did so.

The back wall was full of magazines, the top shelf all the lurid colors of porno, half obscured by a plastic plank laid over them.

"I didn't think anywhere even *sold* those anymore!" Sam said, laughing.

"What?"

"Those!" Sam pointed upward.

"They've always sold those here," Dennis muttered.

"But who *buys* porn anymore? With the internet?"

"How should I know?"

"I'm just saying…why are you getting so wound up? I thought it was funny, how old-fashioned this place is."

"Can I help you?"

Sam jumped. The man stood so close behind her she felt his breath on her hair. "We're just looking," she said.

"We're about to close for the day, so if you don't mind seeing yourselves out?" He held his hand toward the door. Sam checked the time on her phone and saw it was three forty-three.

Dennis folded his arms across his chest and smiled at the man. "I want to buy my magazine and get our groceries. Isn't that OK?" Dennis stood half a foot taller than the old man. The light coming in from the window behind him made him like a shadow, stretched long in the afternoon sun, featureless and dark.

"We haven't got what you're looking for. You might want to try someplace out of town."

"You sure you don't have this month's issue of *Men's Health*? It's a good one, I'm in it." He flashed his teeth.

"Don't sell that stuff round here. Now, I'm afraid we're closing. Have a nice day." As the man turned to walk away Dennis took a long step forward.

"We've got every right to shop here, anywhere we want," Dennis said.

"As much as I've got the right not to serve anyone I want in my store."

"Let's just leave it, let's go," Sam pleaded. Outside the dog stood with its paws against the glass.

"Dennis, we don't want trouble and we don't want you round to cause it. We were all sad to hear about your father but you need to sell that land and get on out of town. There's no place for you here."

From behind the counter they heard a scuffling that made them turn. A woman came out of the back room, leaving the door open behind her. In her hand was a small revolver, shining silver. "Everything OK, Bill?" she asked.

"Come on, please, *please*, let's go. It doesn't matter." Sam started to move toward the door. She thought about leaving Dennis there and wondered if she would feel guilty if he was shot. She had never wanted anything as badly as she wanted to get out of that store.

"Fine. Fine," Dennis said. His hands were at his waist, fingers spread. "Be seeing you around, Bill."

Sam jumped as the dog brushed against her calves and skittered over the wood floor, and felt the warmth of the sun on her cheeks as she walked out into the suffocating air. Behind her Dennis was laughing.

"No wonder these little stores are heading for extinction," he said, slamming the car door so hard that Sam felt it in her eardrum. For a moment she sat still in the driver's seat, closed her eyes and tried to keep her hands from trembling in her lap. "Well?" Dennis said after a while, "Walmart?"

22

Sam was OK on the empty roads leading out of Red River but when they came to the traffic that surrounded the megastores and strip malls outside of town she felt overwhelmed by all the colors and movement. She started to panic, the world blurring behind tears that she tried to hide from her husband.

Once they'd parked, Sam went to the Walmart restroom to gather herself and came back to find Dennis missing. After several stressful minutes pacing the aisles she found him in the home section, throwing pillows and blankets into two shopping carts.

"What's all this?" she asked.

"For while we're staying here. I don't think there'll be any spare stuff. Where are the inflatable mattresses?"

"We're staying in the house?" Sam tried to keep her voice light but it came out shrill with anxiety.

"What's wrong? It's only for a couple weeks. Besides, I thought you were *sick of living in hotels*."

Sam didn't know how to respond. She remembered what it was like in that house, the smell of illness and rot. She wondered where Lionel had shot himself, whether they had people who cleaned it up or if the floor would be stained with the contents of his skull.

"It's kind of…messy there," she said. She felt embarrassed, as if she were criticizing him somehow, even though he hadn't been to the house in twenty years.

"It was always messy," he said, turning back to the shelves.

"No, I mean…it smells weird and…" She didn't know how to ask about his father's suicide without sounding offensive.

"And…?"

"Nothing," she said.

"We'll clean up a little. It'll be fine. We'll be gone before you know it."

Sam already felt the same itchy unease she'd felt the first time she went to the house, but she wanted to be supportive, even if she couldn't understand why he would want to go back there. Maybe, she thought, he's in denial. Sam bet as soon as they arrived he'd want to go to a hotel. He didn't realize, yet, how bad it was.

"Can you cook?" Dennis asked her, swinging the shopping carts around and pushing one to her.

"What?" Sam was hardly paying attention, daydreaming of the hotel she hoped they'd be staying in that night.

"Cook. Can you?"

"I suppose," she said. "I mean, basically, yes."

"You're not filling me with confidence here," he said, laughing.

"You know what I mean," she said, pushing him playfully. "I'm no Gordon Ramsay but—"

"Who?" he asked.

Sam linked her arm through his and talked about Gordon Ramsay as he filled the shopping cart with food. Would they have to throw all this out when they got to the hotel? She told herself it didn't matter. For now, she was happy that they weren't arguing. If he wanted to believe that they would stay in the house that night, she would let him.

The house was surrounded by more mess than there had been the last time she was there. In the short time that the house had sat empty, unguarded, the peeling white walls had been sprayed with red words: "MURDERER," "CHILD KILLER." Dennis retrieved the house keys from the hospital-issued bag full of his father's effects and walked toward the house. Sam lingered by the car.

"We'll paint over that tomorrow," Dennis called back to her, pointing at the wall. Sam shifted her weight and rubbed her bare arms. The house gave her goose bumps. After a couple of trips to and from the house, Dennis stopped to ask Sam if she was going to help at all. She nodded, taking a plastic bag in each hand, and walked as far as the porch before placing them down by the steps and the rickety, makeshift disabled ramp that bent under her foot as she tested it.

"OK," Dennis sighed. "What is it now?"

"I don't know what it's like inside. Like…where he died."

"What?"

"Where he died."

"Oh," Dennis said, softening his voice. He smiled and took her hand. "You mean where he shot himself? Over there." He pointed to a metal shed with a rusted door to the side of the property. Spider webs stretched across the corners, shivering in the breeze.

"Really?" Sam asked, clutching his hand.

"Yeah, really. I guess because that's where Mom did it? Maybe it was sentimental, maybe he didn't want to make a mess inside, who knows?" Sam stared over at the garage, so old and ramshackle it looked as though it might collapse with a push of a finger. "Feel better?" Sam nodded limply. "You want me to carry you over the threshold? I guess that's something we never did."

"No! No, I'm too heavy!"

Dennis rolled his eyes. "You're not too heavy. Come on." She made to run away but he had a hand around her wrist before she could go. Giggling, she attempted to pull away while he reeled her in, hand over hand up her arm, before flipping her legs out from under her and carrying her into the house. She didn't feel heavy. She felt the way she had always wanted to, like those girls who were always cold, or else fainting in afternoon heat, delicate and vulnerable. Sam laughed honestly, a noise she hadn't heard in so long that she didn't recognize it. It was a loud, goose-honk laugh that echoed in the miles of woods that separated them from the rest of the world.

When they were inside Dennis placed her back on her feet and kissed her gently. "It's only for a couple weeks, I promise."

He went back to the car to get the last of their things while Sam looked around, still feeling as though she was doing something she shouldn't.

In the living room, dust floated in the beams of light streaming through the gaps in the boarded-up window. The air inside was stale. Sam walked from the living room to the master bedroom: shelves cluttered with junk blanketed in dust; the bed with a flat, yellowed pillow at the head; a dresser covered with bottles of medication. The walls were all wood paneled, making the house seem dark even during daylight. When she looked up she saw the silhouettes of dead insects inside the lampshades. There was Dennis's old room at the end of the hall, the door closed. She walked past the bathroom, glancing through the crack in the door.

In the kitchen, the sink was full of stagnant water and a cockroach skittered over a dirty plate. The lino beneath her feet was bubbling up, peeling away from the cabinets. A broken window had been taped up. Sam covered her nose and mouth with one hand and tried to open the back door, but it stuck in its frame. There was nothing beyond it. Just the wilds behind the house.

"It's not great, I know," Dennis said behind her as he put down a couple of boxes filled with cleaning products. He pushed against the back door but it still stuck in its frame. He leaned back and kicked. It swung open and snapped back, clattering against the frame. "Would you mind getting started in here? I'm going to clear out the sitting room, make some space for us to set up our bed." He pulled her in, arms looped around her lower back, and pushed his mouth against hers. "I love you," he said breathily into her lips.

When she was alone Sam closed her eyes, leaned against the counter and smiled. Maybe staying here wouldn't be completely terrible, she thought. Dennis had seemed different since they arrived, like something inside him had loosened. Perhaps it was that they were, finally, alone. Sam thought of the miles of trees around them and all the space and the time that they had just for themselves, finally.

It was pointless to clean the crockery that littered the kitchen, so Sam put on her rubber gloves and threw everything into heavy duty trash bags, enjoying the satisfying crash as each thing smashed against the last. She pulled the plug in the sink and watched as the rancid water was sucked down, leaving the remnants of rotting food in a slushy pile at the bottom. Her whole body felt dirty. She needed to pee but was afraid to see what the bathroom was like up close. After sweeping the crumbs and God knew what else from cupboards and surfaces she squirted bleach over everything until her eyes burned and flooded with tears. She had to step out into the backyard for air.

Outside, she wiped her eyes with the back of her

wrist and blinked the tears away. The world was a blur but she thought she saw something move at the side of the house. She squinted. Suddenly it seemed to take a step toward her. She felt fear hit her like cold water and shouted for Dennis, stumbling back into the kitchen, still half-blind from the chemical fumes.

"What is it? Oh, it's looking way better in here, nice one."

"There was someone out there just now, at the side of the house," Sam said.

"Really?" Dennis frowned, his voice steady but concerned. He went out and looked around. "Did they say anything?"

"No. I think they were hiding, I couldn't see properly because my eyes are watering."

"Are you sure?"

She could tell he was starting to doubt her. She was certain. "Yeah, it was creepy."

"It's probably those kids who spray-painted the house. It's nothing. Call me if you need me. You're doing a good job here." He winked.

She returned to work, scouring at the sticky patches and spraying every surface with a last layer of disinfectant. When she was done she looked around, proud of the transformation. She had never once tried this hard in her own house. Mark always used to complain about the huge pile of laundry she left in a heap in the spare room. She thought about how her sink was always full of dishes stained with pasta sauce and how the bin was constantly overflowing. When she'd left it long enough Mark would inevitably roll up his sleeves, sighing, and start cleaning, as if she was someone who needed to be saved. Now she enjoyed the cramp in her arms that she had earned from scrubbing and the knowledge she was saving someone else. It felt right, like growth.

By the time Sam had finished it was dark. She went to look for Dennis. On the floor of the sitting room a double mattress was inflating itself, the plug trailing across the room and into the wall. The old furniture was almost all gone, leaving just the sofa and a lamp against the back wall, a fraying armchair and the TV on a unit in the corner. Everything else was piled outside in the yard. Sam couldn't see or hear any sign of Dennis. She called to him a few times but there was no answer. So much for being alone *together*, she thought.

Sam entered the bathroom apprehensively, peeking around the door and revealing the room an inch at a time. It was as filthy as she had predicted. She gathered all the things from the kitchen and made a start there.

23

After dark, the air became thick with the noise of cicadas, and moths bounced off the screens at the windows. Sam wandered the house, noticing how the boards bent beneath her feet. In the hallway, on top of a table piled with unopened letters and beneath a nicotine-stained telephone that hung on the wall, she found a modem and router. The relief was instant. While typing the Wi-Fi password into her phone she heard the back door screech against the floor. She froze. From the corner of her eye she saw a man in the kitchen and heard the pounding of heavy boots on the floorboards. "Dennis?" she shouted. "Dennis? Is that you?"

"Yeah," Dennis shouted. Sam held a hand over her chest to feel her heart slow down.

"Where were you?" she called, but he didn't answer. As he walked past her on his way to the bathroom he stopped and kissed her on the head. He closed the door behind him and she heard the shower running.

When Dennis emerged, he was wearing just his boxers, and clutching a towel at his side. Sam asked if he was ready to eat and then, on her way to the kitchen, asked again, "Where've you been? I cleaned the bathroom too."

"I noticed, thanks," Dennis said. "I went to look for whoever was hanging around. I knew it was bothering you so I checked it out. I couldn't find anyone, so try not to worry about it."

"Thanks, that's sweet." Sam smiled to herself, taking the brand-new pans from the cupboard. The oven was broken so she had to do everything on the stovetop and some things went cold while she over-cooked other things. It was Dennis food: chicken, brown rice and broccoli. Boring, dry food. Utilitar-ian. "Eat to live, don't live to eat," as Dennis was fond of saying. Sam chewed and swallowed, tell-ing herself how good this was for her.

Dennis ate everything in minutes, thanked her and sat back on the sofa to read the *Men's Health* that he'd picked up at Walmart. Sam sat with her legs across his lap. Every now and then she heard a scratching noise, which seemed to be coming from all around her. Rats, she thought, until what sounded like the wail of a baby made her jump and bury her face in Dennis's armpit.

"Shh," he said. "I think it's in the crawl space. It's just an animal! Don't worry, let go, get off, I'll go check."

She followed him outside into the yard. She watched him crawl on his belly under the house, her eyes scanning the surrounding trees for anyone who might be watching her. Something scurried past her, brushing her leg. She screamed.

"Jesus CHRIST, it's a raccoon, for fuck's sake, a raccoon! Hang on..."

Sam climbed back onto the porch, shaken and embarrassed. The wailing had stopped and Sam wondered what Dennis was still doing under there. Beneath her she could hear him talking quietly, cooing.

"There's a cat under here. She's got kittens... Hey, hey there! Hello! She must have been fighting that raccoon. She doesn't seem hurt... Sam, get a can of tuna from the house."

Sam returned with a bowl of tuna and a bowl of milk.

"Leave it here; we need to make her trust us. She can't stay out here. No milk! They can't have milk." Dennis poured the milk into the long grass and handed her back the bowl.

Dennis went inside and got some old towels, which he placed under the porch and shaped into a makeshift cat bed.

"I used to have such a great cat. He showed up like this one, all stray and with this sick infected eye. I fed him and let him come and go and eventually he just stuck around. I had to fix his eye because we couldn't afford a vet. I had to disinfect it and he hated it—he scratched the shit out of me. It was worth it though, when the pus all dried and the swelling was gone. I think he went blind in it; his eye was all milky. I called him Ted. He was always fighting, with cats, with possums, whatever was around."

"How old were you?"

"Seven? I had him until I was about fourteen. He got hit by a car on the road out there. Whoever hit him just left him. I went looking and I saw his tail sticking out from the grass. He was stretched out and stiff, all the fur was scraped away on one side of his face and one of his ears was missing. There were just holes where his eyes were. I think that the birds ate them. If I knew who hit him, I'd have killed them. How could they just leave him there? Sick, people are sick."

Sam thought about her old cat, Tiger, and how many times he'd disappeared. She remembered how worried she used to be until he'd show up a day later as though nothing had happened. She hated worrying about him, and she resented it. It was too hard loving something that much, something that had its own life and its own mind, and could come and go as it pleased. It was almost a relief when he died. Now she barely thought of him at all. Already she worried about the cat and her kittens under the crawl space: Were they cold? What if it rained? Would the raccoon come back? Did raccoons eat kittens?

They slept poorly that night, lightly, wondering if the cat would be there when they woke up. In the morning, they checked the crawl space again and saw the cat was still curled around her kittens. They drove out of town back to the superstores and bought boxes of cat food, kitten food (though they were so young they wouldn't need the food for weeks yet). Proper cat beds and toys that jingled. They went home and put out the cat's lunch and a bowl of fresh water. Dennis did the same in the afternoon and he and Sam waited on the porch, talking gently so they didn't scare the mother off.

"I hate to think of her under there all night," Dennis said.

"Me too." Sam swung a leg over his lap and felt a rush of affection at seeing this new side of her husband.

"Sometimes my dad would kick me out of the house and tell me not to come back in. I'd have to sleep under the porch. There were snakes and spiders. Sometimes I'd find bones from the things that crawled under there to die." Sam didn't know what to say. "I can't leave that cat under there."

"What will we do when we leave here? Will we take them with us?"

"I think so. We'll have to see where we go."

They were quiet for a while.

"I really need to get a start on some of this." Dennis gestured to the yard. "The dumpsters I rented will be here tomorrow and I'll need to run some errands in town soon, too."

"Town?" Sam said anxiously, remembering the incident in the general store.

"Don't worry, you don't have to come. I can always get a cab. Besides, I won't cause any problems. It's just funeral stuff."

After dinner, Dennis threw on some sweats and told Sam he was going for a run. Sam tried to busy herself by rearranging the clothes in her suitcase, taking them out and folding them back in again.

Occasionally, she'd go out to check on the cat. She still wouldn't come out, so Sam crawled under the porch, sliding on her belly and clicking her tongue to get the cat's attention without startling her. The cat tentatively stepped toward her, stretching her neck to Sam's outstretched fingers and sniffing delicately, the air from her nostrils tickling Sam's hand. Sam tried to stroke her but she backed away to protect her squeaking kittens. Sam was excited to tell Dennis that she had made some progress while he was out.

Two hours passed and Dennis still wasn't home. It grew dark and every noise was suspicious and loaded with potential danger. In the bathroom, she kept the door slightly open so that she could see down the hall and listen for Dennis's return. As she wiped herself she saw, through the small frosted window behind the bath, a moving shadow. Sam turned to look at it full on and saw clearly the shape of a head ducking, followed by the thump of feet on the discarded plywood that littered the side of the house. Clutching her underwear around her thighs she was frozen, unsure what to do first. She kicked the bathroom door shut, yanked her underwear up with one hand and slid the bolt shut with the other. Sam looked for her phone to call the police but she saw it, in her mind's eye, resting on the arm of the couch. She turned the light off and on again and stuffed a towel under the door; then she realized that was for a fire and that she had never learned what to do if there was an intruder.

Sam didn't know exactly how long she was in

the bathroom, with her back pressed against the wall, her eyes darting between the window and the crack under the door, waiting for the shadows of approaching feet. It was long enough for her legs to go numb beneath her and her back to start seizing. She thought of a knife pressed to her throat, or the click of a trigger, or a fist colliding with her cheek, the feeling of snapping bone.

She heard the noise of the back door, its rusted scream. She held her breath at the sound of approaching feet. Then someone was rattling the handle, pushing against the locked door. Sam crawled into the gap between the bath and the sink and squeezed her eyes shut.

"Sam?" Dennis's voice. "You in here?" She slid the bolt open and threw herself at him. He smelled like grass and something else, something metallic that made her teeth ache a little. She pulled back and told him about the shape at the window, that there was definitely someone there this time.

"This is ridiculous. Get out, I need to shower," Dennis said.

"No, I'm serious, there was someone looking in," Sam insisted, knowing how she must sound to him.

"There wasn't. Come on, I want to shower."

"I don't want to be alone."

"So stay here. I don't care." Dennis peeled off his damp shirt, his trousers and a pair of Nikes he got from the magazine shoot.

"Weren't you wearing your old trainers when you left?" she asked.

"What?"

"Your old…sneakers, when you left, those white ones."

"No." He pulled his boxer shorts down and stepped out of them, sliding the glass screen of the shower and turning on the water. Sam watched him, how his body moved and the soap ran down his back. He turned to grab the shampoo and she leaned to get a better look at him.

"Don't look," he said.

"I'm not."

"Liar."

Sam smiled.

"Hand me the towel," he said, reaching for it around the side of the glass. She handed it to him, almost forgetting the fear she'd felt a moment ago and instead thinking of sex, of grabbing him and pushing herself against him, of making him want her.

"It's like prison all over again, some creep watching me shower," he said, pulling on his fresh clothes.

"I'm serious, I promise you, there was someone definitely outside."

"Fine, I believe you."

"It doesn't scare you?"

"No. It's probably just some kids coming to see the old Danson place. They probably think it's haunted."

"What if it's someone who still thinks you're guilty? What if they want to hurt us?"

"You're being so dramatic." With this, he strode from room to room to show her they were empty and then patrolled the yard with a torch. Sam followed, looking nervously over her shoulder as they went. Dennis stamped on the wood beneath the bathroom window and asked Sam if it was the same sound she had heard earlier. She said no, then maybe, then that it might have just sounded different from inside.

"Mm-hmm," he said, shining the light up to the guttering and tutting at the amount of debris crammed in there, the plastic pipe sagging under the weight of the leaves. "You know what you need?" he said.

"What?"

"You need to see that there's nothing to be afraid of around here. It's not spooky, or haunted, or full of bad energy." He wrapped his arms around her waist and kissed her on the nose. "Come on." He pulled her legs out from under her and flung her over his shoulder. She was laughing, playfully beating her hands against his back. "Let's go to the garage," he said.

Sam stopped laughing. His shoulder was pushing into her sternum and making it harder to breathe. "No, no, please—I don't want to go in there," she said.

"You've got to beat the fear. It's irrational."

"No, I really don't want to. You're scaring me now, it isn't funny, please." She tried to push and wriggle away from him but Dennis had hold of her hamstrings and lower back and she could only move in convulsions. "Please, please!" Sam started to cry. Dennis opened the garage door and carried her over the threshold. He set her down and gave her a push that made her stumble a few steps before she lost her footing and hit the floor with a thump. Dennis was already back outside and the last she saw of him was his silhouette as he swung the metal door shut and plunged her into darkness. "Please! Dennis!" She was sobbing and banging her palms against the door.

"It's just a little blood," he shouted. "There's nothing more to it. Probably don't touch the walls, though."

"Dennis, *please*!" Sam had never screamed like this before; it was a sound she didn't know she could make. It scratched up her throat and reverberated against the metal walls surrounding her. In nightmares, she could never scream.

As her eyes adjusted to the dark she started to see outlines: tools hanging on the walls; gardening equipment draped with sheets; things that looked horribly like a corpse, a body sitting in the chair, a shotgun shape protruding from one side, the head dangling limp toward the other.

"Are you still there?" She stayed close to the door. "Dennis?"

The door finally opened and she pushed past him, her palms smacking him hard in the chest. Dennis made a small "oomph" noise, which made her want to hit him again, harder, but she kept running straight to the house. Once inside, she looked for her keys, pushing letters onto the floor and throwing sofa cushions across the room. She heard Dennis come in behind her and she searched faster, sweat rolling down her neck; then she ran into the kitchen and slumped onto the floor, hugging her knees.

"Hey," he said softly. "I was just kidding. You OK?"

"No!" Sam glared at him, thrusting herself away from him.

"I didn't think you would get that freaked out by it," he said, as if it were her fault.

"I asked you to stop! I was screaming!"

"Girls scream." He shrugged. "I thought you were playing."

"I wasn't!" Sam didn't know if she believed him. "Why are you still… Why not just say you're sorry?"

"I'm sorry," he said with a sigh. Sam felt another flush of anger: Was it that he didn't understand why she was upset? Or that he didn't care?

"You don't mean it."

"For f—I'm sorry, OK? I took it too far." Sam relented and let him hold her. "I shouldn't have said that. About the blood and stuff. It was a bad joke."

"Is it really like that in there?" Sam checked her hands and clothes for stains.

"No, he didn't kill himself inside there. I'd never have… It was against the garage wall. Outside. They already cleaned it."

"Why would you trick me then?"

"I don't know, I don't. You were so freaked out by it, I was only teasing. I didn't think you actually thought he killed himself inside there. But you've been acting like it's haunted here or something. It's kind of, I mean, it's real to me, it's not a county fair ghost train."

Dennis looked away, his jaw tense. Sam thought he looked as if he might cry. She reached out to touch his face and turned him gently to look at her.

"Den, I'm sorry. I don't think that. I don't. I know it's real to you. But, I did see someone, honestly. Not a *ghost*, just someone. I think someone's watching us."

"OK." He kissed her, keeping his lips on hers for a moment before pulling away. "If you're really that worried, I'll take care of you."

Dennis made Sam a green tea, which she hated but drank anyway, just to show that she appreciated the gesture. He stroked her hair and lulled her into a passive state, just on the edge of sleep. They heard a mewing from outside, looked at each other and rushed to the door. Dennis gestured for her to stay back. He walked as slowly and softly as he could, opening the door millimeters at a time. He crouched and the cat approached hesitantly. In the porch light Sam could see that she was small, with long gray fur and a white belly.

"You can tell she was looked after," Dennis said, combing her fur with his fingers, "until she got pregnant. Someone probably drove her out here and left her on the side of the road."

"I don't understand how people can do things like that," Sam said.

"People do worse things," he said. The cat stretched to his hand. She rubbed her face all over Dennis's fist and turned around, her tail sticking straight up to the sky. Sam brought over a bowl of cat food and they watched her eat. When they checked the porch they saw that she'd placed her kittens in the cat bed. They huddled together like balled-up socks.

Sam and Dennis picked up the cat bed together with the kittens inside and took it into the house, waiting for the mother to follow. The cat was anxious at first, mewing and pacing, but eventually calmed down and picked at some food that they had placed near the bed. All night there was noise, the squeaking of kittens and the shuffling of them moving around and being gathered back to the bed by the mother.

24

Dennis was up with the sun. He propped the door open again so that the cat could let herself in and out. He hit the bowl with a spoon to summon her for breakfast and watched her eat with a smile on his face.

"You're so good at this," Sam said. "You'd make a great dad." Dennis grimaced and she wished she hadn't said anything.

The mother returned to the bed to feed her kittens. One struggled to get in the crush, clumsily stepping over the others, uncoordinated and small. "He's the runt," Dennis said. "I hope he gets bigger soon."

Instead of going for his morning run, Dennis stayed inside and trailed a laser pointer across the floor, watching the cat's frantic movements as she chased it. "We need to name her," he said.

"Smudge?"

"No way. Tuna?"

"Maybe."

"Tuna."

The morning was slow and hot. Dennis threw knickknacks and clothes into trash bags and put them in a corner. Sam suggested taking them to Goodwill but Dennis dismissed the idea, showing her the chipped ornaments and the yellowed armpits of the shirts. "Who would want this shit?" he asked, not waiting for an answer.

The sound of an engine drew close and Dennis wiped his forehead. "That'll be the dumpsters."

He carried one heavy bag in each hand, his arms straining with the exertion. Sam looked out of the window and saw a police car, with three men inside. The driver was a young man, thirty, and the other two seemed to be in their late seventies, not wearing uniforms. One of the older men seemed familiar and as Sam's eyes met his she realized it was Officer Harries. His face was drawn and he looked puffy, unwell, as though he'd been drinking heavily. Dennis dropped the trash bags by the front door and stood, leaning against the frame watching as they walked nonchalantly up the yard to the house.

"Morning, Dennis," Officer Harries said.

"My God, Officer Harries, is that you? I almost didn't recognize you."

"Yes. And this is Officers Gacy and Cole."

There was something in Harries's voice that made Sam edgy, something that told her this wasn't good news.

"Sam, come here. These guys were cops when I was in school."

Sam hovered behind him and waited for what was coming.

"Know why we're here, Dennis?" Harries said.

"You want autographs?" Dennis said.

"Where were you last night, Dennis?"

"Here. Actually, we're pretty glad you stopped by, because Sam's been a little freaked out. We think someone's been creeping around here, peeping through the windows. Know anything about that?"

"Was he here all night, ma'am?" The youngest, Officer Cole, leaned round to ask her. Sam nodded. "You sure about that?"

"I'm sure, yeah," Sam said quietly. She cleared her throat and said again, with what she hoped sounded like certainty, "He was with me, here, all night."

"So what's this about?" Dennis stretched his arms over his head and held on to the top of the door frame. Sam noticed the sound of the wood splintering as he pulled down.

"Bill Landry called us early this morning. He found his dog dead outside, said she'd been eviscerated. He was very upset. Never seen anything like that myself."

Dennis tilted his head. "What does 'eviscerated' mean?"

"The dog was gutted, torn apart. It looked like an animal did it."

"So did an animal do it?"

"No, an animal did not do it, Dennis. We looked around nearby and there was a burned-out trash can containing the dog's skull. Bill said that he'd had an incident with you, a couple of days ago, in his store."

"You mean when his wife threatened us with a gun because we tried to buy a magazine? Sure, that happened."

"Not quite how he tells it. He says you were threatening him." He paused. "You kill the dog, Dennis?"

Sam watched Dennis's back, how his shoulders tensed beneath his shirt.

"This is just like old times, isn't it?" Dennis said finally. "Of course I didn't kill any dog."

"You sure about that?" Gacy said.

"Sure, been here the whole time, trying to sort through my old man's effects. I've got to get out of here before I go nuts like the rest of you people."

"This kind of stuff seems to follow you around, Dennis. It would be great if you could make your business here swift, get out before people get really upset."

"Listen, you're blocking the driveway and I'm expecting dumpsters soon, so you'd better go before the truck arrives. You want me out of here, fine, but I've got to do this first."

"You haven't changed at all, Dennis," Officer Harries said. "See you around."

"It's been a pleasure." Dennis turned and walked back inside.

"Ma'am," Harries said, holding back. Sam waited for him to keep talking. "I don't know how much you know about Dennis or his situation…"

"I know everything," she said.

"There's a lot of history around here and I'd ask yourself why he wants to come back someplace

where everybody hates him when he could be anywhere he wants."

Sam stopped herself from telling Officer Harries about the house, how they were cleaning and
fixing up the place, because even she didn't understand why they needed to be there. They had
enough money to pay others to do it for them. The
house itself was worthless; the wood was rotting
and the roof was leaking. Better to knock it down
and leave the land to grow over.

Just as Harries turned to leave she asked, "The
dog—why would you think it was Dennis?"

Harries sighed. "It's not the first time something
like this has happened to someone who pissed Dennis off. Seems like too much of a coincidence to
me." He looked over her shoulder and nodded. Sam
turned to see Dennis standing in the window, still
and tense, a look of intense concentration on his
face. "If you think about it and remember he wasn't
with you last night, just give the station a call." Harries passed her a card, which Sam took reluctantly.

"He was with me," she said again, fixing her
eyes on his. "All night."

Harries smiled.

"You're all the same," he said, walking toward
the car.

Sam ignored the bait and stood firmly waiting
for him to look back, knowing he wouldn't be able
to resist flinging one last threat or insult before he
left. But he didn't. Harries bent and lowered himself into the car, with a slowness that showed his

age, and closed the door behind him. Sam watched until they'd driven away.

Back in the house Dennis asked her what Harries had said.

"He wanted to ask again where you were last night."

"What did he give you?" She pulled the card from her pocket and he laughed.

"Should I throw it out?" Sam asked.

"Do whatever you want," he said, and continued swiping everything off the shelves into the trash bags.

"I know you wouldn't do what they're accusing you of," Sam said. "But…"

"But?" He stopped and dust rose behind his head, settling on his hair.

"You weren't here last night."

"Yes I was."

"Not all night. You went for a run."

"Around here. How would I get to town and back without a car?"

"Of course, I know."

"You want points for lying or something? I was here. I went for a run around the woods, that's it. They're just bothering me like they always did. The dog was probably hit by a fucking car or something."

"But they said the head…"

"They're lying. They're trying to scare you."

"I guess…" Sam said.

"Guess? What, you don't believe me?"

"Of course I do," Sam said.

"It doesn't seem like it. You know, you're either on their side, or you're on mine."

"I am on your side," Sam said. Suddenly she felt terrible, as if she'd betrayed him.

"You're my wife," he said, his voice softer. "I need you to trust me."

"They just scared me," she said. "I'll always be on your side."

25

Sam needed to get away so she drove out of town to a donut shop, where she chose two luminous iced ring donuts and a giant iced coffee. She took a picture of them and uploaded it to Instagram with the hashtags "paleo," "clean eating," "health." She smiled at herself and ate, sticky and sated and a little sick.

She pictured Dennis and Tuna, how gently he called her and how he held the kittens in one palm, putting his nose to their heads to nuzzle them. She knew he wouldn't have hurt an animal. Sam thought again of the figure she'd seen, someone lurking around the house. She knew there had been someone there; she'd felt their eyes on her even before she'd seen them. The gaze like fingernails dragged gently down her spine. How many creeps were there in this town? she wondered.

Two weeks, she decided, and then she would leave.

When she arrived back at the house there were three yellow dumpsters lined up along the front, one already half full with the black bags and broken furniture which they'd piled in the yard the previous day. Dennis had painted over the graffiti on the side of the house, though the red lettering showed through the white paint. There was also a flatbed truck she didn't recognize and a boy of about ten—skinny with dirty knees—sitting sullenly on the steps. As soon as she stepped out of the car she heard a raspy smoker's laugh and the rise and fall of Dennis's voice beneath. The boy didn't bother to look at her as she passed. He sniffed a watery-sounding mucus through his sinuses and coughed it out, spitting onto the grass.

"I'm back!" Sam called to Dennis.

He didn't answer. Sam heard the laughter of two people in cahoots, one obviously a woman. Dennis was in the kitchen, his clothes dotted with white paint, leaning back against the counter holding a sweating bottle of Pellegrino in one hand. Standing across from him, her spine curved and her crotch thrust toward Sam's husband, was Lindsay Durst.

"What's up?" Lindsay said.

"Wow, hey, how are you?" Sam said, trying to keep her voice cheerful.

"Pretty good, pretty good. It's awesome to see this guy again. Didn't think he'd be back here in a hurry."

"You met Lindsay, right? When you were filming?" Dennis asked.

Why was he pretending they hadn't spoken about her before? Sam gritted her teeth and smiled. "Yeah!" Her voice was too loud, too shrill. She told herself to reel it in. "Briefly. It's so nice to see you again."

The plastic bags stretched from her hands, her palms were sweating, the plastic was beginning to cut into the skin. She stood there, still and dumb, and watched as Lindsay and Dennis shared a smile. She looked down at Lindsay's flip-flopped feet. Her nails were painted cherry red and Sam noticed her little toe curled inward and under the others, ugly and gnarled. She must have felt Sam's eyes there as she shifted the foot behind her, out of sight.

"You want to put those down or something?" Dennis said, gesturing to her white knuckles around the handles of the bags. She started to lower them. "Not in here," he went on. "We're busy in here. Why don't you take them to the living room?"

Mortified, Sam left the kitchen. She imagined Dennis and Lindsay sharing a look, silently mocking her. She pictured a smile smeared on Lindsay's face and Dennis's malevolent smirk, its ugliness masked by his beauty. Outside the front window the boy was scratching marks into the wooden floorboards with a sharp-edged stone.

Sam walked back into the kitchen and interrupted their conversation. "Is that your son outside?"

"Yeah," Lindsay said casually. "I couldn't leave him at home, he's got the flu." Then she added, "He's not *doing* anything."

"Yeah, just leave him. He's fine," Dennis said.

"I was…" She paused, mouth dry. "…only asking. Why doesn't he come inside?"

"Oh no," Dennis said, "he'll touch things and he's contagious right now. I have too much to do to get sick."

Lindsay shrugged. "Fresh air will do him good."

Sam stood and there was a silence where she sensed them waiting for her to leave again. In the end she turned and went outside.

"Hey, you OK out here?" Sam asked. The boy turned, startled. "Are you hungry? Do you want a drink?" He nodded. "What do you want? Food or drink?"

"Both." He wiped his nose on his arm.

"I can make you a sandwich if you want?"

"Whatever," he said, working the stone back into the wood.

He was dirty and his manners were appalling. She reminded herself to tell Dennis this later, how it was a sign of a poor upbringing. Sam knew getting the sandwich was just an excuse to hang around the kitchen again but the conversation stopped as soon as she went in.

"You're not making something for Ricky, are you?" Lindsay asked. "He eats all the time. He's like a garbage disposal. He'll eat everything you got in there if you're not careful."

"Does he eat meat?" Sam asked.

Lindsay laughed. "Uh, yeah."

"Is he allergic to anything?"

"Nothing we know of."

Lindsay watched Sam as she put together a sandwich with deli turkey slices and Swiss cheese. She took an organic cola made from cactus juice from the fridge, the only soda Dennis hadn't sneered at when she picked it up, and took them back out to Ricky. He looked from the sandwich to the can to Sam and shook his head.

"I don't eat the brown kind." He pushed the paper plate back to her with one finger.

"We don't have anything else." She gave him the soda, which he turned about in his hand, frowning at the unfamiliar logo.

"What is this?"

"It's a Coke. But made from cactus and something. They're OK, honest." Sam put the paper plate and the sandwich down on the floor and sat next to the boy. He wrinkled his nose and started to hand the can back to her when she said, "It's either that or water. Dennis doesn't let us have real Coke in the house."

"Why not?"

"He says it's full of corn syrup."

Ricky shrugged.

"I love it though. I always buy it when I'm out." They fell quiet and behind them Sam could hear muffled laughter from the kitchen. The can hissed as Ricky pulled the tab and took a hesitant sip.

"It tastes like Diet." Ricky looked disappointed.

"Yeah, it's not great. Better than nothing though."

"I guess." He drank it in huge gulps, wincing as he swallowed. The end of his nose was red and raw and he wiped it again on the back of his hand.

"How long have you been sick?" Sam asked eventually.

"Dunno. All week."

"Have you been to a doctor?"

"No," he said with a snort. "I don't even know why we're *here*. It's creepy here." He looked up to her quickly. "Sorry."

Sam sighed. "I think it's creepy too."

"Everyone thinks it's creepy. One time, I was here with my brother Aaron, and he dared his friend to go up and touch the garage, but he wouldn't even do it. And he ate a worm once."

"A worm?"

"Yeah. He does anything if you dare him."

"He sounds kind of gross."

"He is." Ricky started to giggle. Sam could hear the bass rumble of fluid in his chest. After a small coughing fit he asked, "Did he really do all that stuff?" His eyes looked at Sam all wide with hope and horror, wanting to hear a ghost story but not wanting to be afraid.

"Dennis?" Sam asked. "He never did anything. That's why he's not in prison anymore."

"People at school say that there are bodies here. That if they could find the bodies he wouldn't be allowed out of prison, but he hid them really well."

"There's nothing like that here. Those people are just trying to scare you. The police looked all around here. They searched everywhere. There's nothing here. No one could hide them that well."

"What about out there?" He pointed to the back-woods, so dense with foliage that Sam couldn't imagine how vast it was.

"They searched there too."

"What if…" He stopped, shook his head. "Some people say he ate them."

Sam looked him in the eye. "That's just not true. Are you scared of him?"

Ricky shrugged again.

"You shouldn't be scared of him. Dennis hasn't done anything. He wouldn't." She wondered how she could prove to him that it was all just stories and myth. "Besides," she said, "I'm married to him. I'd *know* if he was a bad guy. He'd never hurt anybody."

Ricky looked at her and nodded weakly.

She took the uneaten sandwich and went back inside, stopping to eavesdrop on their conversation in the kitchen. "Remember Alex?" she heard Lindsay say. "Well, he was running a video store in town but the police raided it in like…ninety-seven, ninety-eight? And he had all kinds of illegal videos back there, kids, animals, rape."

"Ugh, I knew it."

"Right? Anyway, he was out by two thousand two, lived in Fiddler Park for a while and now he's back in town. No one gives him shit. You see what I'm saying?"

"He was always a creep."

"And he's out there now, people don't bother him, and you're like some kind of p-puh-puh…"

"Pariah?"

"Right! Oh my God, I was trying to be *smart*. I'm so embarrassed!"

"It's good to see you try."

"Aw, thanks." Her laugh was rusted with years of cigarette smoke.

Sam strode into the kitchen as if there were no one else there, holding the uneaten sandwich in front of her like a shield.

"Oh hey, Sam! He didn't eat it?" Lindsay said.

"No." She dumped it in the trash can. "I don't think he's well enough to be out, really. Maybe you should take him to the doctor?"

"For the *flu*? He'll be fine in two days. He's just trying to get as much time off school as he can. I have to make sure he's not having too much fun or I'll never get him back there. Like Aaron. I tell you about Aaron yet, Dennis? My God, he's so much like you. He got himself suspended for two weeks for fighting, and for telling the teacher to go fuck herself. But she was manhandling him and I told him if any grown-up laid their hands on him, he needs to fight 'em off because only your own blood can lay a hand on you."

Dennis smiled.

"I named him after you. Not his first name, obviously." Lindsay laughed again. "Just his middle name. He's Aaron Dennis."

"Aaron Dennis Durst?" Dennis asked, eyebrows raised.

"Yep." She turned to Sam. "Den was such a big part of my life. I always tell the boys he's their uncle because he was like a brother to me. Well. Kind of." Lindsay winked.

"You're the worst." Dennis shook his head, letting Lindsay paw at him and punch him playfully. "You're just awful, Linds, you're the *worst*." Lindsay wiped imaginary tears of laughter from under her eyes, her heavy makeup smudging ever so slightly. Sam could tell she loved the attention, the teasing.

"Well," Lindsay said eventually, out of breath. "We should go, but I'll see you Sunday night?"

"Sunday?" Sam asked.

"They're releasing the first episode of the show," Dennis said, irritably. "You know this. It was supposed to be the premiere."

Sam tried to ignore Lindsay's smirk as she pulled her handbag over her shoulder. Sam noted how tatty and worn it was. A bunch of oversized plush-animal key rings swayed from the handle.

"Oh, and don't worry," Lindsay said to Dennis, tapping the side of her nose with her index finger. "I haven't forgotten." Dennis didn't reply but Sam just caught him mouthing something to her before he realized she had seen him.

Sam watched them both as Dennis walked Lindsay to the door, his hand resting on her lower back, knowing that their intimacy was built on a history that she would never be a part of.

26

As soon as the sound of the engine died away Sam asked Dennis, "What was that about?" She tapped her nose, her face pulled into a sneering caricature of Lindsay. She knew it was an ugly thing to do but she didn't care.

"She's looked after some personal items for me while I've been away. So that my dad couldn't sell them. Is that OK with you?"

With that he went into the next room to continue stripping the house. Sam stood and listened to the sounds of furniture being snapped and stomped into pieces. She didn't know whether she was in the wrong or not. Mark always said she was clingy, that she was paranoid and possessive and unpleasant. She imagined herself as a different person, the kind of woman who laughed and said *shut up* and pushed men playfully, instead of sulking and fighting. And why couldn't she be that person? Sam wondered. Perhaps she should try.

Dennis was in his old bedroom. The room was mostly untouched, as if Lionel had preserved it, not so much out of sentimentality but as a curiosity, a morbid museum from which he selected items to sell when he was strapped for cash. Sam watched as Dennis sorted through the shelves that lined the top of the room. Junk was crammed in so tightly that he had to hold it all back with one hand while carefully edging something loose with the other.

Without turning to her he asked, "What do you want?"

"I'm sorry," she said.

"Fine."

"I really am. I don't trust you enough. It's difficult for me, seeing how you are with Lindsay because...we're not like that, I guess."

"I don't know why you're jealous of her."

"I'm not, but I see how you two joke with each other and have so much history."

Dennis sighed and stepped down from the bed. "We're just friends, OK? I think you'd like her if you got to know her. You aren't so different. She just likes male approval, you know, like you."

Sam watched his face for clues that he was joking but his eyes were behind those lenses and his face was motionless.

"Do me a favor." He held her hand and she leaned in to him, her head against his shoulder. "Check if the paint is dry and we can add another layer yet?"

"What's the point of this, Dennis?" Sam asked.

"Of what?"

"All the cleaning, the painting. What are we doing here? Are you planning to sell the house?" Sam couldn't imagine anyone wanting to live out here. Certainly, she couldn't imagine anyone local wanting to buy the house.

"I don't know yet," he said irritably. "It's what you do. When someone dies you deal with what they leave behind. You don't just leave it all out to rot. And I don't want to live with that fucking graffiti on the wall anymore. Do you?"

Sam didn't. "I'm sorry," she said. "I get it."

It was sticky-hot outside and mosquitoes stuck to Sam's moist skin in beads of sweat. She slapped one hand against her neck and brought away a black smear of an insect on her palm. She ran a fingertip over the paint: still wet. Not wanting to go back inside and clean, she sat on the porch and daydreamed about where she and Dennis would go next. New York, she hoped, but she knew he wouldn't agree to it. Maybe a house in the Canyons in LA, with an infinity pool that made their hearts pound with the cold when they first stepped in, lit up green in the night while they wrapped themselves together and listened to the water move around them.

It was possible to change. It had to be. *You aren't a bad person, because you want to be good.* If she was bad, she thought, then she wouldn't lie awake at night as she remembered Mark's cry, the shatter of glass and that awful noise that echoed in her skull.

On the porch she sipped a bottle of sparkling water when something flew past her ear and cracked the window behind her. For a second she sat still and asked herself what on earth could have done that. Then another struck her on the shoulder and rolled down her body, a small rock, followed by another ricocheting off the long-dead bug zapper. Shielding her face with her hands she ran inside and called to Dennis. The spot on her arm where the rock hit her stung, turning red. "There's some-one out there again, throwing rocks. They hit me!"

Dennis wasn't in his bedroom. Sam walked back through to his father's room, to the kitchen, to the bathroom, but he was gone. She heard the back door open before Dennis clomped around the cor-ner, a shotgun hung over his shoulder, a strap with the American flag printed all over. He held out one hand to her, gesturing for her to stay against the wall and keep quiet. She watched him unhook the gun and stride through the front door. It felt as if she were dreaming until two gunshots made her jump so much she hit her head on the wall behind her. She put her hands over her ears and braced herself for more but nothing came.

Dennis reappeared and leaned the gun against the wall. "Kids," he said.

Sam waited for more but he had gone to wash his hands in the kitchen. "What happened?" she asked him, voice shaking.

"I fired a couple shots into the air. They ran out of the bushes, probably pissed their pants."

"Wh-where did that come from?"

"The gun? I finally found my dad's stash. He never had a license but he's got about ten of those things in a trunk under the bed. You scared? Don't be, they won't come round peeping on you anymore." He hugged her. "Get cleaned up. We need to go to the store and then we can go out to dinner."

The runt of the litter still wasn't feeding well so Dennis bought some cat-milk formula and a feeding syringe before dinner. They would keep him, Dennis decided, and Tuna, but they would try to rehome the rest before they left. Sam knew Dennis was being kind to her. He insisted on going to a burger place even though he hated it. He ordered a chicken burger without any mayo but it came with mayo anyway. Sam watched him peel the limp, mayonnaise-soaked lettuce from the chicken and wrap it in a napkin.

"You can send it back," Sam said, feeling guilty, like it was somehow her fault.

"It's fine," he said. "Really, don't worry about it."

The waiter returned with a side order of broccoli, limp and overcooked. Dennis looked disappointed but didn't complain. He even talked about where they might live after this was done, smiling politely when she described the house in New England she had always dreamed of. She knew he felt bad about scaring her and she admitted she felt a little better knowing those kids wouldn't be sneaking around anymore.

When they got back home she watched him as he held the kitten, so small he could carry him in one hand. His breath came in little huffs, tiny inhalations followed by a short, hard exhalation. Sam loved how gentle Dennis was with this fragile thing, his patience as he fed the kitten formula with the syringe, wiped his mouth with the cuff of his shirt. Whoever had killed the dog, she knew it wasn't Dennis.

"It isn't looking promising for this guy," Dennis said, holding the kitten close to his face and touching his nose to its head.

"Should we call a vet?"

"We'll see how he feels tomorrow." He put the kitten back in among the crush of his siblings. Sam noticed how much smaller and less mobile he was than the others. The kitten curled up tight and continued his labored breathing. "Hopefully he'll start to improve by tomorrow."

Sam cleaned her teeth and looked at herself in the mirror, at the freckles that had sprouted after a day in the sun.

"Oh God…" Dennis said from behind her.

"What?" She turned and spat, shielding it from his view with one hand.

"You're using my toothbrush…"

"Oh? Sorry." She turned it over in her hand. He was right. She rinsed it off and put it back in the holder.

"What am I supposed to use?"

"Just use this one. I'm sorry, OK?"

"It's disgusting, I can't use that."

"Don't be ridiculous. We're married, and it isn't a big deal."

"It gets food out from between your teeth. We need to go back to the store so I can buy a new one."

"What?"

"It's still open. It's open all night. Let's go."

"I'm too tired, I've been working all day…"

"You worked for about two hours. And it's not like you do anything else. What do you *do*? Besides taking pictures of everything you eat and posting it online?"

Sam stared at him. All day she'd done her best. She'd been quiet and nonjudgmental and cooperative. He'd fired a shotgun, she thought. At *children*, for fuck's sake. And she hadn't bitched at all.

"Do you hate me?" she said eventually.

"Huh?"

"Sometimes I feel like you hate me."

"Look, forget it. I'm just a little worked up today."

He took his toothbrush from the holder and held it under the water for a long time. Standing behind him Sam saw the same stubborn reluctance to apologize that she was guilty of herself. Instead of fighting she looped her arms around his waist and apologized for using his toothbrush. He grunted an acceptance and she went to settle on the airbed in the living room.

He appeared a few minutes later, still silent but not as tense. Without speaking he folded his glasses and rested them on the coffee table, shuffled up to her awkwardly and pulled her into him. They kissed softly; she could hear him breathing and the squeaking of the mattress underneath them. She started to slide a hand down his shorts but he jerked away from her.

"Sorry," he said. They kissed and she tried again, her hand sliding over him.

"No, don't," he said, rolling over.

"I just…"

"Stop it. Not yet." He turned onto his side, his back to her.

It almost hurt, how much she wanted him. She molded herself to his back, and he took her hands in his and held them around him. Part of her wanted to ask him what was wrong. She thought of him in prison, eighteen years old and beautiful, of those months in general population before he moved to Death Row. Had something happened then? Or was it earlier? She remembered how he hated his father. She pictured the late nights, drunken footsteps down the hall, coming closer. She held him tighter. It wasn't something she thought she could ask.

Eventually Dennis relaxed and she fell asleep against him. When she woke up later in the night he was gone and though she tried to stay awake until he returned her eyes closed and she drifted off, waking in the bright morning to see him lying beside her, smelling of outside, his T-shirt slightly cold to the touch.

27

The next morning Sam asked where he had been in the night, but he shrugged.

"Needed to get out, couldn't sleep."

When he went running she set the laptop on her knees in bed and searched for news in the Red River area. The dead dog was the top story, though they said it had been killed in a break-in and there were no details about the head, nothing about evisceration. The police had been lying, Sam thought, just as Dennis had said. The report suggested the dog had been hit with a baseball bat. She couldn't read further. It upset her too much. Instead she lay back and thought of Dennis, imagined his hands inside her dress, fingers pulling her underwear to the side.

"Busy day," Dennis shouted as he came back in. "I have to plan the funeral, we need to fill these dumpsters for pickup and then we better get something together for when Lindsay comes over for the premiere." He made his way into the shower before Sam could respond.

They settled into their routine, Sam cleaning the rooms that Dennis had cleared, winding cobwebs around a duster, using an old toothbrush around the yellowed light switches. No matter how much she cleaned it all looked soiled, the dirt and misery soaked deep into the surfaces. All the wood felt soft and tacky to the touch, as if it were rubbing off onto her own skin until she was covered in the same invisible layer of filth.

The sound of a car outside made her start. This time there were two of them, Officer Harries and the same young cop in an immaculately pressed brown uniform, walking slowly to the door. She went outside before Dennis did and the young man tipped his hat and smiled perfunctorily.

"Morning. Is your husband home?" Dennis came from behind her and squeezed her shoulder with one hand, sending bolts of pleasure and anxiety through her back.

"What now, guys?"

This is about last night, Sam thought. And she looked at everyone, deciding what she would do or say if they asked her where he had been.

"We had reports of some gunfire here around four-thirty yesterday afternoon. You know anything about that?"

Sam breathed out in relief.

"Nope." Dennis shrugged. "You hear anything, babe?"

"Nothing." Sam raised her shoulders elaborately, palms up. It was an absurd gesture, she realized.

"Got some kids who were pretty shaken up. Said you fired a couple off into the air when you caught them snooping around."

"Sounds like it could have been a lot worse. What about the whole Stand Your Ground law? Maybe they should be more careful where they mess around. Some people around here take that kind of thing very seriously."

"You got a license for that weapon?" the younger cop chipped in.

"I'm just speaking hypothetically, of course. There's no weapons here. Maybe those kids got lost. They could have been at some other house around here."

"No other houses out here. Not for a couple of miles."

"Well, maybe they're just telling stories."

"We can get a warrant, Dennis," Officer Harries said. "Or you can let us in and we'll just take the weapon. I know your dad might've had more than just the one he used to shoot himself with."

"Look, we'd love to have you guys in but we're kind of stretched today. Maybe another time?"

"We'll see you again, then. Just be safe, now." Harries looked at Sam, and gave her a small nod.

When they'd gone, Dennis slammed his palm against the wall of the house, over and over, until the cracked window spat out a shard of glass onto the porch. "You see? They just want me back inside. They can't let it go."

"Maybe we should get everything sorted as quickly as possible and just leave. Look at how stressed it makes you."

At this Dennis became agitated. He reeled off a long list of chores that needed to be finished be-

fore they could run him out of town, told Sam she
was being unsupportive, and started to dismantle
his bed in his old room with a renewed ferocity,
muttering under his breath about funeral directors
and coffins and goddamn reverends. He brought
his boot down onto the frame, snapping it in two,
and threw the pieces to the side. Sam picked them
up and took them to the dumpsters, which were
nearly full, stopping for a moment to think again
how her life had changed so much in one year and
how different it could have been.

Sam had often thought that if Mark had been interested and available from the start she wouldn't
have pushed so hard. They had almost nothing in
common, and she remembered with bitterness the
hours she'd spent watching him play *Call of Duty*,
talking into a headset while she marked practice
exams on her lap beside him. He was no Dennis;
he was pudgy and indistinct. There were a billion
Marks, walking around in their faded movie memo-
rabilia T-shirts, *Jaws* and *Star Wars* and *Back to the
Future*, brown hair kept short, telling women they
didn't want a relationship but really, Sam knew,
just holding out for something better to come their
way. And something would because women were
so stupid. They thought a man like Mark would appreciate them more, that because he was dull and
ugly he would love them just for loving him. But
it wasn't how it worked; she knew this now. Even
the fat and boring ones thought they were entitled
to more.

With Dennis she felt more secure. Women mostly

seemed invisible to him, even the truly beautiful ones who moved like cats around him while he spoke. There was only Lindsay who seemed to hold something over him. Lindsay, whose old eyeliner was smudged beneath her new eyeliner, whose face was mapped with hairline wrinkles, the smell of stale smoke trailing her as she walked. They shared some history, something old and buried deep, but she felt it. She felt it the way she could feel the train before it arrived, an energy that traveled through her bones.

Sam walked around to the back of the house and took a seat on an old, rusted chest freezer. She looked out into the dark woods. It was like a whole different world. She considered the way Dennis had grown up, how his life had been on pause for over twenty years while he'd been on Death Row. There were times when she forgot he wasn't something to be worked out, a narrative to be unraveled, but a messy, confused person. Just as she was.

"You ready to go to dinner?" he asked, making her jump.

"Sure." He held out a hand so she could pull herself up. Inside she grabbed her bag and rooted around for the keys.

"Here," he said, shaking the keys from a finger. "Seriously. What would you do without me?"

28

Lindsay arrived on Sunday evening while Dennis and Sam were laying out plates of carrot sticks and hummus for the premiere of the first episode. It felt, to Sam, like the first time they'd done something that a regular married couple would do. It was the kind of scene she remembered from her childhood, watching from the stairs as her mother and father laid out plates of party food wrapped in cling film. But the illusion was shattered as Lindsay leaned on her horn in the driveway until Dennis jogged out to speak to her through the car window.

When he came back he was carrying something inside a brown paper bag. It rattled. Dennis peered inside and exhaled, before wrapping it back up. When Lindsay came in she put down two six-packs and hugged Dennis tightly. From over his shoulder she opened her eyes and looked at Sam for a second before closing them again.

Dennis disengaged himself and walked quickly through the living room, his footsteps disappearing to the right, to the bedrooms at the back of the house. Sam continued placing bowls of nuts and edamame on the coffee table around Dennis's Mac-

Book. Today they would premiere the first episode of *The Boy from Red River*; the rest of the series would be released the following Friday. Carrie had called to say how sorry she was they couldn't be at the premiere. Sam knew she meant it. The rest of the production crew had barely called at all since the incident on *Today's Talk*. Sam thought of how quickly they'd tired of their Death Row pet.

Dennis came back without the bag Lindsay had given him and sat between Sam and Lindsay on the sofa. As they watched the preview he held the sickly gray kitten, wrapped in a hand towel, milk formula hanging in drops from his chin.

"You think he's gonna make it?" Lindsay said, extending a finger to stroke his forehead.

"Maybe," Dennis said.

"If he isn't doing better by tomorrow, we're taking him to the vet," Sam said, using the corner of the towel to wipe his chin.

"Well, if you're looking for homes for the others, I'm game. Think a couple of kittens would be great. Teach the boys some responsibility."

"There's four left to choose from; go take a look," Dennis said.

"Do you know which ones are boys? I don't want them coming home pregnant one day."

"No idea."

"You have to get them neutered, either way," Sam said.

"No point if they're boys," Lindsay said, tipping her head back and pouring in some cashews.

"Uh, yes, there is," Sam said. "Everyone has to

get their cats neutered. That's how it works. Otherwise some other cat is going to come home pregnant and get dumped like this one."

Lindsay rolled her eyes. A powerful sense of righteous indignation rose within Sam and suddenly she felt as if this was her cause, this was what she had always truly believed in. "You can't have the kittens. You're obviously not responsible enough."

"Ha! Fuck *you*! I'll just get them from the fucking pet store, then. Sorry, Dennis, I'm not responsible enough for your kittens."

"She's kind of right though," Dennis said, and the smirk faded from Lindsay's face. "Sorry, Linds, but you're kind of the problem."

They watched in silence for a while. The first episode, to Sam's disappointment, was mostly focused on the core details of the case. It didn't feature anything about their relationship or any of the footage she'd shot with Carrie. Suddenly, young Dennis's face filled the screen. It had the flickering and bleached look of old VHS home videos.

"Oh my God, Dennis," Lindsay said in a hushed voice. "You look so *young*..." She leaned closer to the laptop. It looked as though she might reach out to touch it. "It's so...it's so..." Lindsay started to cry. She covered her face in her hands. Sam didn't know where to look.

"Don't cry, Linds," Dennis said. He tucked the kitten under one arm and hugged Lindsay with the other.

"I'm sorry, I'm really sorry. This is so stupid," Lindsay said, her cries emerging like hiccups.

"I'm here now, aren't I?" Dennis said. Sam wished she hadn't been so mean to Lindsay about the kittens. She wished she knew what to say now.

"I know," Lindsay sniffed. "It just freaked me out for a second. When I think about how long you were…" She lowered her head again and continued to cry.

Sam looked for tissues to offer her but realized they didn't have any. She left the room and returned with a roll of toilet paper, apologizing as she handed it to Lindsay.

"It's fine. Thank you," Lindsay said. "I'm so embarrassed."

"Don't be," Sam said sincerely. "I do this kind of thing all the time, right, Dennis?"

"She's not lying," Dennis said. "She cries over everything."

Lindsay forced out a laugh. "It's crazy though, right?" she said. "I thought you'd never be here again. And here you are."

The credits rolled over a piece of moody piano music and black and white images of Holly Michaels and the river and Dennis's mug shot. Lindsay and Sam applauded and Dennis grinned.

"It'll be huge," Sam said.

"What have people been saying about it?" Lindsay asked. "You know, on Twitter."

Sam had purposely avoided looking all day and was instantly irritated with Lindsay for bringing it up. Dennis got his phone and started to read through the reactions. As Sam had expected, there was a lot of negativity.

"It's only the first episode," Sam said. "And they used so much old footage. It's just that people were expecting something new. Wait until the rest of the series is released."

"Listen to this one!" Dennis said. "'This is the whitest story ever told.' What does that even *mean*?"

"Ignore that," Sam said.

"OK, what does being white have to do with anything?" Lindsay said. "I'm sorry, but that's just racist."

"Right?" Dennis said.

"Not really," Sam said. "Wait, what are you typing?"

Dennis was tapping at his phone furiously. "Nothing," he said.

"Seriously, don't respond!" Sam pleaded.

"Why not?" He looked at the screen for a moment and pressed once.

"What did you say?" Lindsay asked, giggling.

"I asked her what being white has to do with it."

"Delete it," Sam said. "You don't get it. She isn't saying that—"

"She replied!" Dennis said. "'Check your privilege.'"

"She can't explain it because it's bullshit," Lindsay said.

"Just say you understand what she's saying but… What are you writing?"

"'I was the poorest kid in town, my dad beat me, but I am privileged?'"

"Oh God," Sam said.

"He's right though. You don't think he's *right*?" Lindsay said. "Does this shit look like privilege?"

Dennis continued typing. Sam got her own phone and read as he posted: "One year I was the only white guy on my block in Death Row. Not privilege."

The girl replied: "Uh, my point exactly. Please get out of my mentions."

Dennis tweeted on his own feed: "No such thing as white privilege where I am from. Stop bringing it up. If you don't like me, don't watch #BoyfromRR."

"Dennis," Sam said, losing her patience. "You need to delete that! Now!"

"Forget it. I'm allowed to have my opinion on the shit they say."

"But you don't *get it*!" Sam said.

"I don't think *you* get it," Lindsay said. "Dennis came from nothing."

Lindsay left when the beers ran out, bored of watching Dennis bent over his phone. To Sam's disgust she climbed unsteadily into her beat-up truck and crawled out of the driveway into the dark back roads, honking her horn goodbye.

"It's just what people do here," Dennis mumbled without looking up.

"She could kill someone!"

"Probably just another drunk."

"I don't want to drive here at night again, not if they're all off their faces like this."

"Whatever."

Carrie called him repeatedly. Nick called. But Dennis rejected all of them and continued to argue his point. But the more he fought, the more he lost, and he couldn't understand it. He was like a thirsty man drinking from the sea and Sam couldn't make him stop.

Dennis carried on late into the night until his battery eventually ran out. He tossed the phone across the living room. It bounced off the inflatable mattress and skidded under the TV unit.

"Sleep on it," Sam said, rubbing his shoulders. "Look, in the morning it won't seem so bad." She hoped that was true, that it would blow over or that Nick would have the right words to make amends for the evening's madness.

Dennis picked up the kitten and tucked him back under his arm.

"It's not that I don't understand what you're saying," Sam said. "But I think you don't understand what they're saying either. In a way, you're both right. You don't need to take it so personally. They don't know you."

"I'm not taking it personally," he said irritably.

Dennis stood and made his way to the bathroom. Sam followed, still trying to reassure him as he sat on the edge of the bath, watching the water run. He looked tired. Sam felt a rush of love as he kissed the kitten on the head and slid him into the front pocket of his hoodie.

"It'll be fine," Sam lied. "Tomorrow there will be something else everybody will be mad about and no one will remember any of it."

Dennis smiled wearily and ran his toothbrush under the water.

"I love you," Sam said.

"I love you too."

Sam went back to the living room and started to take off her makeup. With a hand mirror she inspected her pores and her eyebrows, plucking errant hairs as she found them. She checked her phone and wondered why Dennis was taking so long.

"Den?" she shouted. "Are you coming to bed?"

He didn't answer.

"Dennis?" She got up and looked toward the bathroom, the door slightly ajar. She knocked with one knuckle. "Dennis?" She pushed it open. The sink was full, the faucet dripping. Dennis stood with his back to her, facing the bath. "What are you doing?" she asked, gently touching his shoulder. He jumped and something fell into the tub with a soft thud. "What's—" Sam recoiled. The kitten was still, his body limp, lifeless. "What happened?"

"He died," Dennis said. "I was holding him and he just…"

"But he seemed fine. I mean…"

"His breathing got worse. I was holding him and he was struggling. Eventually he just—stopped."

Sam tried to look at the body but Dennis moved in front of her.

"Is he wet?" she asked.

"What? I don't know. Don't look at him, you'll upset yourself."

"He just stopped breathing?"

"Yeah, after a while. Like I said, he was struggling. It got worse before he stopped."

Something didn't feel right. Sam had thought the kitten was getting worse but she didn't think it would happen so fast. Unless he'd been sicker than she'd thought.

"I feel terrible," Sam said, starting to cry.

"We did the best we could," Dennis said. "This happens."

He hugged her and as he did he turned her, so she wasn't facing the bath. As he twisted her hair around one of his fingers she felt the cuff of his hoodie against her cheek, damp. She shivered.

"Do you think we were selfish? Trying to keep him alive so long? I'm worried he suffered."

"What else could we have done?" he asked.

"The vet could have put him to sleep," Sam said.

Dennis let go and looked at her, suddenly his face tight with anger. *Put him to sleep?* he said. "How would that have been any kinder?"

"At least he wouldn't have suffered," Sam said uncertainly.

"How do you know that? How do you know it wouldn't hurt? Would you have let them just put *me* to sleep?"

"That's not what I was saying…"

"You don't know if that hurts. You don't know that it would have been kinder than…"

Than what? Sam thought. What had happened?

She looked back at the body in the tub but Dennis pulled her back into him and hugged her tightly.

"I'm sorry we couldn't save him," he said. "We'll bury him tomorrow. You go to bed; I'll find somewhere to keep him until then."

Dennis kissed her and, deftly, maneuvered her out of the bathroom, closing the door between them. She told herself she was being paranoid, that she was upset. But something about the silence behind the closed door gave her chills and she pictured the kitten as she thought she'd seen him so briefly, eyes glassy and fur slick against his tiny body, water pooling around his head.

29

The next morning, when Dennis left for his run, she felt herself let go, as though she'd been sucking in her stomach all night. She'd had bad dreams that flashed through her brain like fireworks, each one quickly replaced by the next. She saw Dennis holding the kitten underwater. Next she could see him holding a dog by the scruff of its neck while it yelped, the flick of a knife through its windpipe. Finally, she saw Dennis on top of Lindsay, holding her hands above her head, looking deep into her eyes.

She needed to see the kitten, his body. She needed to know that she'd been wrong, that his fur was dry and his eyes were closed. It was absurd, she told herself, to believe that Dennis could have drowned him. Even if he was doing it to end his suffering, as she believed he had. But searching the house she found no sign of the kitten. In the bathroom she checked every corner, to see where Dennis could have hidden him while she had been lying awake, listening and running the scene again and again in her head.

As she wandered from room to room that morning she saw the crumpled brown paper bag that Lindsay had brought to him. It was placed carefully among his old belongings in his childhood bedroom, as if he was putting it back where it belonged. Sam knew she shouldn't look but she was drawn to it. If Lindsay had been looking after it all these years then surely it wouldn't hurt if she had a look at it, too. She carefully opened the paper bag. Inside was a metal box, rusted green. It looked, to Sam, like a kind of army-issue lunchbox. It rattled when she lifted it. Even though it was obviously locked, she slid her nails into the seam and tried to lever it up. When it didn't work she banged it against the wall and groaned in frustration. She shoved it back into the paper bag, ripping it as she did so, and shoved it back among the other things. *Fuck him*, she thought, *fuck his secrets. Fuck Lindsay. Fuck them both.*

When Sam calmed down she felt sick with a binger's remorse. This wasn't how she'd wanted to be: the crazy wife snooping through her husband's possessions. Paranoid fantasies about drowned kittens and affairs with old girlfriends. It stopped, now. Why was she so hell-bent on destroying everything that made her happy?

The bag was torn and she couldn't hide it. So she wrapped the box back up as carefully as she could and placed it back where it belonged. This was a fresh start. When Dennis asked her about it she would be honest and they would put it behind them and move on.

But when she heard Dennis return her stomach lurched and she began to panic. Excuses raced through her mind but none seemed believable. She couldn't wait for him to find out; she would have to confront him first. When he'd finished stretching, Sam heard him go to the kitchen and open the fridge. She steeled herself, ashamed and embarrassed. As they met in the hallway, Dennis taking a long drink from a bottle of Smartwater, his head thrown back, Sam started to confess.

"I—"

Dennis's phone rang from the living room. He unplugged it from the charger and answered. "Carrie, I'm sorry, I was going to call…"

Sam let out a long breath and went into the kitchen, where she could eavesdrop in privacy. She heard Dennis try to defend himself but eventually he fell quiet and Sam envied Carrie for being able to get through to him in a way she could not. Finally, he started to speak again.

"You're right. I fucked up. I'm sorry," Dennis said. "I guess I should accept they don't see things the way I do." His voice came closer. "OK. Talk soon. Yeah, you too. Sam," he said, holding the phone out to her. "Carrie wants to speak to you."

"Are you as pissed with him as I am?" Carrie asked.

"It was a…weird night," Sam said, making sure Dennis was out of earshot. "I tried to stop him but he wouldn't let it go." Sam wondered how much she should tell Carrie about last night.

"He's stubborn when he wants to be," Carrie

said. "It's not great for the series, to be honest, but..."

"How was the premiere?" Sam said.

"There were protestors. It was kind of a shit show. Probably better Den wasn't there. Or at least I thought that until I saw Twitter."

"I'm so sorry," Sam said. Everything felt as if it was going wrong.

"It doesn't matter. Dennis is out; you're happy. Right?"

"Yep," Sam said half-heartedly. "Yeah, we're mostly good. I mean... I hate it here, to be honest. I'm lonely. That Lindsay girl is here all the time."

"Ugh..." Carrie groaned.

"They have this weird brother-sister thing going on but they're also kind of flirty?" Sam realized how she sounded but she had to talk to somebody. "Or I might be imagining that. But she's here. All. The. Time. She was here last night, getting him all riled up over that stupid tweet." Sam explained what had happened. She stopped at the part where Lindsay drove home drunk.

"If it's any consolation Dennis told me how he can't wait to get away from Red River. He says he can't wait to start fresh somewhere with you. He just wants you to be happy."

"He said that?"

"Sure. Whenever I speak to him, you're all he talks about. Listen, I have to go. But I'll be at the funeral. We can talk more then."

"Thanks. I just want to speak to someone *nor-*

mal. People out here are…" Sam couldn't put it succinctly enough. "Anyway, we'll talk at the funeral."

After hanging up, Sam went to Dennis. He was in the living room, the crumpled and torn paper bag resting on his knees. Sam started to explain but he stopped her.

"Twenty years and Lindsay never even asked me what was in here. Do you know why?" Dennis asked.

"Because she trusts you?" Sam remembered the night before and felt queasy.

"No. Because she wants *me* to trust *her*. Do you not want that?"

"Of course I do," Sam said.

"Do you think there's something in here I need to hide from you?" He rattled the box, pulled a small key from his pocket and tried to turn it in the lock. The key no longer fit, the lock rusted shut, so he fetched a screwdriver, which he wedged into the seam of the box, and levered up the lid. It popped open.

"Here," Dennis said. Inside were photographs, of himself as a baby, of his mother and grandparents. There were the deeds to the land, a movie ticket stub, a small silver-plated crucifix with a broken chain, an address book. Slowly he took each item out and laid it on the empty sofa cushion next to him. Things of no real value, Sam realized, just things he'd miss if they were gone.

She couldn't even tell him she was sorry. Instead, she knelt on the floor next to him and picked up the photographs: there was a picture of his mother holding him in the hospital, another of him as a boy, not more than five, standing barefoot on the steps of the house. Lastly there was a snapshot of him as a teenager, his arm around a young Lindsay, who wore a crop top and wide flares, her hair plaited into white-girl cornrows. Sam smiled. And there was someone else, a boy who rested his head on Dennis's shoulder, with long thin hair and a wispy teenage moustache.

"Who's that?" Sam asked.

"Howard," Dennis said, taking the photo out of her hand. He looked at it for a moment before putting it back into the tin.

"That was a nice picture," Sam said. "You looked happy."

"I think we were," he said. "I can't remember."

30

Dennis wanted to bury the kitten in a place away from the house, in the woods beyond the fence. Just after lunch, he came into the living room holding a shoebox that Sam knew must contain the kitten's body. He put the box into a plastic bag and passed it to Sam while he got ready to leave. It was almost weightless, she noted sadly, remembering how small and fragile he'd been. Her stomach sank; she was glad when Dennis took the bag back. They set off into the trees, Dennis telling her that he wanted to bury him next to his old cat, Ted, in a place that would be meaningful.

The ground sank under her feet, and she felt the soles of her shoes disappearing into the layer of moss and weeds that covered everything. Dennis told her to stick right behind him, as he tested the earth with a long branch, poking for areas where there were holes who knew how deep, or the roots of trees on which to trip. Everything was covered by a blanket of green.

They'd been walking more than half an hour and, looking over her shoulder, Sam could no longer see the house, or any signs of civilization. Dennis swore he could remember the way, and was leading her confidently, stopping every now and then to get his bearings. But, Sam realized, if he left her there she didn't know how she would find her way back.

They'd started on a diagonal trajectory, bearing right, then turning a sharp left before sidestepping down a steep decline, before heading straight on once again. There had been no distinguishing features since the decline, and soon paranoia started to grip her. He would leave her there, Sam knew, and as it got darker she would fall and be trapped in a hole, left to die in some bottomless pit.

The air was thick, as moist and claustrophobic as a swimming-pool changing room. Still, she walked silently behind him, her clothes sticking to her body, sipping from a bottle of piss-warm water, watching a Rorschach of sweat spread on the back of Dennis's T-shirt as they weaved between fallen trees and heavy foliage.

"Almost there," he said eventually. "I remember all of this."

Sam didn't think anyone could possibly remember something as chaotic as this but Dennis was more at home here than she had ever seen him. She looked around her, disoriented, and stumbled, her ankle twisting underneath her, stuck in a tangle of roots. The pain was immediate and she cried out.

Dennis turned back to her. "What is it?"

"My foot. I think I've broken my foot."

"Shit. Why didn't you stay behind me?" He dropped his branch and slid off her shoe. "It's OK,

I'm just seeing if you really broke it, or if it's a sprain." He cupped her heel in his hand and moved her foot to the right. Instinctively, she pulled away from him and he supported her foot so it didn't fall to the ground. He repeated the motion to the left and she cried out again.

They sat on the ground for some time. Dennis asked Sam for updates on the pain, a scale of one to ten, and eventually she felt it subside a little. He found another branch for her to use as a walking stick and persuaded her to continue the ten minutes to Ted's grave. "It's just a sprain," he said. "You wouldn't be up right now and walking if it was broken."

Each step sent a shock of pain up Sam's leg and into her core. The branch splintered in her hand and she nearly sobbed in relief when he finally said, "It's here!"

At the next clearing Sam could see a blue plastic sheet wrapped around one tree; underneath was a flat stone with a blue-painted inscription: "Ted 1990." Around it hung decorative objects such as a crow might collect: chunks of bottle-green glass swinging from string; a ceramic cat, faded from the weather; shapes made out of bent twigs and tied with bent wire, stars, hearts, diamonds. Dennis crouched next to the stone and pulled up the weeds that had grown around it.

Sam's ankle ached and she looked around for something on which to sit. As she took a step backward she felt the edge of something beneath her heel, and looked down to see the corner of another

slab, overgrown with a tangle of what looked like
veins—bits of undergrowth, dark red and green.
She ran her toe over the stone and pulled the vegetation back to see a date, also in paint, "1987." She
began to notice more of the glass shapes, wink-
ing as they twisted and caught in the light. Sam
moved around, trying to find a place to sit down,
and she tripped on other flat rocks, each with a
date, some with "Dog" or "Rat" written on them
in paint that seemed to fuse with the stone's surface and some where details had been carved into
the rocks, the lettering filled with more paint. More
caught her eye in the disarray of nature, little pockets of human interference. To her it looked almost
like a shrine. She shivered.

"Dennis?" She leaned against a tree to take the
weight off her right ankle. "What are all these?"

He looked around as if he were seeing it for the
first time.

"Were these all…pets?"

"No. Just animals I saw around."

"Dead animals?"

He was kicking a cut of wood the size of a desktop. As it fell back insects skittered in all directions,
some of which he crushed under his boot.

He shrugged. "Everything deserves its own
grave. Even my father, right?" He smiled at her
and she stared back, unsure. There must have been,
at a glance, thirty or so little graves.

Beneath the wood was a rudimentary toolbox,
also crawling with insects. He pulled out a rusted
old trowel, found a spot on the ground near Ted's

tomb and started to dig. The earth was soft, as spongy as cake, and Sam watched him meticulously scooping the dirt and piling it at the side of the hole. Eventually he clapped his hands against his jeans to clean them and picked up the shoebox. He took the lid off and just looked at the kitten for a while. Sam turned away; she'd seen the kitten's body curled stiff, face screwed up tight as if bracing himself for a punch, and she didn't want to see it again. She heard the dirt hitting the lid of the shoebox and looked back. Dennis sniffed and wiped his nose with the back of his hand. She wondered if he was crying.

Dennis asked her to help him look for a stone but after limping over the treacherous terrain for a while she decided to rest up for the long walk home. She found a fallen log, sat down and looked at her phone: no signal. She listened for Dennis, but he was out of earshot, and was away long enough for her to worry he'd left her there.

He returned carrying a rock with both hands. It wasn't flat like the others but had a smooth surface, and he buried it until only the smooth side emerged from the earth. From his pocket he took a bottle of Sam's nail polish. Sam watched him paint a lurid red "2015" and then "S+D." She wasn't sure whether to feel flattered or creeped out.

Dennis spent some time bending and tying twigs together, twisting wire around the joints, while Sam watched the sky starting to gray through the trees. If it rained it would only make the journey home even harder and she willed him to finish quickly so she could get back to the house and take some painkillers. Soon there was a low rumble of thunder and heavy drops of rain hit her cheeks and rolled down like tears.

"Shit," Dennis said. He stepped back to look at the grave and then patted the earth by the kitten's headstone. Before leaving he covered the toolbox with the plank of wood and beckoned for Sam to follow.

Sam walked slowly, trying not to put too much pressure on her right ankle. "How much further is it?" she asked, raising her voice to be heard over the sound of the rain hitting the large leaves of palms around them.

"Over an hour," he shouted back.

"Which way is the road? Is there somewhere else we could go?"

He shook his head and pointed at the forest ahead of them. "That way's just woods for miles. *That* way is back where we came. And that way's the mangroves and the lake, and too close to bear territory."

"Bears?" Sam said, voice shaking.

"Don't see too many here but yeah, bears. Best we stick to this route."

The closest Sam had ever been to nature were the Center Parcs holidays her family took when she was younger. There she rode a rented bike along a heavily signposted trail and had a picnic under a redwood tree. It was hard to imagine a forest in Britain large enough to get lost in, to be somewhere

so vast you could walk for two hours to a place un-
disturbed for over twenty years.

He turned back to her. "Can you do this?"

"I don't know," she said. "I don't think so."

With a sigh, he turned and crouched, patting his
back, and she was suddenly shy, reluctant to climb
onto him and no longer feeling vulnerable but
vast, stocky, immovable. Ignoring her hesitance,
he hooked his arms behind her legs and started to
lift her, forcing her to cling to him to stop herself
falling backward. And eventually she was up, legs
around him, trying not to choke him with her arms.

It slowed them down so that the sun was setting
by the time they arrived back at the house, pulling back the broken chain fence and navigating
the debris scattered around the backyard. Dennis
placed her down once the ground was flat, and as
he stretched his back she limped into the house and
went straight to take off her shoe.

Her ankle was swollen and what looked like a
faint bruise was spreading like ink on water. Unable to get into the shower by herself, she asked
Dennis to help her, which he did without looking
at her body. As she stepped out, he held out a towel
and looked down to the side, which only made her
feel worse.

The pain did not ease with a Tylenol, nor could
she lie next to Dennis in bed as each movement
sent shock waves up her leg.

In the night, she woke him up. "It must be broken. I need to go to hospital..." but he urged her to

wait until morning, to give the swelling a chance to subside. But by morning it was worse.

"Should I call an ambulance?" she asked. "I don't think I can drive."

"I don't have a license and you know the cops around here are looking for any excuse to harass me. But you can't call an ambulance just for a sprained ankle. Can't you just use your left foot?" Dennis said, walking down the hall and returning with the car keys. He wouldn't be able to go with her, he explained, as he needed to meet the funeral directors today. "Don't worry, Lindsay will give me a ride."

Before she left he asked her not to tell the doctor where she hurt her leg. "That spot in the forest is kind of my place, you know what I mean? You're the only person I've shared it with. I don't need people trampling it up trying to sell a story about me. Can you say you hurt it while we were working on the house?" Drowsy from her lack of sleep and eager to get going, she agreed.

It was clear she shouldn't be driving as she jumped her left foot from brake to gas, often catching the edge of one pedal with the side of her shoe while her right foot lay throbbing to the side.

An hour later she was back in the hospital in which they'd watched Lionel die. It was louder in the ER. She filled out the forms on her lap with a shaking hand and her name was called much quicker than she was expecting. She glanced back guiltily at a young boy curled tight to his mother, hair plastered to his forehead with fever.

It wasn't a break, the doctor said, but a severe sprain, with some damage to the ligaments. He wrapped it tightly with gauze and told her to rest it as much as she could.

"Come back in eight weeks if you're still having trouble," he said, writing a prescription. This she relayed to Dennis by phone, in a Vicodin bubble, leaning on a crutch outside the hospital. Her insurance had expired months ago and the shock of the medical bill was cushioned only by the orange bottle of painkillers they handed her, along with a script for two refills. The car would have to be collected by the rental agency from the hospital parking lot and she would need to find her own way home. For a minute she was horrified at the thought of Lindsay coming to collect her but instead Dennis said, "I'll get you a taxi," and hung up without telling her when it would arrive. On the drive back she dozed and dreamed of leaving Red River. When this was over, she thought, Dennis would be different. It was something about this place, as if it changed him, and she could feel it changing her, too.

31

Now that Sam was incapacitated, Dennis relied heavily on Lindsay to get to the store and organize the funeral. Sam managed her frustration by taking her Vicodin every four hours, the pills dulling everything around her, making her sleepy and warm.

On the day of Lionel's funeral, she decided she would take her dose when she was in the hearse, hoping to ride out the service on an opioidal wave. The suit Dennis wore was tailored, and had been given to him on one of their first days together. He'd never worn it and to Sam he looked like someone new. She became shy around him and awkwardly attempted to fix his tie while he slicked down a rebellious lick of blond hair at the back of his skull. She was still surprised by how handsome he was, even after all the months they'd been together. The kick of desire she felt still hurt as he brushed away her hand.

Outside the sky was a troubling gray. Hurricane warnings were in effect and the old house trembled in anticipation, a teasing current of air trickling through the cracks and gaps in the windows and roof. How the house had weathered so many storms before, Sam didn't know. Maybe this would be the one that leveled it to the ground so they could leave. Dennis didn't believe in hurricane warnings and said they'd discuss it after the burial.

As they waited outside for the funeral car, Dennis looked straight ahead, his jaw working on another stick of cinnamon gum. She leaned in and kissed him, her lips tingling from the spice of cinnamon.

The car arrived, late, and the funeral director in the passenger seat got out to hold the door open for them, shaking their hands as they climbed in. Sam looked over her shoulder at the coffin behind them, which seemed absurdly small, until she remembered that Lionel was an amputee. Relieved it was a closed coffin, she took a pill out of her clutch bag and opened one of the bottles of water that sat in the cup holders either side of them. Dennis watched her from the corner of his eye. As they rounded a bend, the car jumped and jarred on the uneven road, disturbing the flowers in the back, shaking them out of their perfect arrangement. When the car hit a pothole there was a sliding sound and a soft thump as if Lionel's body had shifted, his head bumping against the end of the coffin. Sam became a little queasy. Reaching around Dennis, she opened the window a crack and leaned in to the fresh air, breathing in shallow gasps.

The driver apologized profusely at the end of the journey: his funeral cars just weren't suitable for roads like that, he said as the director rearranged the flowers. The church was tiny, white, with a large wooden cross hanging over the doorway. Outside Sam could see Carrie and a few of the film crew talking among themselves. There were a few people Sam had never seen before, and some uniformed police officers.

"For fuck's sake…" Dennis murmured, extending his hand as Carrie came to greet him, Dylan teetering behind her in high heels that sank into the soft ground as she walked.

"Fucking antagonistic pricks, right?" Carrie said. "I can't believe this. It's your father's *funeral*. Ugh, anyway, you guys OK?" She hugged Sam tightly.

"Nice to see you two again. Sorry it's not under better circumstances," Dylan said.

"I'm so glad you're here," Sam said. Seeing people she cared about made her aware of how lonely she'd been.

"What happened to your leg?" Carrie asked.

"Sprained it while I was out in the yard," Sam said.

"You poor thing!"

Sam gestured toward the crutch and made a gesture as if she was *coping*. The truth was that she was almost enjoying being injured: the likes she got when she posted a picture of her ankle on Facebook, the way Dennis held out his hand to her each time she stood. The ritual of wrapping her ankle each morning, admiring the tie-dye bruise in all its yellows and purples as it changed day by day. The pills.

"Really painful. It's so hard when I'm up and about like this but the pain medication helps." Behind them, the group of people Sam didn't recognize watched Dennis with hostile expressions.

Dennis greeted mourners before leading them into the church. Carrie, Sam and Dylan sat in the front row. A few others sat further back: people who must have known Lionel; the rest of the crew. Sam felt depressed as she looked at all the empty seats.

The reverend walked in, leading the pallbearers and holding a red Bible to his chest. Behind him walked Dennis, his corner of the coffin resting on his shoulder. The other pallbearers were from the funeral home, strangers who nodded solemnly at Dennis as they put the coffin down on a cheap stand at the front by the altar. A red curtain hung around it but the gold wheels protruded at the bottom.

The reverend began. Dennis took his seat next to Sam and held her hand. She gazed at him and he turned to her and mouthed, "What?"

Sam lifted his hand to her mouth and kissed it.

There were some prayers; then Dennis stood to give the eulogy.

"Thank you all for coming," he said, reading from a folded piece of paper in his hands. He looked up and smiled before lowering his head again. He read steadily. "My father was an alcoholic who burned most of his bridges while he was alive. He was not an easy man to get along with. If he knew I was giving this eulogy right now he would probably shoot himself all over again." He paused for laughter but the church was quiet. By Sam's side

Carrie and Dylan smiled at him, and he continued. "Anyway. We didn't have a great relationship, but he was the only family I had left, so, obviously, you know, this is not easy. I didn't know who would even be here today—there were only a few people I could invite. But I'm lucky to have friends and a wife who care enough to be here, so thank you." Sam mouthed, *I love you*, and he nodded.

"The only thing I could think to say here was this: He wasn't a great guy, he wasn't a kind man, he pissed most people off and he never achieved anything. But"—Dennis pushed his glasses up his nose—"he was the only father I had. Thanks."

People coughed and shifted in their seats, then some conversation started at the back of the room. The reverend added some lines about how fathers are irreplaceable and it's hard to put into words the loss we feel when our parents pass on, but the whispering continued in the back pews.

Shortly afterward, they were back in the church-yard, where the police officers still stood, shifting on their feet and casting their gazes at the spectators along the edge of the grounds, as if in anticipation of an attack. Sam scanned the faces for Harries but she saw no one she recognized. This, at least, was a relief.

"I don't even know how these people knew about this. I didn't put anything in the paper," Dennis said.

"Rubberneckers," Carrie said.

"Ignore them," Dylan agreed.

The funeral director and the pallbearers wheeled

the coffin over to the side of the open grave in the small cemetery to the side of the church. The crowd moved closer and started to chant something.

"The fuck are they saying?" Dennis asked. Everyone craned their necks to see what was happening.

As the crowd got closer they started to make out the words. "Where are the girls? Where are the girls?" One woman held a picture of Lauren Rhodes above her head; underneath it read, "Lauren's parents buried an empty coffin!!!"

"Unbelievable," Carrie said. "Fucking nut jobs!"

"Where are they, Dennis?" a man shouted. "Where are *they* buried?"

The police watched but didn't move forward to break it up.

"I've had enough of this shit," Dennis said, starting toward them.

"Dennis! Stop! Don't do anything stupid," Carrie said, running after him. Sam watched as Dennis approached the man at the front of the group and began pointing in his face. The man was clearly frightened and instinctively stepped back, but forced himself to stay facing Dennis, bolstered by the approaching police officers.

Carrie started to pull Dennis back, pleading. A police officer stepped between the two men and the protestor fell back into the group. An argument ensued between Dennis and the officer, until the police formed a line between the protestors and the funeral party. He and Carrie returned to the graveside and Dennis nodded to the reverend, who stood, nervous, his hands shaking as he held his Bible in front of him. Sam tried to hold Dennis's hand but he pulled it away and balled his fists by his side.

Afterward, Dennis had booked a table in a restaurant just outside of Red River. Lindsay showed up as they all sat down to eat and ordered a double vodka and Diet Coke. Carrie leaned in and asked, "Who shows up to the wake but skips the funeral?"

"Isn't that weddings?" Dylan said.

"I think she's putting the drinks on our tab *and* she'll probably drive home after…" Sam said. She and Carrie smiled at each other.

"Oh my God…" Lindsay said, so loud that everyone froze with their forks halfway to their open mouths. "Look," she said, pointing to the window. The table turned and looked at a man who had cupped his hands to the glass, peering in. He was skinny, unkempt, with long black hair that receded from his forehead. When Dennis looked up the man waved slowly.

"Is that…Howard?" Lindsay said.

Dennis pushed his chair back and stood up, suddenly pale. He excused himself and the group watched quietly as he passed the windows around the outside of the restaurant. When he saw Howard, he extended his hand but Howard didn't accept it. Carrie looked away, uncomfortable, and started to talk quietly to Dylan. Sam felt she shouldn't be watching but she stared as hard as Lindsay did, trying unsuccessfully to read their lips. Howard was clearly angry about something, but it was impossible to say what it was. Dennis stood still as Howard ranted, before finally Howard pushed him once, and walked away quickly as Dennis stumbled back a few steps,.

Dennis put his hands in his pockets and looked at them in the restaurant. Sam and Lindsay both quickly turned back toward their plates, though they knew he'd seen them watching him. He returned a short time later, a layer of moisture on his skin, his eyes rimmed red. When they asked him what was wrong he told them it was nothing, but Sam noticed a gentle tremor as he picked up his drink, and Lindsay gave her a knowing look across the table.

"How long are you staying?" Sam asked Carrie as they left the restaurant,

"We're flying back tonight… This storm…we can't risk it."

"But you two should definitely visit!" Dylan added.

"Mm, definitely. But, um, we've got some stuff left to do on the house…" Sam said.

Carrie looked over at Dennis, who was standing by Lindsay's truck. The pair of them were talking intensely.

"You can always come out by yourself, you know."

"I think he really needs me right now? He's having a hard time."

"I'm only thinking about what *you* need. This

situation here is…not great. You don't seem well, not yourself."

"I'm fine! It's these painkillers. I'm tired."

"I don't want you to worry about a few stupid haters, OK? They're a very loud but very small minority, remember that."

"I know," Sam said, though she believed otherwise.

"Thanks for coming," Dennis said from behind her. "It was great to see you both. We really appreciate it. Are you sure you can't stay?"

Around them the sky was dust-gray and Dylan's hair blew across her face, wrapping itself around her neck like a rope.

"We'll be lucky if this flight isn't grounded as it is," Carrie said. "Supposed to be a big one, this hurricane."

Dennis laughed. "They always say that and it comes to nothing. You Californians could do with experiencing a little weather now and then."

"All the same, I think we'll pass, Dennis," Carrie said, hugging him.

"We'll be finished up here soon and then we'll come visit, I promise."

Sam wondered what he meant by "finished." As time had passed it had become less and less clear what the point of the visit was. She had hoped that once the funeral was over Dennis would realize how futile it was to clean the house to try and sell it. Whatever he was doing there, it seemed only he would know when it was done.

* * *

Dennis helped Sam into the truck, threw her crutches into the bed, and slid in next to her so that Sam was pushed up close to Lindsay as she drove. On the way back to the house she rested her head on Dennis's shoulder and semi-dozed.

"She seems pretty out of it. What's she taking?" Lindsay said, not attempting to lower her voice.

"I don't know. Painkillers. Let it go, Linds. She hurt her leg pretty bad."

"Whatever. I'm only asking."

Sam felt his hand squeeze her shoulder, and listened to the sound of the engine as they drove the rest of the way home in silence. The bumps in the road woke her up as her bad ankle bounced in the footwell of the truck. From the driveway she could see grass cuttings and bits of trash from the dumpsters were strewn across their garden. Blown by the wind, wrappers and cardboard tumbled over the grass. The mess made the place look abandoned, as if the people inside had left in a hurry.

"Shit," Dennis said, opening the door and reaching back in to help Sam onto the grass. "Coming in for a minute?" he asked Lindsay. Sam faltered in his arms.

"Sure." Lindsay pulled another six-pack from the bed of the truck and offered one to Dennis and Sam. He shook his head and she shrugged.

They sat on the porch, Lindsay tapping her ash into her empty can of beer as she drank the next.

"Howard though. Can you believe it?" she said after a while.

"Didn't think I'd see him again," Dennis said.

"I've seen him around. He never says hi. Always with his dad. It's pathetic."

"Do they live together?" Sam asked.

"Until recently," Lindsay said. "Two grown-ass men, never had any women there, never had any company at all."

"Where is he living now?" Dennis asked.

"The trailer park where the old factory used to be. Oh shit!" Lindsay pulled her feet up onto the bench, hugging her knees. Sam clutched at Dennis.

"What?" he said, scanning the garden for intruders.

"Look at the *size* of that bastard!" Lindsay pointed to the floor as a large brown spider ambled past.

Sam shrieked and brought her feet up onto the bench. Lindsay laughed until her laughter descended into coughing. Dennis took the cigarette from between her fingers and leaned down to the spider. He touched the cherry to its body and the spider stuck to the glowing tip of the cigarette, its legs wriggling as it tried to free itself. Dennis watched it, then put the cigarette to his lips, the spider still wriggling on the tip, and inhaled. The spider's legs curled inward, twitching, and then it was still.

Sam watched, appalled, as the smoke poured out of Dennis's mouth and nostrils. The spider burned, turning black, shrinking.

"*Gross*, Den," Lindsay said. He smiled and offered her the cigarette back. "Ew! No fucking thanks."

Sam felt ill. As he took another puff she thought less of the spider in its death throes than she did of the fact Dennis didn't cough when he inhaled. It was as if he'd smoked all his life and she'd never known. She felt suddenly very alone, as though the person she married had never existed and she had woken up to a life she didn't recognize, in the middle of a story she didn't understand.

32

That night the wind picked up and bullets of rain dashed the windows.

Dennis set about securing the dumpsters in the front yard, strapping huge sheets of plastic over the piles of junk that could be blown from the heap and hit the house. The kittens mewed incessantly, while the mother sat, ears back, emitting a low growl as she watched the screen door waving in its frame.

From the garage Dennis produced two huge water containers, yellowed and dusty, rinsed them in the bath and filled them with water from the faucets.

"I guess this storm's been upgraded," he said, raising his voice over the weather that pounded the walls. "Might be best to stick this one out in the storm shelter."

Sam didn't like the way the shutters banged open and shut in the wind, or the way the rain lashed the windows, so she didn't question what Denis said. She only nodded, and allowed herself to be led to the back door and down the steps, soaked the minute she was outside, her clothes clinging to her skin.

Still there was the constant pressure in the air that never seemed to break, even after the heaviest rain.

At the bottom of the steps, Dennis kicked back some weeds to reveal a trapdoor made of wood that led under the house. He lifted the door and she peered into the darkness, unable to make out anything inside.

"There's no electricity!" Dennis shouted. "We need flashlights. I'll take you down there and then I'll go get the stuff!"

"I don't want to go in there," Sam said.

"You want to get crushed when the old place falls down?"

"I thought you said these storms are never that bad."

In the distance Sam could hear the crack and groan of trees bending in the wind. She looked at Dennis again.

"Trust me," he said, "You'll be safer down here."

Inside, the air was cool and dank. As her eyes adjusted she could see the detail around her: a cot on one side, a slumping, lumpy-looking sofa on another and a large plastic bucket in the furthest corner.

"I'll bring you something dry to wear. What else do you need? We could be here all night," Dennis said.

"My pills," she said, quicker than she had intended. "And, um, my Kindle. Um…" Dennis was becoming impatient as he hovered at the foot of the stairs ready to leave. "Can I wear your jumper? The one I like, the gray one."

"Sure, whatever, anything else?"

"Be quick, please. It's weird down here."

"Sure."

As Dennis left he shut the door behind him and Sam found herself sitting in a darkness so thick she couldn't see her hand in front of her face. She forced herself to breathe slowly. It occurred to her he had never mentioned the storm shelter before. For a second she worried, *What if I never get out?*

Sam stood and held her arms in front of her, taking tiny steps, feeling for the stairs. If she could make it up there, she might be able to open the door. She reached the wall, the concrete smooth under her fingertips. The stairs weren't there. She felt disoriented. Panic started to set in. She'd never known she was afraid of dark, enclosed spaces. She realized she'd never been in one before. The walls were thick; the sound of the storm above was a whisper. If Dennis were to lock the door from outside, no one would ever know she was there, no matter how much she screamed. She asked herself why she was thinking this.

Finally, the door opened, and Dennis returned with a bag and a lamp that wound up with a crank on the side and buzzed like a hornet.

"What were you doing?" he asked her, helping her back to the sofa.

"I freaked myself out a little," she said, embarrassed.

This time he left the door open as he brought things down: water bottles, a box of food, the box of mewing kittens, their writhing and angry

mother, a litter box and finally a sack of cat litter. Sam folded her damp clothes and changed into
what Dennis had brought down: his sweater that
smelled of him and which hung over her hands and
made her feel petite. She pulled the neck up to her
nose and sniffed.

"Stop stretching it," he said.

Sam looked at the time on her Kindle and
was dismayed to see she still had two and a half
hours until she could take another Vicodin. Dennis changed from his damp clothes, his back to
her. Every time she shifted on the sofa the rusted
springs beneath her creaked.

"Stop fidgeting," Dennis said.

The kittens were clumsily exploring the room,
while Tuna sulked halfway up the stairs, ears flat.
Sam checked the time again and felt a surge of irritated misery. Eventually she decided she would
take just one extra tablet for now, to tide her over
until later.

Dennis was pouring cat litter into the bucket.
"If you have to go, go here. Then pour cat litter
over it. OK?"

Sam nodded, though she was already dead set
on not drinking for the night. Thankfully the pills
made her constipated and she felt safe in the knowledge she wouldn't have to shit in the corner while
Dennis complained about it from the other side of
the room.

"It gives me the creeps down here," Sam said.

"You get used to it," Dennis said. "My dad
locked me down here once. I got caught taking

some things at the old folks' home. When he found out he beat me, threw me in here. Left me down here over a day, no light, nothing."

Above them, the world was raging. In their quiet and airless room, she felt it trying to burst in.

Every now and again came these reminders of the horrible life Dennis had led before her, and it made her feel like shit that she couldn't do anything to take away all that had happened. No, worse than that, she hated herself for the things she did to ruin the life he had now: whenever she didn't trust him, whenever she started an argument, whenever she tried to make him be something he wasn't, or do something he didn't want to.

"I'm sorry," she said.

"For what?"

"For being pushy, for trying to force you to… you know, when you aren't ready."

"Samantha."

"No. I'm always pushing you or I'm starting these fights. I always do this, always."

"It's OK…"

"It isn't OK! I always fuck things up! I don't know what's wrong with me."

"There's nothing wrong with you."

"But there is. I'm a terrible person. I've done awful things but I think this is even worse."

"Even worse than what?" he asked.

She shook her head, wishing she hadn't said anything but also wanting to say everything, finally, to someone who wouldn't lie to her.

"Worse than what, Sam?"

"I…when Mark broke up with me I…"

"Your ex-boyfriend?"

"We used to argue, a lot. I was jealous. Sometimes he really messed with my head, you know? One minute he said he loved me and the next he was saying how he didn't want a relationship. It had been three years! When I think about it now, I don't know if I even loved him. It's like I was insane. One night I was driving us back from dinner. He was supposed to stay at my place but now he was like, 'I don't know if I should stay over, I feel like we need some time apart…' He's saying all this after a whole evening of, 'What's wrong?' 'Nothing.' 'What's wrong?' 'Nothing.' You know? He's telling me now, in the car, I've had a glass of wine, I'm tired.

"I asked him, 'Why? Why now?' He says, 'I can't keep hurting you.' Can you believe that? As if he's doing me a favor. I'm like, 'Fine, fine,' and he asks me to drop him back at his house. He lived with his parents still. He was always saying he was saving money but… He was a real mother's boy. She never liked me. It drove me crazy. So I drove him there. I thought I could handle it but when we got there…he got out of the car like it was easy for him. I could tell he'd never loved me, he'd been lying the whole time. I followed him to the door, I was screaming. He was worried the neighbors would hear, I guess, so he let me in. I get in there and his parents aren't home, which just makes me scream even louder.

"Then, I don't know, I went up to his room. He

was so precious about his stupid room. He had all these *toys*. Figures. Things he painted himself. I started breaking them, I was like, 'Tell me, be honest. You've never loved me, have you?' and eventually he says it, he says, 'I don't love you, I'm sorry,' and then he says, 'And I met someone new, OK?'

"I didn't expect it. I'm standing there, I'm looking for something else to break, just to try and hurt him, just a little, and I pick up this glass of water and I throw it. It hits the shelf and it explodes, glass everywhere. He screams; he's holding his face. I panic. I try to pull his hands away but he won't let me near him, like he's scared of me. There's blood rolling down his neck. I keep saying, 'I'm so sorry! I'm so sorry!' but he tells me to get out. He says he's going to phone the police and I beg him not to. I didn't mean to hurt him like that, I really didn't. I'd just wanted him to feel something!

"I promise I'll go if he lets me see his face. He can't open his left eye, and there's so much blood. I tell him he needs to go to hospital but he won't go with me. Instead he calls an ambulance. I wait because I don't want him to call the police. He asks me to go, again, he says if I go and leave him alone, if I don't call him again, he'll say it was an accident. So I left. I drove the car to the corner and I cried. I waited until I saw the ambulance and then I left."

Sam took a breath. It didn't feel like a relief to say it all, the complete story. It felt dirty and wrong.

"A few days later his mum rang me. She said that he was going to lose the sight in that eye. She'd wanted to call the police but he stopped her—I think because he was afraid of me, more than anything. Not because he cared about me."

After a while Dennis spoke. "Is that it?" he said.

"Yeah," Sam said, confused.

"Listen. Lindsay tried to run me over with her dad's car when I told her I just wanted to be friends. Lauren threw a beer bottle at my head. This is just what girls do when they get pissed off."

"Lauren?" Sam said. For the first time since it had happened, she started to feel a little better.

"Yeah. Lauren Rhodes. I told her I didn't want to go to this dance? She said she wanted to go so I told her to take someone else. I guess it was the wrong thing to say because she threw her beer at me. I guess it could have broken and I could've been just like—what's his name?"

"Mark." Sam laughed in spite of herself.

"Right. No big deal. It was just an accident."

"You don't think I'm crazy?" she asked.

"I think all girls are a little crazy," he said.

It was something Sam wanted to believe. Since it had happened, all she'd felt was shame and guilt. Now she felt absolved, relieved.

"You've never talked about Lauren before," she said after a while.

"Not much to say, really. At the time we barely knew each other. I don't know why she flipped out so much."

Sam thought of how Dennis must have looked back then and of Lauren: the cheerleader and the football player. It made perfect sense to her, and she understood why Lauren would be driven mad by him.

"Anyway. After she... I can't talk about any of this stuff without people making something of it."

"Wait... Lindsay tried to run you over?" As Sam laughed he fell onto the sofa next to her and pulled her into him.

"Like you can talk," he said, teasing. He held her close and kissed her head. She shivered. "You're so cold," he said, holding her tighter, moving his lips to her neck, biting her skin. He ran his hands up her thighs and under her clothes. She stayed still, letting herself enjoy it, not pushing him. He kissed her ear, cupped her breast, ran his nails over her skin and down her back. She turned her face so he could kiss her, and he bit her lip slightly too hard, and she pulled back but he pulled her forward. She put her leg across his lap. Then it stopped, his hands still.

"Do you want a drink?" he asked, getting up to grab a bottle of water from the corner.

"No," she said, her whole body hot with warm, rushing blood.

He didn't return to the sofa. He lay back down on the cot, his back to her, too still to be sleeping. She listened to the faint sounds of the storm purging the air. She imagined opening the hatch in the morning and finding the air crisp and unburdened but she knew that it wouldn't be. The air would already be full, the pressure rising in anticipation of the next storm.

33

The light was dazzling when Dennis eventually opened the door to the storm shelter the next morning. They ran inside the house, desperate to clean their teeth and get into fresh clothes. At first the faucets ran brown, then clear, and Sam hesitated before running her toothbrush under the water. Tired and sore from the night in the damp shelter, Dennis suggested she lie on the bed in Lionel's room instead of their air mattress. It was the only thing left in the otherwise bare room. Sam resisted, but Dennis made the bed with clean sheets and she was too tired to argue. Before leaving her to sleep, he placed a cup of green tea on the floor by the side of the bed. She was determined to learn to like it. Instead of coffees with four pumps of sugar syrup she would drink the flavorless green teas Dennis enjoyed. It was cleansing and she knew she needed to be cleansed. Inside she was black as a smoker's lung, the jealousy and the hate and the lust all seeping deep into every part of her.

When she woke up the tea had been replaced by a glass of water and two Vicodin, stacked one on top of the other. She leaned over the edge of the bed and looked at them, held one between her fingers. She remembered the night before only hazily and wanted to be clearer today. But her head was aching, her leg was sore, and—promising herself she would cut down later—she threw both pills into her mouth. As she swallowed, one stuck at the back of her throat and she gagged. With another gulp she loosened the pill and lay back down.

She'd been aware of a general amount of noise since she'd woken up. The sound of chat shows on the TV. It seemed strange that Dennis would be watching television, she thought, let alone a chat show. Then it dawned on her that Lindsay might be in the house. Hesitantly, she limped out of bed and into the hall.

Around the door she saw the side of Lindsay's head, flyaway hairs clinging with static to the cheap material of the sofa. She was scooping up Doritos that left the tips of her fingers stained with orange dust.

Sam considered turning back, but before she could Lindsay had seen her. "Fuck's sake, you scared me. What were you doing?" It had a high-school twang to it: *What are you staring at? Are you, like, obsessed with me?* Sam felt it bone-deep; she wanted to hurt back, but she didn't.

"Where's Dennis?" Sam asked.

"Running, I guess. He said not to wake you up. That you were, like, sick."

"I'm OK now."

"Thank *God*." Lindsay raised an eyebrow and turned back to her chat show.

"Did he say when he'd be back?" Sam asked.

"Nope." Lindsay tipped the bag back to her open mouth to catch the debris and dust at the bottom. Her can of beer had a crescent of orange below the lip. She looked at Sam out of the corner of her eye, and sighed. "You can, like, leave, now. We're done here."

Sam turned, but then caught herself. "I don't have to leave. This is my house."

"*Excuse* me?" Lindsay forced a laugh, her eyes livid.

"It's our house, mine and Den's. And he's my husband. So you can't tell me to leave." Sam took a step closer to the sofa and crossed her arms.

Lindsay let the empty packet she was holding fall to the floor. "Fine," she said, turning back to the television. "Don't leave. Do whatever you want. Like I give a shit."

"What's your problem? I mean with me." Sam tried to keep the tremble out of her voice. She only argued with people she knew intimately, those with actions she could predict.

"My *problem*?"

"Yes. You're always trying to come between us. Me and Den."

Lindsay rolled her eyes. "You mean your husband?"

"But it won't work," Sam said. "We're leaving soon."

"When?" Lindsay asked, looking uncertain suddenly.

"Soon," Sam said, wishing she had a date.

"Whatever. Dennis and I, we have history. It doesn't matter where he goes, he always comes back."

Sam wanted to wipe the complacent smile off her face. "Well, it's funny because actually he told me last night about how you went psycho when he told you, flat-out, that he only wanted to be friends." As soon as Sam said it she wished she hadn't. It felt like a betrayal.

"What did he say?" Lindsay was up from the couch, so close now Sam could smell her breath, the tang of beer.

"I'm sorry," Sam said, backing away.

"What the fuck did he say?" Lindsay said, grabbing Sam's arm. "Tell me."

"He…he was only joking. He said you tried to hit him with your car, that's all. He said it was funny."

"We're friends." Lindsay's grip tightened. "We're practically blood. You think this marriage of yours is deeper than that? He don't like you that much, believe me. I've seen it all, I know what happens when he likes somebody and, guess what, you don't want it."

"What does that mean?"

"It means I'm the one still here. That's what it means."

Sam tried to twist free, but Lindsay dug her nails into her forearm. They froze when they heard the back door. Dennis had returned.

"You're threatening me!" Sam said, loud enough that she hoped Dennis would hear.

"Shut up," Lindsay hissed. "Don't try to make anything out of this." She let go.

Sam rubbed her arm. Lindsay's nails had left deep crescents in her skin. Lindsay sat back with her eyes fixed on the television, as if nothing had happened.

"You need to take me to Target and Whole Foods," Dennis said as he walked through the house from the kitchen. "Not now, later. I've got stuff to do here first. I got a call from…" Sam looked at her arm; she thought about running straight in to Dennis to show him. *Look, look what that bitch did, she's crazy.* But something stopped her. The way Lindsay looked so serene, like someone had flipped a switch. It was as if the whole thing hadn't happened.

"Sure," Lindsay was shouting back.

"Oh, hey," Dennis said as he walked into the living room. "You're up." He sounded, Sam thought, almost disappointed to see her.

34

That evening, before they left to go shopping, Dennis helped Sam get showered and dressed, made her a sandwich and tipped out another two Vicodin. "You're running low. I'll pick more up at the drugstore for you," he said, kissing her on the head as Lindsay rattled her keys impatiently in the background.

As the truck lights disappeared around the corner and the noise faded, Sam rolled off the sofa and heaved herself up onto her crutch. She was bored, antsy. She limped from room to room, lonely and searching for something to occupy her thoughts.

In the kitchen, she saw Dennis's MacBook out of the corner of her eye. When she opened it she felt her stomach sink. It was protected with a password. She asked herself why, if he had nothing to hide, would he need a password? She tried to ignore the feeling but it nagged at her, just as it had in the past. *You're bored*, she told herself. *You're paranoid*. But before she realized what she was doing she was sitting at the kitchen table trying to figure out how to unlock it.

She tried "PASSWORD" and "password" and

"Password" without expecting any of them to work, but still felt a sense of disappointment when they didn't. She tried her name, tried variations, and felt a renewed sense of insecurity as each failed. She tried Lindsay, and exhaled when it was rejected. Then she tried his name, she tried his birthday, and she tried his name and his birthday and suddenly the screen was on, just as she was about to start typing again. In a moment of horror she couldn't remember what she had typed. Had she used a capital D? Was it just his birth year? And then she remembered and tore off a piece of a nearby envelope and wrote down "Dennisdanson1975," slipping the paper into the pocket of her cardigan. She felt a little ache in her chest at his lack of imagination.

On the screen was his book, the memoir he was writing for his publisher, the cursor blinking away in the middle of a paragraph. She scanned the page for her name, but found herself reading:

The years I spent as a child in the woods, playing solitary games and talking to myself for company, would in many ways prepare me for the solitude of Death Row. In my cell I would remember looking out into the endless wilderness and the feeling of insignificance it would give me...

Promising herself she would read it when it was published, Sam minimized the window and opened his web browser. It was clear. She checked Dennis's history but found nothing there. *When had he learned to do that?* she asked herself.

The desktop had three files, "Book," "Book2" and "Book3," drafts of the autobiography. In his notes was a list of his passwords, which Sam wrote down on the back of the envelope, just in case.

The anticlimax was massive. Sam reopened the Word file, rolling her eyes as she caught the sentence, "I knew to never stop believing in myself because the minute I stopped believing in myself would be the minute I really lost my freedom..." and snapped the lid shut. She looked around her, hoping for something else—anything—to give her a clue as to what he was thinking, who he was, whether Lindsay was right and he didn't like her that much. She went through his case, unzipped every pouch, and found things that looked initially tantalizing but turned out to be boring: a folded receipt for the dumpsters, a handwritten letter from his editor in New York, a Moleskine notebook that turned out to be empty aside from his name and telephone number written in the front and a promise of a twenty-dollar reward for turning it in.

She went to his old bedroom and opened drawers and wardrobes, all empty, until she saw the box that Lindsay had taken care of all those years. The lid was broken and now there was an elastic band stretched around the box to stop the contents from spilling out. Sam slid the band off and put the photographs out onto the floor one by one as she finished looking at them again. It was different this time, she told herself. She'd already seen everything, so this wasn't exactly snooping.

Midway through the pile she came to a page

ripped from a magazine. It was a full-page picture
of them both from the photo shoot just after he was
released. Dennis was behind her in a white shirt
with the collar left unbuttoned, his sleeves rolled
up and his arms over her shoulders, smiling. She
felt terrible, then. Sick and guilty.

She started packing away the photos hurriedly,
and was stretching the elastic band back over the
tin when the rusty yawn of the back door struck her
in the chest. She was trying to get the tin behind
the board games again as silently as possible but
heavy footsteps were making their way quickly to
the bedroom and she knew she'd been caught out.

"I'm so sorry. I was bored. I was thinking we
hadn't cleaned this room yet and—"

The man who stood in the doorway was large,
with long black greasy hair that started closer to the
back of his skull. As he took another step closer,
she registered the look of anger in his eyes.

Sam's scream came out clear and sharp as broken glass. Howard's hands shot to his ears and
Sam picked up her crutch and thrust it into his
stomach. He tipped sideways and cowered against
the bookshelf. Sam launched herself forward on
her bad foot, fueled by adrenaline. She struggled
down the porch steps, her crutch sinking into the
too-soft grass. She glanced back every now and
then, expecting to see him behind her. For a moment she thought she had really hurt him and then
reminded herself that she had meant to hurt him,
that it was OK.

It was dark on the road, and Sam couldn't see

much behind or ahead of her but she kept going, breathing too loud to hear whether Howard was approaching or not, unsure where she was heading.

Her ankle started to throb, and soon Sam had to slow down. She was sure Howard was close, expected to feel his hands around her throat, but there was no sign of him. She had to walk up the middle of the road, as the sides were deep puddles of mud. The road was unlit but the moon was full, and Sam looked up into a sky with more stars than she'd ever seen in her life. Something buzzed by her ear and she flinched, losing her footing and falling onto her hip in the mulch of the roadside.

She stayed on the ground for some time, the seat of her leggings now soaking with what she knew would be filthy water. She felt a tickling sensation on her neck, slapped at herself, dug her crutch into the ground and pulled herself up. She screamed and it cut the dark. She carried on, not knowing whether Howard was pursuing her, or if he was waiting for her back at the house. Her ankle throbbed harder, the compression bandage soaked.

Sam heard the engine before she could see any car. She stayed in the center of the road, waiting to see lights emerge in the black. They appeared ahead of her, blinding her as they came closer so she couldn't see who it was. As the vehicle approached she waved with her free arm, then raised her crutch when the truck showed no signs of stopping. It was coming too fast, even seemed to be speeding up, and she froze in disbelief before hopping clumsily to her left, diving into the grass and lying facedown. The truck swerved, its tires skidding on the loose ground, and the engine stopped. Sam heard the sound of laughter that got louder as the window rolled down.

"Sam? What are you doing?" Dennis leaned out of the window.

"You didn't stop!" She sat with her legs outstretched in front of her.

"Why are you out here?" His voice more serious now, something that bordered on concern but wasn't quite.

"At the house… Howard was at the house. I was cleaning and—"

The engine started abruptly, the car moved forward and Sam scrambled up to her feet.

"Wait! Don't leave me!"

They drove away quickly, the lights disappearing in the distance. Sam stood still in horror. It could be another prank, she thought, but with every second this seemed less likely, and her body started to ache with hatred. Lindsay, who thought it was funny to pretend to run her down. Lindsay, who sped off, leaving her in the dark again. She wondered if Dennis had laughed and told her she was *the worst*.

The crutch was hurting her arm, every hop pinched and bruised her skin, and her head was starting to ache. Just as she'd resigned herself to walking the whole way back to the house, she heard the truck again, approaching slowly, and saw the lights that flashed to show her they had seen her too. The passenger seat was empty.

"He told me to come get you," Lindsay said.

"Where is he?" Sam pulled herself up into the truck.

"I don't know. Hurry up! Fuck."

"Was Howard still there? I hit him."

"Not hard enough, obviously. He's gone."

"Well, where is he? He wasn't following me on the road."

"No shit." Lindsay turned around, the truck bouncing off the road and back on again.

"He came from nowhere. There was no sign of a car—"

"He knows this place as well as Dennis. Maybe better, now. There's a shortcut from the trailer park, if you don't mind getting dirty."

"Through the woods?"

"You can cut through, save you walking the road. Takes maybe half the time."

"I think he's been watching us," Sam said, realizing it was the first time she had admitted this. "There's been noises and once there was someone staring through the bathroom window."

"Howard's creepy, all right."

"Is he...like, a rapist?"

Lindsay started to laugh. "You thought he was going to *rape* you? Oh my God. Dennis will love that."

Sam held her breath. She imagined grabbing Lindsay by the hair and pulling it out in handfuls. "Then what was he going to do?" she asked.

Lindsay sighed. "He doesn't give a shit about you, I can tell you that much. He's always been totally obsessed with Dennis. Like some kind of fucking puppy. It's sickening, really."

"Obsessed?"

"He was probably trying to get hold of some of his things. He used to do that a lot, at school. Take stuff, mostly Dennis's."

"What does Dennis have that Howard would want?" Sam said.

Lindsay seemed to be thinking for a while.

"Howard was great to have around because he would just do whatever you wanted. His dad gave him *so* much cash. So he was always getting beer or buying gas or whatever we needed. But once Dennis started to get a life outside of Howard, it was like Howie couldn't stand it. He just wanted him to himself. Looks like nothing's changed."

35

Being back at the house made Sam uncomfortable. Though it still looked the same, with the lights left on, and the television flickering on mute, it had the feel of a place altered, as if everything had been moved a centimeter or so. She walked down the hallway and glanced into Dennis's old bedroom.

"Howard took his memory box," Sam said, noticing it was missing from the junk that littered the floor.

"His what?" Lindsay said from behind her.

"The tin, the one you were looking after."

"Better hope Dennis catches up with him or he'll be pissed."

"What's so important about it, anyway? It's not like there's anything special in there," Sam said.

"You looked in there?" Lindsay's eyes were wide with shock.

"He showed me," Sam said. "Old pictures. There's some deeds to the land but it's not worth anything." Sam stopped and watched Lindsay, who stared past her, face tight with anger. "You never looked?"

"Never. He asked me to take care of it. He asked me never to open it, and I promised I wouldn't."

"You were never even curious?"

Lindsay shrugged. "It was locked."

Sam wondered at this. In the same circumstances she knew she wouldn't have kept that promise. After he was sentenced, what had stopped Lindsay from opening it? The lock was flimsy enough; Dennis had prized it open with a screwdriver easily. Again she thought of how innocuous a thing it was to be so secretive about.

"I promised," Lindsay said again, before making her way to the kitchen.

Sam could tell she was rattled, jealous that Dennis had allowed her to see what he had kept from Lindsay. As she started to stack the items back onto the shelves, she smiled. It was desperate, she thought, how subservient Lindsay was.

Dennis returned, the back door crashing against the wall with the force of him. He had the box. Sam was relieved until she saw how upset he was, his skin pale, his eyes red. He threw the box onto the sofa and Lindsay stared at it before tearing her eyes away.

"What happened?" Lindsay asked.

"Nothing," Dennis said.

Sam noticed the grass stains on his jeans. "I'm sorry," she said. Dennis fell back onto the sofa and she saw him shaking slightly. "Your hands…" Sam looked at his knuckles, the skin peeled back, shades of red and purple.

"It's nothing," he said absently. "His teeth…"

"We need to clean that up," Sam said. Dennis nodded slowly and stood.

In the bathroom, Sam ran cold water over his hands and watched blood creeping to his wrists.

"Come here," he said, pulling her to him suddenly. She felt his sweat on her skin.

"He scared me," she said, apologizing.

"I know." He kissed her hair.

"Do you think it was Howard looking through the windows? Hanging around?" Sam asked.

"I'm sure it was," Dennis said, holding her tighter. He kissed her again. "It's fine now."

Instead of going out for a run the next morning, Dennis stayed in. He toasted Sam a bagel and layered it with peanut butter and blueberries, placing her Vicodin neatly on the side. They dabbed his wounds with antiseptic.

"I think human mouths are even dirtier than a dog's, or something," she said, wrapping his knuckles with bandages, trying to keep it loose enough so he could still bend his fingers. "You need to be careful this doesn't get infected."

There were bruises that appeared on his arms, as though Howard had grabbed him hard and held tight. Sam thought of how lucky she'd been, and feared that he might come back.

"I'll be here," Dennis reassured her. But she was edgy, every noise made her jump, and she felt eyes follow her around the house.

Midmorning, a car screeched into the driveway, and Howard's father, Officer Harries, stepped out, leaving the car door open and the engine running. This time he was alone, and there was no need for him to feign civility.

"Danson," he yelled, though Dennis was already standing behind the screen door, waiting. "You ever lay a hand on my boy again…it'll be the last thing you fucking do! Hear me?"

Sam watched from the living-room window.

"Your son ever lays a hand on my wife again he'll get more than a beating. You hear me?" Dennis mimicked Harries's drawl.

At this Officer Harries stepped toward the house, close enough that Sam could see the sweat rolling off him and the scatter of broken veins that made his nose and cheeks light up red. "He did no such thing. You mark my words he won't be back here, not again. But he did not touch anybody."

"Samantha?" Dennis asked.

"It's true," Sam said, opening the window slightly. "He crept into the house yesterday and grabbed me from behind. I hit him to get him away." She waited for a response, but none came. Harries looked at her, face twisted.

"See?" Dennis said. "I told her she needs to protect herself round here."

"Liars. You and she deserve each other." Harries spat onto the grass. "Fucking liars." The car door slammed behind him and, with the growl of the engine, he drove away.

Dennis came into the living room, put his arms around her, and told her she was good.

"I thought he was going to arrest you or something," she said as he ran his nails down her back.

"He won't, don't worry."

As he kissed her, his hand moved up and down her back over her T-shirt, his fingers catching the strap of her bra. When he let her go she felt drunk, warm.

"Wait here," he said, "I just need to check on something quick."

She lay down on the air mattress and ran her fingertips over her stomach, thinking of him. He was gone a while, but she could hear him outside: the rusted yawn of the storm-shelter hatch being lowered, the sound of debris being kicked around. When Dennis came back in she closed her eyes, pretending to sleep. She heard him undo his belt, his shoes being kicked off, his jeans sliding to the floor, the sound of his glasses being placed on the table. He lay down beside her and pressed himself against her.

"I know you're awake," he whispered. She smiled. "I can tell." She let him curl around her, still keeping her eyes closed, and let herself ache until she fell asleep.

She was dreaming, pushing herself against him while he thrust. Then she wasn't dreaming, and he was pressing back into her. She reached back to pull him closer, deeper. He rolled her onto her stomach, her arms trapped underneath her, her face in the pillow, his weight on top of her. Was she dreaming? Limbs heavy with Vicodin, she moaned.

"Shhh." His lips on her ear. He rested his head

on hers, pressing her into the pillow again. She wanted to tell him to slow down; she tried to turn but he put his hand into her back and whispered, "Stay still."

She was sore. Dennis pushed himself deeper inside her and she felt a strange mixture of pleasure and pain. Then his body tensed and his breath caught; she felt him twitch inside her, and stop. He lay on top of her for a while, breathing, his fingers in her hair. When he rolled off her she turned on her side. He held her against him and she sank back into sleep, sore and smiling, not even sure it had been real.

The hot afternoon woke them up. Sun pouring in directly over them as they lay there. They peeled away from each other, confused with sleep.

"I never nap," Dennis said, putting his glasses on, recoiling from the midday sun like a vampire. "I need to make some calls."

Sam felt it warm and sticky on her inner thighs. She wiggled back into her underwear and stayed curled in the sheets. She touched herself; she was still sore. It had finally happened. It was all she wanted.

Lindsay arrived late afternoon while Dennis was emptying a box of magazines into a metal trash can outside, ready to burn them. Sam was sitting on the porch bench, flicking idly through her phone.

"You didn't answer my text," Lindsay said, shading her eyes with her hand.

"I was asleep," Dennis said, crushing down the trash to make room for more.

"At eleven?"

"We fell asleep," he repeated.

"Did you need a ride to Whole Foods? We could do something."

"Not really, Linds. We're kind of busy." He gestured to Sam. *We*, Sam thought. It felt good that Lindsay wasn't a part of it.

"I'm going that way anyway so if you need anything?"

He wiped his forehead. "It's OK, really."

"Fine." Lindsay's keys rattled in her hand. "See you tomorrow. Call if you need anything."

"Sure will," he said. They watched the truck pull away. "She gets so clingy and weird."

"Yeah, that was weird," Sam agreed.

"Like she doesn't have anything better to do."

"Doesn't she have kids? What happened to them?" It made Dennis laugh and she felt a kick of pleasure. "I actually feel bad for her."

"I don't," Dennis said, and they laughed again.

It had been a perfect day, she decided later, brushing her teeth. In the wastebasket she saw the bloodied cotton balls she'd used to dab at his torn knuckles. She picked one out and held it in her palm. The blood was turning brown. She remembered it vivid red, as it came fresh from him in that moment. She held the cotton ball in her fist, deciding to keep it, to start a box of her own, to remember days like this one.

36

For a few days, Sam felt as though they were the only people in the world. They sat in silence on the porch, her legs on his lap, watching the light fade ahead of them, the sky like a bruise. Dennis worked with renewed energy, emptying the garage, emerging with cobwebs in his hair that made him look gray, and Sam pictured them growing old together, and wondered where they would be. Dennis told her they would be in LA by the end of the month and, sensing that since the night Howard broke in he was as eager to leave as she was, she believed him.

The house became bare and cavernous. "Will you sell it?" she asked as he hauled a rusted ride-along lawnmower out of the garage.

"I think we should just tear it down," he said, "and plant over the foundation. Before it becomes some kind of morbid attraction. It'll be like nothing was ever here."

Something had changed him, Sam realized. It had happened the night Howard had broken in. Whatever he'd been holding on to here he had finally decided to let go of it.

Dennis took a sledgehammer to the garage, the tin roof sliding down toward his throat like a guillotine. He jumped back, grinning, laughing at his near miss. Trucks came and took away the dumpsters. Dennis tipped the drivers folded hundred-dollar bills, and they smiled to Sam and called her "Miss." It made her think of her life back in England, all the teenagers who raised their hands and called to her for help. She didn't miss it at all.

In the heat of the afternoons Dennis worked indoors, emailing his publisher, arranging the final details for the release of his autobiography. Because of the backlash he would no longer be doing a tour, and it seemed they would be promoting the book in his absence. A negative *Buzzfeed* article about the new documentary series, "23 Things *The Boy from Red River* Left Out," was shared widely. In small print at the bottom they claimed that they'd tried to reach Carrie for comment but hadn't received a response.

"I responded," Carrie said in a phone call. "I told them to go fuck themselves."

Dennis found he was calling his manager, Nick, more than Nick was calling him. He did a *Reddit* AMA, a telephone interview for a successful podcast and got paid ten thousand dollars for taking an Instagram photo in a T-shirt from an athleisure range with the caption "Ready to get on it." It got only three thousand likes.

Frustrated with the lack of viable opportunities, Dennis agreed to film a pilot for a reality show, focusing on his and Sam's move to LA and their adjustment to a celebrity life. It would be aspirational while remaining relatable, with structured real-life events. Sam remembered the comments she'd received when he was first released.

"I'm not sure I want to," she told him.

"I didn't graduate high school," Dennis said. "I can't even work at McDonald's without people staring at me like I'm some kind of freak. At least if I'm on TV I don't have to *see* them staring at me. Unless," he added, "you want to go back to teaching?"

"God, no," Sam said, remembering how it felt to get up every day to do something she hated. Wasn't this what everyone wanted? Fame, money, an easier life? Eventually she agreed and Dennis gave Nick the go-ahead, telling him they would be back in LA in the next couple of weeks.

One afternoon, as they sat in the living room while Dennis replied to emails and made arrangements for their departure, a telephone rang. They looked at each other. It was the house phone, hung on the wall of the living room, an old corded phone, once white but now yellowed, with the grubby gray marks of a handprint around its middle. It was an old, rattling buzz, as though it hadn't spoken in years and its throat was dry. She picked it up and gestured to Dennis, who turned and frowned. It hadn't rung the entire time they'd been there. In fact, Sam thought, she couldn't remember the last time she'd answered her own house phone.

"Hello?" Sam answered, smiling at Dennis, cherishing the weirdness of the moment. No one said anything. "Hello-o?" she repeated. She heard breathing on the end of the line, uneven. The smile fell from her face. She thought she heard a sob. "Who is this?"

Dennis moved closer. "What is it?" he asked her. She gestured for him to lower his voice so she could listen. "If it's some creep just hang up. I thought this place was unlisted—"

"Shhhhh!" she hissed. The person on the phone had cleared their throat.

"You tell him," the voice said, the words choked up. He cleared his voice again. "You tell him that if my boy doesn't get in touch soon that I'm coming for him."

"Who is this?" Sam said just as Dennis took the phone from her hand.

"Listen," Dennis started, before falling silent. After some time he lowered the phone from his ear and let it hang at his side.

"Did they threaten you?" Sam said.

"Yeah," he said. "It was Harries. Howard's missing. He didn't come home last night."

"Oh," Sam said, not knowing what to say. "Well, you've been with me this whole time. I can tell him that."

Dennis wrapped the wire around his hand and ripped it from the phone, then threw the receiver into the trash bag beside them.

"I know," he said to Sam. "Thanks."

He seemed despondent and the silence made her feel as if she should say something else.

"Do you think…" she said, hesitating. "Maybe he killed himself?"

"What?" Dennis stepped toward her and she had to stop herself from taking a step back. "Why would you say that?"

"Well, you know. He's a forty-year-old man living alone in a trailer park. It must be kind of depressing."

Dennis picked up the trash bag and walked away without saying anything. Sam watched through the window as he pushed the bag into the trash can, the rain darkening the shirt he was wearing. For a moment he just stood there, his head bent as though he were praying. Abruptly, he turned and walked back to the house. Sam shifted out of sight, hoping he hadn't seen her watching him.

After the incident with the phone, Dennis became short-tempered and distant, and stared into his phone, reading out tweets from people who irritated him.

"Look at this one. 'I used to think Dennis was innocent but now I feel like he's definitely got some creepy vibes going on…' I mean, it says it all, right?"

"What?"

"'I used to *think*…now I *feel*…'?"

"I don't follow," Sam said, putting down her own phone.

"When did people start to value feelings over thought? It's like, 'Yeah, I used to look objectively at things and make informed decisions but now I just go with whatever I feel like.' It's stupid."

"Right," Sam agreed. "Why don't you just delete your account, Den? It only makes you miserable."

"And then there's this one…" he continued.

Lindsay came by that evening and Dennis spoke with her in the hallway, their voices too low and soft for Sam to make out their words. She imagined he was telling her about the phone call, that Howard was missing. When they came back into the living room Lindsay was quiet and pale. She sat on the sofa, her dirty feet curled under her, chewing her nails incessantly and staring blankly at the television.

Dennis seemed similarly distracted. Neither complained when Sam changed the channel, though they usually protested bitterly about anything she wanted to watch. Dennis told them he was going to check something out back and Lindsay didn't seem to notice him leave. They sat together in silence while he was gone and when he returned Sam could bear it no more.

"It's so sad about Howard, right?" she said, looking from Dennis to Lindsay, hoping they would let her in on what they were thinking.

"What do you care?" Lindsay said.

"Well, I'm worried about him."

"He's probably fine," Dennis said. Sam didn't think he sounded convinced.

"You didn't even know him," Lindsay said, sitting up straighter. "In fact, didn't you sock him in the gut? Didn't you accuse him of— Wait, Den, you don't know, do you?" She turned to Sam. "Tell Dennis," she said. "Tell him what you thought Howard was going to do."

"Shut up," Sam said.

"Sam thought Howard was going to *rape* her. Can you imagine that?"

Sam expected Dennis to laugh, but he didn't. She saw his eyes darken and the smile fall off Lindsay's face.

"Why is that funny?" he asked.

"You know," Lindsay said. "Because Howard's a total fag, right?"

Sam waited for Dennis to say something. He stared hard at Lindsay.

"Come on, Den. He was, you know... He's, like, obsessed with you," Lindsay added nervously.

"And you're not?" Dennis said.

Sam watched Lindsay's cheeks redden.

"Fuck you," Lindsay said. "You can find some other bitch to take you to Walmart. I'm done." She slammed the front door as she left. Instead of satisfaction, Sam felt a slimy sense of guilt.

"That was kind of harsh, Den," she said.

"Leave me the fuck alone," he said, turning to storm out of the house. The cats were mewing, winding their way around his legs as he walked toward the kitchen. "Hey," he snapped at them. "Get the fuck out of the way." Then Tuna got between his feet and he tripped. The cat yowled under his foot and Dennis collided with the door frame. "Fuck!" he yelled. "Fuck off!" He kicked Tuna and she skidded across the floor.

"Dennis!" Sam shouted. "Don't!" She ran to the cat to pick her up but Tuna cowered against the wall. "Get out!" she told Dennis, but he was already leaving, the door slamming behind him.

Sam tried again to approach Tuna, extending a hand, but the cat was shaken and wanted only to be left alone. So she went back to the bedroom, which still smelled of piss, antiseptic, cigarettes, even with the window open all hours. This time she knew what she'd seen. The cruelty had shocked her but, looking back, she wondered whether she should have been shocked at all.

Lindsay returned the next evening, quiet and anxious after their argument, all her usual bravado missing.

"So did you still need a ride or…" she said while Dennis remained stony silent.

"Sure," he said. And Sam sensed this was a fight they'd had before, that whatever it was between Lindsay and Dennis and Howard meant there was no need for apologies; it ran deeper than that.

When they left, Sam waited five minutes and searched the kitchen for the key to the storm shelter. At first she'd dismissed the thought as madness but something about Howard's disappearance kept nagging at her, and seeing the flash of cruelty that had come so naturally from Dennis the night before had made her wonder what else he might be capable of.

And Dennis had been spending so much time in the shelter lately, always closing the hatch behind him as he went. Sam remembered how she'd felt when she was down there, so hidden, so alone. She had to check, just once, to make sure Howard wasn't down there. As stupid as she thought she was being, she *had* to see it now, just to prove to herself that he had nothing to hide.

Before opening the hatch Sam knocked. Feeling ridiculous, she called out, "Hello? Is anybody down there?"

When there was no answer Sam took a torch and went down the stairs, sitting, sliding off each step and landing on the next with a bump. She shone the torch over every corner of the space, and exhaled. Of course she hadn't expected to find Howard. It had been a stupid idea, even given Dennis's outburst the previous evening.

Even so, Sam wondered why Dennis would want to spend so much time down there. It was basically empty now. The cots had been removed, thrown into the dumpsters, and the only thing left was the memory box. She couldn't imagine why he had moved it in here. Was he hiding it from her? But she had already seen it; he had showed it to her himself. Out of curiosity, she opened it again and spread the pictures across the floor. She looked for meaning in them, the reason why they were so precious to Dennis, but came up with nothing.

Defeated, she picked up the box and started to collect the items to put away. As she lifted it, there was a noise, a feeling, of something moving inside. She shook it a little and heard it again, the sound of something shifting. She tipped it upside down, rattled it, tapped it on all sides. Eventually she threw it, facedown onto the concrete. The bottom came loose and more Polaroids scattered out, facedown, onto the floor around her.

Shaking, Sam crouched down and touched the backs of the photographs. The room had filled with something else, and she knew whatever was in the pictures was something she didn't want to see.

Carefully, she took the corner of one of the Polaroids and turned it over. The girl in the picture was young, Sam realized, only sixteen at most. She was naked from the waist up and lying on her side, eyes closed, like she was asleep. There were more, similarly posed, in various states of undress. They were curiously unsexy, Sam thought, though she knew with a twist in her gut that these were pictures Dennis had taken with ex-girlfriends. Not so weird for him to have these when he was younger but did he still look at them now? Sam wondered at the morality of this as she flicked through them.

Then one picture made her stop. The girl in the photograph was naked, her arms out and palms up, her feet crossed at the ankles and her hair spread around her head like a mane. Sam couldn't immediately tell what was off about it, but when she looked again she saw there were no nipples. Instead, just red lumpy tissue and fat.

She flipped the pile of photos and spread them quickly, her eyes scanning every one for something logical, only to find herself more confused. There was the girl again but her lips were gone and she was grinning. There she was again but her body was gone, her spinal cord protruded from her neck and the ends of her mousy hair were stained red. Then a different girl, someone blonde, and her face was swollen and her arms and legs were tied behind her, making her pelvis stick obscenely into the air. The next girl had plastic cable wrapped around her throat; her hair was short and dark, her skin was purple and the cable looked as though it would go right through her. Sam realized that she was holding her breath and that her fingers were on the girl in the picture's throat, as if she could untie the cables and let her breathe again.

She looked up, retching and gasping for air. Why would he have these? How did they look so real? They couldn't be real, could they?

Sam seemed to be moving before she'd made any conscious decisions. She fixed the bottom of the tin in place, gathered all the objects and put them back inside, then tucked the Polaroids into the waist of her trousers. They felt cold against her skin, as if they were oozing something toxic and contaminating her. She remembered a corner of the playground in her primary school, where she'd found a magazine with lurid colors and a woman's legs spread open. A boy had kicked it at her and she'd cried, feeling as though touching it somehow made her a part of it, guilty and ashamed.

Making sure everything looked as if she'd never been there she crawled back up the steps of the storm shelter, closed the door and covered it up. In the kitchen, she hung the keys on the hook. She looked around for somewhere to place the photos, wishing now she'd left them down there. She needed to hide them, quickly, while she decided what to do next, but there was nowhere to put them. Everything in the house had been stripped clean.

There was only her suitcase, and she was sure that would be the first place he'd look if he noticed they were missing.

Sam stopped and tried to calm herself. She would have to call the police. There was no other way. She grabbed her phone and twice typed in the wrong passcode with shaking hands. But when it came to it she found she couldn't dial. Instead, she looked at the pictures of Dennis she'd taken, pictures they'd taken together. It didn't make sense. And she looked at Carrie. It made her chest hurt, thinking of her. All the years dedicated to proving Dennis was innocent, fighting for him. What would it do to her if it turned out that Dennis had...?

Then she heard them, unmistakably the sound of an engine approaching in the quiet, and she panicked, unzipping the sofa cushion and stuffing the photos inside. Quickly she switched on the television and lay down, wiping sweat away from her forehead and trying to steady herself, trying to work out what she was doing and if she wanted to be doing it.

"They didn't have any avocados!" Dennis shouted from the door. "Can you believe that?"

"You were quick," Sam said, trying to sound bright.

"Well, they didn't have anything. We need to go back tomorrow; they were sold out of fucking everything."

Sam's stomach flipped. If they went tomorrow she could put the photos back, call a cab and leave. "What time are you going?" she asked.

"Why?"

"I don't know," she said. "Maybe I'll go with you."

"Not too late," Dennis said. "We need fresh produce, probably better to go in the morning."

She needed a specific time. If she booked a taxi she couldn't risk it passing them on the road as it came. "So…ten? Earlier?"

Dennis considered her for a moment, his glasses shielding his eyes.

"You OK?"

Sam nodded. "Yes!"

"You're being weird," Dennis said.

She ignored him, though she knew she should say something. The part of her that wanted to survive this told her what she needed to do; it urged her to get her shit together, just until morning, and then to run like hell. But there was a sadness and disappointment so deep she wanted to die. When she thought of how betrayed she felt it made her want to tell him everything. She wanted to tell him she hated him, she wanted him to hit her to the ground and press her throat until she was dead. But the thought of those hands on her skin made her feel sick. All that time she'd longed to be held by him, kissed, touched. Had she been pressing herself into the grasp of a monster? How hadn't she known?

"I was just about to call Carrie," Sam said with her phone in her hand.

"Tell her I say hey," Dennis said.

Sam paused to see if he would leave and give her privacy but instead he sat next to her on the sofa and started looking through his own phone. Outside, Sam could see Lindsay standing on the porch, the tip of her cigarette glowing in the dark.

Why hadn't she just called the police when she had the chance? Suddenly it became very real. It was no longer a case she was following from a computer screen, or love letters that arrived on yellow legal-pad paper. The story the Polaroids told wasn't one she was supposed to know.

Whatever she decided to do, she wanted Carrie to be a part of it. She owed her that much.

"Actually," Sam said, "it's late. I think I'm just going to text her and say we'll speak tomorrow."

"Sure," Dennis murmured. He was distracted, tapping out an email in his slow, determined way.

Sam texted. "Hey Carrie. We need to talk. Free tomorrow morning? Will call around 10. X."

Almost immediately, Carrie replied. "Sure! Everything OK?? We need to talk is NEVER good… x."

Sam tried to find the right balance. She didn't want to worry Carrie but she also needed her to expect her call. Now she realized how much she'd isolated herself since moving to Florida. If something were to happen to her that night, how long would it take for anyone to notice she was gone? All she had left was Carrie. "Just need to talk to someone. Will explain tomorrow morning. Dennis out then so can talk properly! Speak then xx."

She sent it and sat back, feeling the weight of Dennis beside her on the sofa and trying not to draw his attention to her. She was scared of the moment he might turn, like a cat bored of being stroked, and attack.

Lindsay sat with them for some time; the TV was on but everyone stared down at their phones. Sam felt the photographs beneath her. She saw the girls; she saw the marks on their bodies. Bite marks, that was what they were. On thighs, on breasts: little purple indentations and broken skin. Sam bit into her own hand and looked at the pattern her teeth left behind. Still so far from breaking the skin.

Had he held them? Had he kissed them up and down until they ached? Did he bite their skin and make them gasp and then bite harder until they screamed? Did he break the bones in their necks when he strangled them? Did they close their eyes? Had they loved him like she did?

Sam wondered how much Lindsay knew. How much she had always known. But when she stood and stretched and said she was going home Sam almost didn't want her to leave. It felt safer with her there. Lindsay, who had survived when all these other girls had not.

At midnight, Sam switched off the TV and said she was going to sleep. Dennis lay down with her and pressed against her back. She tried to control the urge to pull away. Lying still, she pretended to drift off. After some time, he whispered to her, "Are you awake?" But Sam stayed still, breathing softly, eyes closed. All night she was rigid with fear, waiting for him to stir.

As the sun came up he was still next to her, letting out a small sigh now and then as he exhaled.

Her body ached from a night of tensed muscles and clenched teeth. Sam pushed herself up and watched him for a while. His eyelids twitched as he slept, and there was the slightest wheeze from a nostril as he breathed. He seemed, almost, human.

"You didn't sleep," he said, his eyes still closed.

"I did a little," she said. Her body fizzed with fear again, and she felt stupid, caught out.

"You didn't sleep," he said again, opening his eyes. "I can tell."

37

Sam had spent the sleepless night planning her moves for the next morning. It was stupid to have taken the Polaroids, she realized. It was risky and she needed to play it safe. As soon as Dennis went for his morning run she would go down into the shelter and put them back. She had to get them back before Dennis found out they were gone. If she told Carrie or the police and they didn't believe her she could live with that, just so long as she could survive this.

But Dennis didn't go for his run. "Listen to this," he said, bending and straightening his leg. His knee clicked and popped as it moved.

"All my joints do that," she said. "It's nothing."

Dennis wasn't convinced. He made breakfast and Sam showered quickly, rushing to get back to the sofa, feeling like a nesting bird guarding her eggs. Every time Dennis left the room she braced herself for the squeal of the storm-shelter door and each time he returned she was flooded with a powerful relief. She was safe, for a few more minutes, another half hour; she would be OK.

Lindsay arrived just before ten, and Sam watched

her and Dennis have some kind of exchange on the front lawn, at the end of which Dennis put his arms around her and squeezed, Lindsay holding on just a beat too long after he let go.

"You ready to go?" he said to Sam.

"I might stay here," she said, rubbing her ankle. "My foot's hurting a lot…"

"But you were bugging me yesterday about coming with us," Dennis said.

"Yeah, but I'm in a lot of pain today, I feel like I should just rest it."

Dennis looked at her. "I think you should come with us," he said. "I think it would be good for you to get out of this house."

"I don't think—"

"If it's that bad, maybe I should stay with you, just in case. I mean, if Howard were to come back," Dennis said.

"I'll be fine," she said. "Honestly, I'm just not feeling up to it."

"Then I should stay," he said again, taking a step toward her.

Sam looked at the time on her phone. She could call Carrie when they got to the store. And once she was out, in public, she reasoned that she didn't have to come back.

"You know what?" Sam said, starting to push herself up off the sofa. "You're right, I'm spending too much time here. I'm just being lazy. I'll come."

Dennis was confused, turning between Lindsay's idling truck and Sam, who stood smiling. "So…you're coming?"

"Yes," she said, eager to get out, still unsure what she would do when she did so. "But I need to grab some things first."

He sighed. "Well, hurry up, we're already later than I wanted to be."

She limped to where her crutch was propped against the wall and looked through the window to see Dennis sitting in the passenger seat, door open, talking to Lindsay. She dropped her crutch and crouched to the floor, crawling back to the sofa. She was shaking violently, acting instinctively. She took the Polaroids from the sofa cushion and crawled to her bag. She put them into the zip pocket that ran across the back, which contained some spare coins and used tissues and empty pill packets. She crawled back and picked up her crutch, trying to calm herself as she walked out of the house.

Dennis hopped out of the truck as she approached, helped her into the seat and held her bag and crutch while she shifted over to Lindsay, who stared straight ahead and kept her hands on the wheel. Sam took her bag and put it between her feet on the floor. They drove in silence, the radio off, glass bottles clinking every time they hit a pothole.

Beside her, Dennis looked serene, watching the road through the open window. Sam looked for traces of evil on his face but she saw only the man she had loved. Somehow it made it worse. She hugged her bag to her chest and she thought of all the girls in the photographs. Whatever Dennis truly was beneath the veneer, only they knew.

When they reached the main street Dennis asked

Lindsay to stop. "I need to get something in the hardware store."

Sam looked down the road to the police station.

"I'll stay here," Lindsay said.

"So will I," Sam said, leaning back.

"Fuck it." Lindsay threw the door open. "Fine. I'll go with Dennis."

"How long will you be?" Sam called through the window.

"I don't know, ten minutes? Tops?" Dennis sounded irritated with her again.

Sam watched them disappear into the store and called Carrie but it went straight to voice mail. Irritated, she tried twice more before giving up. It was past ten and Carrie should have been expecting her call, so why wasn't her phone switched on? Sam fought the urge to scream. *Fine*, she thought, *I'm on my own.*

Down the street was the police station. She tried to picture herself inside, introducing herself, *I'm Dennis Danson's wife and I found these pictures in his memory box and I need your help.* She tried to picture her life after this: the police interviews, court, the influx of hate she would receive for her part in getting him out.

Then she imagined another path: getting back to the house and going into the shelter, returning the photos. Making excuses and leaving or sneaking away while he was out running, and going back to a life she didn't want. It didn't seem like much of a choice. She was consumed with self-pity, and disgusted by the lingering flutter in her chest when she thought of Dennis.

Three of the ten minutes had passed and she knew she had to act now. It was obvious to her she wouldn't be able to sneak the photographs back, not now. Dennis would likely be in the house all day, working on whatever he was planning inside the hardware store. If she chose not to move, Dennis would discover what she'd taken and he would act on it. All night, the terrifying consequences of this scenario had played behind her eyelids.

She got out of the truck. Ahead of her was the station. As she limped toward it she started to lose her nerve. What the fuck would she say? How was any of this happening? The world seemed to tilt and whirl and the heat began to close in on her. She found herself veering into the nearest store, a bell ringing above the door as she pushed it open. In the cooler air she tried to gather her thoughts. A woman with gray hair and a kind smile said good morning and Sam nodded, trying to smile back, while the cool air cleared her thoughts.

"Excuse me," a man said as he brushed past Sam, making her jump. She turned and faced a shelf, closed her eyes and tried to calm herself, counting her breaths. *You will get out of this*, she told herself. *Just breathe.*

"Can I help you?" the woman at the counter said.

"I'm just looking," Sam said. "Thanks."

The woman furrowed her brow. "Let me know if you need anything," she said.

Sam looked at the shelf ahead of her but it was

empty. She felt herself blush. At the end of the shelf there was a pen attached to a chain. She looked around the small store: bare walls and plastic chairs lined up along the back. *Where the fuck am I?* she asked herself, disoriented.

The sign above the counter read "Post Office." An idea started to form and before Sam could think better of it she was approaching the counter.

"Do you have any envelopes?" she asked.

Back at the shelf she pulled the Polaroids from her bag and slipped them into the envelope as swiftly as she could, as though the girls in the pictures could cry out in the open air. She sealed them in, pushing hard across the top of the envelope to ensure it was stuck closed and the girls couldn't slip free.

She started to write the address but the pen had run dry. She scribbled and pressed but nothing came out. She looked at the clock on the wall and saw another minute was already gone. If he found her in here, if he saw the envelope…she stopped herself short and limped back to the counter.

"I need a pen," she said.

The woman's smile had long departed and she visibly tensed at Sam's approach. Sam was aware she was sweating, that she was breathless and rude and confused, but these things no longer mattered. She wanted the girls to go away so she could think clearly. One thing at a time. First she would escape; then she would deal with the girls. So she wrote the address as quickly as she could and slipped the envelope to the woman, always looking back at the door behind her, waiting for Dennis to catch her in the act.

When it came time to pay the coins spilled from her purse and scattered on the floor but she left them at her feet and handed the woman a note. When the woman began to fish in the cash register for change Sam waved her away. "It doesn't matter," she said, already at the door. "Keep the change, it's fine."

Back out on the street, blinking in the sun, Sam hoped she'd made the right decision. By taking the Polaroids from Dennis, she had changed her life. And it still hurt, the memory of those first weeks together, of the interviews and gifts and celebrity dinners. She'd never be special or enviable again. In a world where no one was allowed to make mistakes she had made a big one: she had backed the wrong man. It would ruin Carrie, too. They would be figures of hate, the kind of women who lavished praise on a man who killed girls. It was worse than being a killer themselves.

At least the time it would take the Polaroids to arrive would give her space to think and speak to Carrie. After a moment's thought, feeling stronger, she decided to walk to the police station. When inside, she would tell them that she and Dennis had had a fight, that she was scared and didn't want to stay with him. She would insinuate he had hit her but not confirm this, merely ask them to help retrieve her passport so she could stay with a friend for a while. Dennis would have to hand the passport over when the police came to the house, and when he realized the pictures were missing he would have to keep it to himself. By then, Sam told herself, she would be far enough away that he could not hurt her.

If he couldn't get the photographs back, then what choice did he have but to agree to her terms? Unless, she thought, fingers of dread creeping up her spine, he didn't care. Perhaps he would find and kill her anyway, wherever she went.

She was nearly at the end of the street when he called her name and she heard the slap of his shoes on the sidewalk. She stared at the police station, took another step, and stopped, feeling—suddenly—cold.

"Where are you going?" Dennis asked, his voice low, almost as if he knew what she was planning.

"I was thirsty. I was going to buy a bottle of water," she said weakly.

"And? The store is back there."

Sam looked again at the police station.

"Let's go," he said, and put one hand gently on her back to guide her. When she didn't move he put his other hand on her elbow and she moved with him though she couldn't explain why. As she looked toward the opposite end of the street she saw there was a man packing his car and stores were open. If she screamed then someone would hear her, but that seemed to stop her, as if screaming was only for the dark, a secret thing, when no one else was around.

"My ankle," she protested.

"The faster we get to the car, faster we get to sit down," Dennis said quietly.

If anyone were to look at them they would see a woman on a crutch, being helped into a car by a handsome man, another woman waiting to drive them home.

Dennis pushed her into the truck, both hands on her buttocks. Sam almost fell into the seat, her head hitting Lindsay's leg. Then Dennis pushed her further into the truck, sat down beside her and slammed the door.

"Home," he said to Lindsay.

"What about Walmart?" Lindsay asked, a hint of fear in her voice.

"Forget it."

They drove back to the house in silence. Sam could hear the clicking of Lindsay's jaw as she chewed her gum and the rattle of the plastic dash as Dennis bounced his leg up and down. No one asked why she was crying.

At the house, he told Lindsay to leave.

"Dennis?" Lindsay asked, not looking at Sam. "Maybe I should just hang out front a while?"

"Go," he repeated.

"Please don't go," Sam said, but Lindsay turned away.

Inside, Dennis pushed her onto the sofa and stood in front of her. "Where were you going just now?" he asked.

"What do you mean? I was getting water," she said again.

"You were going to the police station," he said. "And you're acting like…" He stopped and looked at her again. "You're afraid of me now."

"You're acting crazy," Sam said. "You *are* scaring me." It felt like a relief to be honest and for a second it looked as though he had believed her.

"Something's changed," he said. "The way you look at me. It started last night."

"You're being ridiculous," Sam said. She didn't say, *You sound like me.*

Then his eyes moved to the left of her, the sofa cushion that she'd left crooked on the seat, the zipper that she hadn't fully closed.

"Don't move," he said when he noticed her looking. He picked up the cushion and ran a hand underneath, like he was looking for lost quarters. Then he unzipped the cover and reached inside. When he pulled his hand out he was holding a single picture and Sam felt her stomach drop.

Dennis looked from the photograph to Sam and she saw a flash of what the girls must have seen, just for a second, when his face changed and he looked like a stranger.

"Don't move," he said again, in barely more than a whisper, though it felt to Sam like the low growl of an angry wolf.

Dennis went to the kitchen, Sam heard him take a bottle of water from the fridge, and the pause while he drank it. Footsteps. She heard the rusted coil on the back door, and sobbed with force. Out front, she saw Lindsay leaning against the truck, smoking. So she hadn't left. For that, Sam was grateful. Sam noticed Lindsay flicked the ash from the tip of her cigarette too frequently and that she tapped one foot compulsively. She heard the clang as the storm-shelter door fell back, silence while she waited for what she knew was coming, the bang as the storm-shelter door was slammed shut, the thud of feet on the rotten wooden steps, and finally the crack of the box as it hit the wall behind her head.

"Where are they?" Dennis shouted, his face white, furious. "Where the fuck are they?"

38

Dennis squatted in front of Sam, resting his elbows on his thighs, trying to look her in the eye. "Where. The fuck. Are they?" He stood up. "This is why you've been acting like this." He shook his head. "You were going to the cops, right?"

Sam sniffed. "I don't know."

"Where are they, Sam?"

"I don't have them anymore." Her voice was high, weak. She felt old.

"What do you mean?"

"I sent them. Posted them. To Carrie… So if anything happens to me—"

"You're lying." But she could hear the uncertainty in his tone.

"If anything happens to me, she'll know it was you! Everyone will!"

He looked at her for a few seconds. "They're still here," he said. "Where's your bag?"

"It's in the truck," Sam said. Dennis hesitated.

"Don't move," he said again before leaving her alone.

Through the window, Sam saw him stop and say something to Lindsay before opening the door of her truck and leaning inside. She knew it was her time to move. If she didn't go now, there might not be another chance. She crawled, knees bruising on the edge of the uneven wooden floor, through the kitchen and out of the back door. The debris that littered the area by the storm shelter cut and dug into her as she crawled, her palms stinging and her knees wet from the sodden ground.

The gap in the chain-link fence at the back of the yard was a foot off the ground. She had to heave herself onto her leg and crouch down to get through. The welcome density of the trees was only a meter away. Once in the woods, she started to run, to the best of her ability, ignoring the pain in her ankle as she hopped and stumbled and fell again and again. She was running in the direction she hoped led to town. After a minute she allowed herself a glance back toward the house, which was obscured by the tangle of leaves and branches she fought through. It fueled her, helped her feel invisible, and she moved faster.

Behind her she heard Dennis call and a new flood of nerves drove her forward. She turned left to avoid a bush and left again when she came upon a pool of black water, impossible to know how deep. She was no longer sure what direction she was going in, or where she should be going. She heard her name, over and over again, *"Sam-an-tha."* She ran away from the voice, into thick mud and fallen trees that rotted and clouds of midges that she breathed into her nostrils and coughed out.

Ahead of her, through the trees, she saw the

white of his T-shirt. She realized she'd been run-ning in a circle, and then the ground left her and she was sliding through mud, still soft from the rain. When she finally stopped sliding she looked up, realizing she was in a hole, the entrance cov-ered with fallen palm leaves. She pulled her feet to free them from the clutch of the soil, one shoe lost in the mud. Above she heard him still, walk-ing right by her, past the hole.

Flies landed on the back of her neck and she had to keep herself from gagging at the stench of rot-ting vegetation. She breathed through her mouth but it didn't help.

She reached back to get her shoe but as she lifted her foot to place it back on she felt something tan-gled around her toes. With her free hand she tried to rip it away. It felt, she thought, so much like hair. She followed it with her fingers and looked behind her. This time her scream emerged as natu-rally as a breath. She saw the glasses and the collar of a shirt, the open neck filling with mud, fingers like claws. Then she was crawling back out of the hole, digging her nails into the dirt to stop herself sliding back. It was Howard, bloated and turning a pale yellow. The muscle had rotted beneath the skin and his face sagged loose from his skull. His cheek started to twitch as if he were attempting to smirk. Insects, Sam realized with a new wave of sickness, insects eating him from the inside out.

At first Dennis's grip was welcome, as she al-lowed herself to be hauled back into the world. "What the fuck is it now?" he asked her as Sam pulled her knees up to avoid the creeping sensation that Howard could reach out and drag her back to him.

"You killed him," she cried, unable to meet his face. It was real then, all at once, and it no longer seemed worth running or fighting.

Dennis looked toward the hole again. Warily, he moved back the fallen palms. "Howard?" Sam heard him say, and then it was quiet. When he came back out he was pale, gentler. "We need to talk," he said.

39

Dennis carried her the way he had over the threshold. He pushed branches out of the way with his shoulders and tried not to let them hit her face; he even apologized when they did. At the house Lindsay stood waiting by the back door.

"Shit, you OK, Dennis? I told you I could watch her," she said as they approached.

"Get inside," Dennis said, pushing past her.

In the living room, he dropped Sam on the sofa. "You just need to be still, you need to listen," he said. He picked up her handbag and tipped out the contents; he pulled out every pocket and pouch and threw the empty bag back onto the floor. "OK, Samantha, one more time: Where are they?" he asked.

"What's she done?" Lindsay asked from the doorway.

"And what did *you* do?" he said, turning to face her.

"What?" Lindsay said, suddenly afraid.

"Howard?" Dennis's voice cracked a little.

"You don't understand," Lindsay said. "He was saying that he was going to confess. Everything. I didn't have a choice."

"When he's getting like that, you come to me, you tell me," Dennis said.

"I couldn't risk it," she said. "I was on my way here and I saw him on the road and he was pacing, he was crazy. I convinced him to talk it out, but he wouldn't stop. I told him if he'd walk with me a while he'd feel better but he took out his phone and he was going to do it this time, I could tell. Besides, you were ignoring my phone calls, you didn't answer my texts."

"So you did this to, what, punish me? What did Howard ever do to you?"

"Dennis, he was going to tell them *everything*," Lindsay said.

"I could have talked him out of it. You didn't need to kill him."

"Why do you care so much? He's a total freak! He was—"

"Fuck you, Linds." Dennis stepped toward her as though he might hit her, but he changed his mind. "Shit!"

Sam realized Howard meant a lot to Dennis. More than anyone, perhaps. She hadn't known he could care so much.

"How am I supposed to tell him his kid's dead?"

"This is all on me," Lindsay said. She spoke eagerly, the words tumbling out fast. "I've thought about it real hard and I'm gonna tell them he came up to me on the road as I was leaving here and I pulled over thinking he needed a ride, but then he dragged me away into the woods and he tried to rape me and I defended myself."

"Defended yourself?" Dennis said. "You nearly cut his head clean off."

"I don't know! I'll just say I was scared, that I didn't know what I was doing, I just wanted to make sure he didn't fucking rape me."

"We're fucked," Dennis said, looking at no one. "Without Howard I... His dad has no reason to keep quiet anymore. The second he finds out his son's dead he's going to show them the yard."

"Look, we can fix this," Lindsay said. She glanced at Sam. "Maybe we should talk somewhere else."

"Oh, it's way past that. Sam just fell right into your shallow grave. So now what? You kill her?"

"If I have to, yeah." Lindsay shrugged, and Sam felt a lurch of pure terror. "Say we text Harries from her phone." She pointed to Sam. "We say, 'Come here, I know what happened to Howard, be quick,' and he comes over, carrying his gun, obviously, because he's ready to kill you by now, and *she* answers the door all like, 'He's out back but you need to be quick...' And when he gets out back I shoot him. OK, now, after I shoot him we take the gun, we shoot her, plant it back on him and we tell them she killed Howard because he was, like, stalking her, then Harries shot her when she confessed and then I shot him in self-defense."

Dennis looked at her, still pale. "Why would Sam let him in and lead him outside if we're just going to shoot her?"

"Because I'll fucking shoot her anyway if she doesn't."

"You don't need to shoot me, please," Sam said quickly, "I won't tell anybody anything. I don't even understand what this is about!"

Dennis sighed and rubbed his tired eyes. "If Samantha's dead… I just don't think it'll play out. I think we need her."

"But she's going to tell the fucking cops as soon as she's alone!" Lindsay said.

"Sam, did you really send the pictures to Carrie?" Dennis asked.

Sam nodded.

"And what did you say? Did you say they were from you?"

"Yes… I said I found them in your things and they were from me…"

"Jesus."

"What pictures?" Lindsay asked.

"Doesn't matter," Dennis snapped.

"Don't tell me you kept those fucking pictures!" Lindsay shrieked. So she had known, Sam thought. Lindsay paced. "But if she's dead you can control the story, right?" Lindsay acted like Sam wasn't even there.

"I don't… No, I don't think I can," he said.

"Fuck… Who's Carrie? The film girl?"

"Yeah. Why, you planning to shoot her too?"

"Fuck you."

Dennis came over to Sam and put an arm around her shoulders. She flinched. "Samantha, I just wish you'd talked to me about this. You've made me look really, really bad. What if I told you they weren't even mine? That I was just protecting Howard. That we had a deal."

"I believe you," Sam whispered. "Carrie will believe you."

"But it's too late. If she gets those pictures, and you've already said they're mine... She trusts you, Samantha."

"I can tell her I was wrong." Sam knew she was bargaining for her life. She took one of his hands in hers. "But if you let Lindsay kill me I can't help. And I want to help."

"I know you do. But you really messed this up." He sighed. "You were different," he said. "When you wrote to me, you weren't like the others. You were so sweet. So *normal*. You were ordinary, and I liked it. When you're with me, it's like, people think: 'He's ordinary, too.' And you stuck by me when everything was falling apart. So I could forgive it when you weren't so normal anymore; when you rooted through my things every time I left you alone. But now... I just don't know where to go with this."

"Just let me go, Dennis. I'll back up whatever you say. Please?"

Dennis sighed again, left the room and returned with two of his father's guns. Sam thought she might vomit.

"Dennis, we can fix this. It doesn't have to go any further." She tried to sound calm, rational.

He handed a shotgun to Lindsay and kept a handgun for himself, tucking it into the back of his jeans. "I'm sorry. This isn't how I wanted it to go."

"No! Please!" Sam cried out.

"You have Harries's number?" he asked Lindsay, collecting Sam's phone from her scattered belongings. "It's locked." He looked at her. "What's the code?"

Sam shook her head and began to cry. He sat next to her again, held her wrist, took her thumb and held it over the home button. The screen unlocked. "Get me his number," he said to Lindsay.

"I don't have it," Lindsay said.

"What?"

"I don't know it. I thought you would."

Sam thought of the card from Officer Harries she'd put in her bag. It was facedown among her things on the floor. She said nothing, waiting, hoping that the plan would fall apart.

"Holy shit." He threw Sam's phone down onto the sofa.

"Dennis, we can get it. We can go to Howard and get his cell phone out of his pocket. He's gonna have his own dad in his contacts, right?"

"Fine," Dennis said. "I'll go. Watch Sam for me." He looked at them both one more time before he left.

"Please," Sam said when she felt Dennis was far enough away. "Let's just call the police. Now, while he's gone."

Lindsay laughed. "You don't think he's going to let you go, do you?"

Sam felt rage swell inside her. "He'll kill you."

"He won't," Lindsay said. "Dennis needs me."

"But you killed Howard. I saw how angry he

was. He won't just let it go," Sam said. But the look in Lindsay's eyes told her that her devotion to Dennis was worth any life, even her own. "And what if he doesn't kill you?" Sam continued, trying to make her see sense. "Even if you come out of this alive, what do you think will happen then? No one will believe your story, it's crazy."

"Dennis has the best defense attorneys in the country," Lindsay said, though Sam didn't think she sounded so sure.

"He might decide you're a risk, that you won't stick to the story. Just think—"

"You think you know him?" Lindsay said, her eyes lighting up in anger. "You think I'm just some dumb bitch who doesn't know what's what but I know him. I know when you think you're in control or you think you understand him that's when you're really fucked. The only way to understand him is to know you fucking can't and be fine with it. You think you're manipulating us right now? You don't have a fucking clue. And he's always relied on me. Always. So I wouldn't get too cozy, bitch."

"You're still afraid of him," Sam said, watching the gun against Lindsay's shaking leg.

Lindsay snorted. She took a cigarette from her pack and went to light it.

"He won't like it if you smoke in here," Sam said. Lindsay shrugged but the flame didn't touch the end of the cigarette before it disappeared.

"Get up," Lindsay said, grabbing her weapon. "Out." Sam led and Lindsay followed, the gun aimed at her back until she was sitting on the porch.

Outside she asked Lindsay for a cigarette and they smoked together, looking into the trees around the yard. Nothing was the same as it had been.

"I'm not pathetic," Lindsay said, blowing the smoke out of the side of her mouth.

"What?" Sam said.

"I'm not pathetic. For caring about him."

"I didn't think you were," Sam lied.

"Yeah, you did. Fuck it. It's not like I don't know what people think. I know what he's done, what he could do. But I also know who he is. Dennis, like, saved me in high school. Nobody cares about that. In school these guys… I was at a party and I got too drunk, I guess. It wasn't rape. I don't know."

"I'm sorry."

"Don't. Anyway, afterward, everyone had something to say about it. Acting like I'm some slut who gets drunk and likes gang bangs. And Dennis and Howard were the only guys who still talked to me like I was normal. They told the other guys that if they ever touched me again they'd fucking kill them. It worked, too. They shut up about it; they wouldn't even look at me. But the girls just kept on. So Dennis told me he could shut them up. He had this little smile on his face when he said it. Then they started disappearing." Lindsay paused and took another puff of her cigarette. Sam heard the crackle of the paper burning as she inhaled. "The first time…the first time I know it was an accident."

"What was?"

"That bitch Donna. Dennis said they were gonna

mess with her. There was this party and… Howard gave her those stupid fucking pills. It wasn't supposed to hurt her. We were gonna spike her drink, take some embarrassing photos with Howie's camera, copy them and pin them around the school." Sam flinched. "I know, OK? You don't get it. She called me a whore; she told everyone I had AIDS. She never let up. We were kids! Anyway, she left the fucking party, just stormed out, so we followed her in my car. She's stumbling along. Dennis rolls down the back window and he asks her if she needs a ride. Of course she says yes—you know, it's fucking *Dennis*. At first she was so out of it she didn't even realize me and Howard were in the front.

"Then she's saying, 'Why do you always hang out with these *weirdos*?' and Dennis is like, 'They're just giving us a ride.' She fell asleep on him. We all thought it was hilarious, you know? She doesn't even wake up when I blow the horn.

"So we go to Howard's house, since his dad is working the night shift. Only when we lie her down and Howard is taking the pictures she starts making this noise…we know she's puking so we put her on her side but it's stuck in her throat. The guys aren't doing anything—they're useless; Howard's just hitting her back like a retard. I stick my fingers in her fucking throat. I tried, I really tried, you know? But she stopped breathing. I was freaking out. Howard was freaking out. Dennis was the only one who could think straight. He told me to leave and they would take care of it, so I did. I didn't know what else to do."

"What happened then?" Sam asked.

"They buried her. Dennis told me later. On the edge of the Harries's yard. We'd all have been fucked, Sam. All of us. It was like Dennis said, they were Howard's pills, it was *my* idea, and Dennis…"

"She's buried in the Harries's yard?" Sam said.

"Howard was too scared to say no. He thought it would all be his fault." Lindsay stopped. "Afterward, he wanted to confess. I told him… I said they'd know it was him, that he'd taken the pictures with his camera, they'd think he was a pervert. I told him they'd put him in the chair for it. Dennis told him, too."

"What about…there were others?" Sam thought of the photographs. Of the girls and their hair and their lips.

"One by one," Lindsay said, "they just disappeared." She turned to Sam suddenly. "I didn't have anything to do with the others, nothing." Sam could hear the fear in her voice again. "Howard told me some things, over the years. Told me him and Dennis…but I didn't want to believe it. I didn't. And Dennis always looked out for me, always. Besides, what could I do? What could I say that wouldn't land me in prison? So I said nothing. It was our secret. We were tied by blood. Dennis protected me. All those years he kept me out of it."

Lindsay rubbed her eyes again and then it was over, her face as before, a shield.

So, Sam thought, there were things Lindsay didn't want to know. When Lindsay talked about the photographs she didn't seem to realize the extent of his collection. For Lindsay it had been about revenge. Sam knew it was something else. Something like desire. And Lindsay didn't want to understand this. It was too late for her.

Dennis came back breathless, eyeing them suspiciously as they sat on the porch.

"I got it," he said, holding up the phone. They walked Sam back into the house, one in front, one behind. This time she unlocked her own phone, knowing it was useless to resist. Sam watched as Lindsay typed.

"It's Samantha, I'm at Dennis's house, Howard is here. We need help. Come quick."

40

They sat in silence, the light outside starting to dim. They watched the phone, waiting for a reply, until the screen turned black. They flinched at the sight of themselves in it.

Then it rang.

"Shit, shit," Lindsay said, getting up and reaching for the shotgun.

"You're going to have to answer it," Dennis said. "Quickly. If it's Harries, just tell him again to get here. Say it's an emergency."

Sam was given the phone, already swiped to answer. She could hear the bark of Harries's voice all rough and whiskey-soaked. She could tell him to alert his fellow officers—if Lindsay weren't looking at her down the barrel of a shotgun.

"Officer Harries? Um, it's Sam... Danson."

"I know it's Sam. What can you tell me about Howard?" His voice cracked at the edges. "Where is he? Where's my boy?"

"He's here," Sam said, looking at Dennis, who nodded.

"Is he OK? Goddamn it! What did Dennis do to my boy?" Harries shouted.

"Nobody's done anything to Howard," Sam said.

"But he's been gone for three days and he's not answering his cell. I know my boy."

"Officer Harries! He's outside and he's yelling something about *bodies*. It's like he's crazy, or something." She stopped, tried to control her breathing as it quickened. "Maybe I should call the police—"

"No," Harries said. "I'm on my way." The phone went dead.

"You did good," Dennis said.

Lindsay watched them, not liking what she was seeing.

"Linds, you need to move your truck. Harries will know you're here. Go park at the side of the house, so he doesn't get suspicious," Dennis said.

Lindsay hesitated. "Fuck," she said, hanging the gun over her shoulder. "I'll be right back."

Sam didn't tell him what Lindsay had said on the porch. She didn't need to: he had already figured it out.

"She'll tell you anything to get you to let your guard down," Dennis said.

"She thinks you need her," Sam said, finding some strength from deep inside. "But I think you need me more. If you help me get out of this, I can get the photographs back."

Sam looked at the crease in Dennis's brow, the way his eyes stayed fixed on hers as they peered over his glasses. He didn't look like himself, she thought. His coldness had been replaced with something that she recognized, instantly, as more human.

* * *

When Lindsay returned, she hid around the right side of the house, obscured by part of the back porch. Sam was to stay in the living room, while Dennis waited in the hall to make sure she didn't back out at the last minute, ensuring she brought Harries inside and through the house. Her head swam with everything she knew, and everything she didn't.

When the car pulled up outside, Dennis slid into the kitchen, his gun in his hand, finger next to the trigger. Harries ran to the house, his car door open, engine running. Sam didn't wait for him to knock, but opened the door as he approached, finding him holding his gun, steadying his grip with his other hand. She swallowed. It would take only one small mistake on her part and her life would be over. Suddenly she very much wanted to live. She would need to stay steady just a while longer. *Then what?* She shook the question away.

"Where is he?" Harries asked her, pushing her aside as he passed.

"I hit him," Sam said. "I'm sorry, I was scared."

"Where is he?" he asked again, louder.

"He's out back," Sam said.

"Go. You first," Harries said, pointing.

Like an executioner she led him along the designated path, through to the back, to the storm shelter. Harries looked around him, but stayed at the back door, checking behind him.

"Where is he?" he repeated, cagey.

"Don't do anything stupid now," Dennis said as

he approached, his hands above his head. Harries immediately raised the gun.

"Where is he?" Harries shouted, his voice booming in the quiet of the evening.

"We had to contain him," Dennis said. "He's in the shelter."

"Open it," Harries said to Sam.

Arms shaking, Sam did as she was told. Harries stayed in the doorway. In that position, Sam knew, Lindsay would not be able to make the shot. *Stay there*, she willed him, *don't move.*

"I'm not going to lie to you, Harries," Dennis said. "He got a little roughed up. You know? Took a knock to the head."

"What have you done to him?" Harries asked, taking a step forward, then appeared to change his mind and retreated into the doorway.

"Nothing, nothing. He's fine. It's just that he might need a little help."

Harries scanned the area again.

"Turn around," he said to Dennis.

"Huh?"

"Turn around! Keep your hands up."

Dennis turned. His gun was sticking out of the back of his jeans.

"You," Harries said to Sam. "Get the gun. Now!"

Obediently she took the gun from him.

"Hand it over," Harries said, taking it from her as she approached and fitting it into the empty holster at his side. "Stand against the wall," he said to Dennis. "Stand *facing* the wall."

Dennis laughed and rested his forehead against

the house. Harries held Sam's arm as he approached the storm shelter, glancing back at Dennis now and then.

"You first," he said, gesturing to the trapdoor.

"Me?"

"Go now," he said.

Sam looked toward the side of the house where she knew Lindsay was waiting, poised. Then she looked into Harries's eyes. They were red, jittery. A man whose secrets kept him awake all night, who loved his son, who had no one else. There was hope there and that was what hurt the most. Sam took a step down into the shelter. She saw Lindsay move into position, her gun pointed at Harries's back.

When the shot came it made Sam falter. Harries's blood hit her cheeks as he keeled over. Frantically, she wiped at her face, her hands coming away with smears of red. He was lying on his front, face turned to the side, blades of grass moving with his breath.

The shot had ripped through his chest, a great hole through which blood bubbled from a burst lung. Still he breathed, noisily, painfully. Sam heard Lindsay whooping in the background, and wished she would stop, and that he would die.

Then he was still and blood pooled sticky beneath him. Sam looked at him, the reality of it hitting her like cold water. He was dead.

Dennis crouched next to Harries's body and retrieved both guns.

Lindsay was pacing in the background, full of

adrenaline, the sight of the blood only exciting her further.

Dennis looked at Lindsay quickly, seemed to make up his mind about something, and surreptitiously handed Sam one of the guns.

"You need to shoot Lindsay," he said. "You can do this." He stepped backward.

Sam held the gun. It was heavier than she'd expected. Could she actually shoot it? But there was little time to think as Lindsay turned to face her, taking aim.

Sam raised her own gun, which shook terribly in her grip. She steadied it with her free hand, as she'd seen Harries do.

"I knew it," Lindsay said as she realized what Dennis had done. "I knew you two would fuck me over."

She began to cry. Sam slipped a fingertip over the trigger, uncertain what to do next. She didn't know whether if she pulled the trigger she'd be met with a click, or if the gun would kick in her hands, or if the bullet would cut air or hit flesh. She and Lindsay looked at each other, each afraid to make the first move, waiting for Dennis to tell them what to do.

Finally, he spoke.

"Lindsay…"

The sound of a car horn was coming closer, sounding repeatedly, long, short, long bursts. The three looked at each other. Sam wondered if it was Morse code, whether a police van was signaling to

Harries. But when the car drew up outside the front of the house, she recognized the buzzing beat of music, of something triumphantly happy.

Dennis gestured to them to wait and went to the side of the house to peer into the garden. When he returned he crouched low to avoid the windows. "It's Carrie," he whispered. "Carrie's out front."

"The film girl?" Lindsay's gun was still aimed at Sam's chest.

Sam heard the door knocking, the chirpy ignorance of Carrie's voice.

"I'm here to rescue you, girl!" she called. "I'm here to take you back to civilization!"

"What do we do with him?" Lindsay gestured toward Harries.

"Hello? Am I being ghosted or something? Hellooo?"

Sam longed to run to her but she knew Lindsay would shoot if she did.

"We need to let her in."

Dennis licked a thumb and wiped Sam's face, looking over her clothes for signs of blood. "Coming!" he shouted.

He went around the house to meet Carrie out front, while Sam and Lindsay stayed where they were, listening to them talk. Sam tried not to think about what might have already happened if Carrie hadn't shown up. Sam heard Dennis telling Carrie that she wasn't here, and Carrie telling him she would wait. Her arms started to ache as she held them in front of her, but Lindsay looked as if she could stand there all day, her gun now aimed directly at Sam's neck.

"Whose car is that?" Carrie was asking.

"Just Lindsay's," Dennis said.

"Lindsay? Dude...you *have* to stop this." Carrie lowered her voice. "...upsetting Sam...commitment...marriage..."

Sam's eyes filled with tears. Carrie was so close. All she wanted was to run to her. The gun felt unbearably heavy in her hand. Suddenly she felt so weak. If she could get out now it wasn't too late. Without lowering her gun, Lindsay started to walk toward the house, until she stood still next to the back door. She stared at Sam but cocked her head as she tried to listen to what was happening out front.

"Nothing is going on. It's fine, don't worry," Dennis was saying.

"Let me in. I'll wait."

Sam closed her eyes and begged Carrie to stay, her lips moving with the prayer. She knew Lindsay wouldn't shoot while Carrie was outside.

"Why not?" Carrie was saying. "Come on, man, I *trusted* you, and now this?"

"There's *nothing* between me and Lindsay." Dennis was louder now. "This is complicated, Carrie, just—"

But Carrie was inside, walking through the house toward them, with Dennis behind her, calling her back. Lindsay raised the gun.

"Stop," she said. The barrel was pointed at Sam. Carrie froze.

"Sam?" Carrie turned. Dennis tried to take her

arm and pull her away but she snatched it from him. "What the fuck is going on here?"

"This has gotten out of hand," Dennis said.

Carrie's eyes were wide and shining with fear. Carrie, who'd always seemed so tough and unshakable. Sam's hope began to fade into despair.

"So what happens now, Dennis?" Lindsay said. "Where do I stand in all this?"

Sam recognized the look in Lindsay's eyes: the tearing of her heart, the anger and the sadness. Now Lindsay was a woman with nothing left to lose. Sam saw that Dennis realized it, too.

"Linds…" he said, reaching to her slowly.

Carrie stepped backward as Lindsay took aim at them, her gun steady now, and said, "Don't move."

Dennis put his arm in front of Carrie, guiding her behind him. He backed away slowly as he shielded Carrie from Lindsay.

"Don't fucking move!" Lindsay screamed.

"Lindsay, please, this doesn't have to go any further," Dennis said.

Lindsay's breath came out in puffs as she tried to hold back her tears.

"Lindsay, I get it," Sam said. "I know how you feel and I'm so, so sorry."

"You don't get it," Lindsay said. "I sacrificed everything for him!"

"Linds—" Dennis said again.

"No! I've had it! You've never treated me right!" Lindsay looked at Dennis with a pure and furious hatred. "I know what you really are. I know."

"What's going on?" Carrie said quietly.

Lindsay looked at Carrie over his shoulder. "You want to know, film girl? Spoiler alert, Dennis—"

The bang was so loud that for a second Sam thought that she had been hit. Carrie's scream sounded distant and faint. She closed her eyes while the sound rang in her ears and when she opened them she saw that the bullet had hit Lindsay through the mouth. Parts of her face slid down the side of the house and stuck to the window, shining red in the fading light. On the ground was a tooth, resting in a puddle of brain and blood. Lindsay's skull was leaking; her one still intact eye fluttered and roved in its socket.

Dennis walked toward Lindsay's body and collapsed. He dropped Harries's gun into the viscera and stared vacantly toward her corpse. The blood that leaked from her open skull was absorbed by the soft earth, like rain after a storm.

Carrie turned and vomited. Sam held a hand out to help Dennis up. He stood slowly, as if all his strength had drained from him, and she didn't feel afraid. She hugged him, holding her head against his chest, inhaled the smell of gun smoke and the tang of blood on his shirt.

"What the fuck just happened?" Carrie said again, shaking.

For some time it was as if everything had stopped around them. The echo of the gunshot faded, engulfing them in silence. Even the wind seemed to have stopped while Sam, Dennis and Carrie looked around themselves, unsure of what to do next. Soon the cicadas started to whine and the leaves of the palms rustled in a warm breeze.

They had to carry on, Sam thought. They had to decide what was going to happen next.

epilogue

Three months later

Sam took her seat at one side of the table, trying not to look at the others by focusing on the vending machine in the far corner. The inmates came in uncuffed and hugged their partners and children. Dennis turned heads, as usual, and received a kiss from Sam without complaint.

"You're back," he said. "How was England?"

"Cold! I think I've acclimatized, finally." She smoothed a thumb over his wrist. She'd been away only a couple of weeks. Just long enough to open a safety deposit box at the bank and arrange for her house to be cleared out into storage and sold.

When she'd opened the front door to her home, the piles of letters and flyers had tumbled out of the doorway like a pile of dead leaves. The air was stale, everything frozen in time. She had rummaged through the post, starting to panic that the pictures had never made it back home. But then she saw the envelope, her own handwriting barely legible.

She had to steel herself before she opened it.

Then, slowly and deliberately, she spread all the Polaroids out and looked at them, really looked, for the first time. Now she had the space, the privacy to think.

The color was faded but she could still envision the vivid red of broken flesh and the blue of their lips. They were posed, their hair purposely fanned around their heads, their arms resting at their sides, as if they were sunbathing, as if they were peaceful. She stared and tried to make sense of any of it. What she saw wasn't the anger of a man who wanted to hurt them, but the sickness of one who wanted to keep them. Then she thought of that day in the woods, when Dennis had bent and lowered the kitten into a grave, had delicately and lovingly patted the earth, of the decorations he'd hung and the nail polish inscriptions.

It wasn't her fault he didn't want her, she realized. It wasn't her body or her teeth. It was the warmth of the blood pulsing in her veins, the rise and fall of her chest, the way she moved against him when he kissed her. She'd put the photographs back, sickened.

"Did you take care of the..." Dennis asked her.

"They're safe," she said, thinking of the Polaroids lying in the deposit box in England.

"Right."

She kissed his hand. They couldn't talk properly here, so she couldn't tell him that she knew, that she understood what the photographs meant.

She'd called the police shortly before she flew home. A pay phone she'd searched miles for, affecting an accent as best she could to disguise her identity.

"There are bodies in the Harries's backyard," she'd said. "Dennis Danson killed them. All of them. Lindsay Durst and Howard Harries are the accomplices." Then she'd hung up, run back to her car and driven to the airport. She'd watched the story unfold from the UK as the bones were raked to the surface.

"I kind of missed this," Sam said.

"Missed what?" Dennis said.

"This." She gestured to the visiting room. "I always loved coming to visit you." It felt safe, she thought, but didn't say. "And it's good we can touch here."

"Yeah," Dennis said, looking down. "They want me to make a plea deal: confess to killing the girls and get life imprisonment without parole."

"Oh?" said Sam. She hoped he would take it. If he fought the charges and lost, Death Row was inevitable. Here he could take his GED, maybe enroll in a college course. His cheeks were bronzed from his hours in the exercise yard.

There were still those who believed he hadn't killed the girls. Carrie's faith had never wavered. Carrie loved him, just as Howard and Lindsay had. And that, Sam realized, was how he controlled them. How he had controlled her.

Carrie swore that she'd seen Lindsay raise her gun before Dennis took the shot. To her, he was a hero.

Sam's own memory of that final evening was

vague, but she knew Lindsay hadn't raised the gun. When she held Dennis after he'd pulled the trigger, she'd rested her head against his chest and listened to his heart beat as slowly and steadily as if he were asleep. It made her cold. Colder still when she noticed the tooth missing from the pool of blood in which it had rested.

"They don't have anything," Dennis was saying. Sam realized she hadn't been listening.

"What?" she asked.

"My lawyer says there's nothing to tie me to the bodies in Harries's yard. They've got nothing."

Sam felt sick. When she thought about him being released, her hand moved instinctively to her stomach, to the baby growing inside of her. *What if it's a girl?* she thought. No. If she needed them, she always had the pictures. They couldn't make her testify against Dennis, not while they were married, but she could say that she found the photographs while she was sorting his things.

She noticed Dennis staring at her growing bump and she smiled. He blushed and looked away. It wasn't something they talked about. Dennis, so much more at ease with the dead than the living.

Sam wished he would do what was best for him. What was best for them.

"Take the plea deal, Dennis," she said, taking his hand across the table.

Dennis squeezed her hand tighter and leaned in to her. "But when I'm out we can be together. Anywhere you want. New York, anywhere." He searched her face for a sign she believed him. "Please," he added. "Samantha."

Sam stared into his eyes, so blue they still took her breath away.

"I'll always visit," she said.

And she meant it. This was the way they worked, she thought, lacing her fingers with his. It had always been better like this.

* * * * *

Acknowledgments

Thank you to the judges of the Daily Mail First Novel competition, Simon Kernick and Sandra Parsons, for your early support of *The Innocent Wife*.

Luigi and Selina, thank you for believing in the book and for all your advice and guidance. I have been so lucky to work with you both. Many thanks too to Alison whose opinion I value greatly, and to everyone at Cornerstone who continues to work so hard for *The Innocent Wife*: Sonny, Clare, Hattie, Matt, Khan, Pippa, Kelly, Catherine, and everyone who has shown so much enthusiasm for this book.

Thank you, Glenn, for the beautiful cover. I absolutely adore it.

Peter Joseph, my book is much stronger for all your fantastic advice. Also thanks to Kayla King and everyone else at Hanover Square Press for your work.

I've been fortunate enough to work with supportive and understanding colleagues who have helped me balance my day job with the commitments of my book. I would particularly like to thank Emma Crocker, who was so kind and encouraging when I needed it most.

Thank you to my Bampi! If you hadn't wrestled me into school I might be illiterate today.

Rhys, thank you for always being honest enough that I can trust your opinion, but not so honest that it stings. I hope that one day I can find the right balance.

Finally, thank you to my dad and to my mum, for always supporting my choices and encouraging me. When I wanted to live as a dog called Rover for several months you made it possible and when, perhaps even more improbably, I wanted to be a writer, you always believed that I could. I love you both.

Questions for Discussion

1. How important do you think the author's focus on true crime is for this novel?

2. What did you think of Dennis? Is he a sympathetic character or a scary one?

3. Why do you think Sam is drawn to a man on death row?

4. By the end of the novel, who do you feel is innocent? Has your opinion of anyone changed?

5. How does Dennis manipulate those around him? Has anyone managed to manipulate him?

True Crime: Stranger than Fiction?

"Watch this," someone will say about a new true crime documentary. "It will make you *so angry.*" People told me that the *Paradise Lost* documentaries would make me angry before I watched them a few years ago and they were right.

Even after the documentaries had finished I couldn't stop thinking about the case. How could three teenagers have been convicted of killing little boys based on such spurious evidence? I trawled the internet, reading arguments on discussion boards between the sides: those who believed the defendants were guilty and those who believed they were innocent. Amateur detectives pointed out discrepancies in witness statements and timelines. I looked until I was exhausted and more frustrated than ever. Where was the truth? Who actually killed those three boys? It was hard to accept that maybe the truth was lost, that the evidence was long gone and that we might never know what happened.

The Innocent Wife was my way of dealing with all those unanswered questions, with all those "what ifs" I asked myself while bingeing on true crime. What if we weren't being told the whole story? What if someone we thought was innocent was not so innocent after all?

As I was writing the book I watched as the true crime genre experienced a huge resurgence. *Serial*, *Making a Murderer* and *The Jinx* were all hugely popular. No longer was true crime a niche interest, something consumed alone, voyeuristic and just a little tacky. Instead it became mainstream watercooler talk. And people seemed to enjoy being angry, playing armchair detectives, being the jury from the comfort of their homes without all that extraneous courtroom procedure that slows down the drama.

This rise in the popularity of true crime in its current form has coincided with a growing mistrust of our appointed leaders, lawmakers and experts. Whereas true crime used to be an insight into the mind of a killer, or lurid reconstructions of gruesome murders and crime scenes, now it is more focused on questioning the verdicts reached in trials, torturing us with the unbearable thought that justice has not been done—that the lawyers and the judge and the police are all crooked or inept or both, and that if it has happened once it could be happening again, elsewhere, to other people and maybe, awfully, one day it might happen to us.

I started to worry that by the time I finished writing *The Innocent Wife* the popularity of true crime would start to wane. I thought we might all be sick of being angry, tired of not getting a satisfactory resolution to the stories these documentaries told and that something else might have taken its place. But as I write this I have recently finished watching *The Staircase*, and looking at people's reaction to the documentary on Twitter confirms interest in true crime is far from over.

When writing *The Innocent Wife*, I wanted the influence of true crime to be evident to others who were similarly obsessed with these documentaries, podcasts and books. I love it when people message to ask if I was inspired by *Paradise Lost* or *Making a Murderer* because they see similarities in the book. The answer is almost always yes, I have used true crime to guide the novel, from the obvious parallels between the *Red River* documentaries and existing true crime docs to more subtle references, such as the names I've used throughout the book.

But I had to be careful as to where I drew the line in following the patterns in true crime. Documentaries spread over a ten-hour-plus series often have a messy and slow-burning narrative. This helps to give them the feel of reality. But would readers accept the same from their fiction? A lot of true crime stories cannot provide a neat and satisfying conclusion because the truth is murky and often harder to dig up than anything contained in fiction.

We can accept all these complications in true crime because speculation is so much part of the experience. The tension comes from knowing that we are partaking in something real, with consequences that reverberate into the real world. We can extend our enjoyment of true crime documentaries by continuing to investigate the case online, or by campaigning for an inmate's release. Some people even go as far as writing to a convict themselves, just like Samantha in *The Innocent Wife*. It's funny to think how none of this seems as strange now as it might have done twenty years ago.

Fiction, however, needs to make more sense than true crime. Good thrillers need to find the balance between the madness of reality and the logic of fiction. If we don't have the tension of real-life consequences to keep people hooked, we need to offer something else. For *The Innocent Wife* I wanted to keep readers guessing, allowing them plenty of space to concoct their own theories, and I love hearing people's takes on the book when they are about halfway through. It amazes me to hear how many different conclusions readers have drawn by that point and how complicated their theories can be. It goes to show how much work we do ourselves when following any narrative and therefore how difficult it is for juries to come to a decision of guilty or not guilty based solely on evidence they have heard in court, without speculating or filling in the gaps in the story themselves. It seems almost an impossible task.

Some madness should be kept in fiction, for good measure. I like messy and complicated characters who contradict themselves and frustrate a reader with bad choices and unpleasant actions. However, even the most complicated characters still won't be as unpredictable and incomprehensible as real people, and maybe that's a good thing. Most of the debate over true crime documentaries hinges on the perceptions of their subjects. Is the man a psychopath or not? What was his motivation? We employ our best pseudopsychology to try to understand these messy individuals. Two people can have radically different opinions of the same person. Sometimes we cannot even agree if a person is sane or not.

I wanted readers to similarly debate over Dennis in *The Innocent Wife*. Even if we can all agree that his behavior is abnormal, I wanted us all to disagree about why he is the way he is. Dennis could believably be a man damaged by a traumatic childhood, someone socially awkward due to decades in solitary confinement, or he could be someone altogether more sinister. To complicate things further, we can only view him through the eyes of other unreliable narrators, characters who all have their own biases and motivations to see him in a certain light. Especially Samantha, who is paranoid and so full of self-loathing we can't be sure if she is projecting onto him. Again, readers seem to quickly make their minds up about Dennis and then make different allowances for him based on their perspectives.

We all want to make sense of the world we live in, and understanding people's darkest tendencies is a huge part of that. True crime has to carve a narrative out of the unformed mass of evidence and circumstance and potential motivations. Sometimes the documentary can opt to leave out any evidence that might muddy its narrative. *Making a Murderer*, for instance, was criticized for what it did not tell viewers. From the beginning of the series we were aware that the story we were being told was of an innocent man wrongly convicted and the filmmakers omitted evidence that did not fit that narrative. Other series, such as *Serial*, took a different approach: instead of trying to convince us of someone's guilt or innocence, *Serial* investigated various leads and scrutinized the evidence, never committing to any particular theory. Still, listeners weighed up the evidence and many came away feeling that they had unearthed the truth.

This is where true crime becomes, ultimately, more chilling than any fiction can be. It reveals so much about ourselves: about the failings of our criminal justice system and our own inability to be objective. It's scary to know that the truth may never come to light, that we might never understand the reasons why people do terrible things or know for sure whether we have locked up an innocent person and the real killer is wandering among us, indistinguishable from anyone else.

At least in thrillers we can make sense of the things that frighten us. For a while we can pretend to understand a little of the darkness that can seem all-consuming if you stare too closely into it.

*Turn the page to read an excerpt from
Amy Lloyd's newest tale of electrifying suspense,*
One More Lie.

Evil Duo Released from Prison

...pair given new identities, cosmetic surgery and full benefits, costing taxpayers over $1,000,000...

...mother of victim says she is "horrified"...

...public anger at resources spent on ensuring the pair remain protected...

...police involved in the investigation say justice has not been done...

1

Her: Now

There is a child staring at me from across the aisle. I turn to face the window and enjoy the warmth of the sun on my face until we pause at a bus stop and the light is blocked. When I look back the child is still staring and I blush. For a second I imagine doing something cute, something like sticking my tongue out at him or crossing my eyes, but I know that when I do these things they are not cute and can even come across as sinister. Maybe it is my shyness. Or maybe I cannot pull it off because people can sense that there is something missing in me, that I am broken.

"Excuse me," someone is saying. They don't say it in a nice way. When I look up, there is an old lady who smells a little like lavender and like her coat has been tucked away for a long time over the summer and she has only just taken it out. I don't know what she wants.

"What?" I say. It comes out wrong. I remember what Dr. Isherwood said about appearing abrupt, cold. I smile with 70 percent of my teeth showing and then relax my face.

"Is anyone sitting there?" she asks.

There isn't anybody sitting there. It's just my bag. Then I realize what she means, and I put my bag on my lap and she sits down with a tut and a sigh. I don't know why people don't just say what they mean. Why she doesn't say, "Please can you move your things so I can sit down?"

I look back to the child, but now it is the mother who's staring at me. It looks like others are, too, and that they are all wondering what is wrong with me and why I made the old lady stand for so long without moving my bag.

Now my stomach is churning. I wasn't worried about my first day of work until all this happened. Two more stops and we'll be on Walters Road. Get off the bus, walk toward the traffic lights, take the next left. I need to go to Customer Services and say, "Hello, my name is Charlotte, and I'm starting here today." I need to ask for Mr. Buckley, the manager.

I can picture all of this in my head as Sarah and I did a dummy run last week. But still I think that I'm remembering wrong and I feel nervous. Sarah said it was fine to feel nervous, that this was a big step and she knew I could do it. Because Sarah normally works with teenagers and children, she talks to me like I'm also a child. Dr. Isherwood says Sarah means well and she's just trying to put me at ease. Secretly I think Sarah believes I am mentally disabled and not just a little strange. She doesn't know who I am, or my real name, or why

I am twenty-nine and need help to get the bus. If Sarah knew who I was, she wouldn't have been smiling so wide. With 80 percent of her teeth and intense eye contact.

My ankle itches. I bend down and squeeze a finger underneath my tag. The skin there is always moist and I can't scratch it properly no matter how much I try. I snap back up, frustrated. Without thinking, I bring my finger to my nose to sniff. Sometimes, if the water gets trapped behind the tag when I shower, it starts to smell a little cheesy. The woman next to me hunches her shoulder away from me. I realize she has been watching and she is making a show of being disgusted. She needn't be; my finger smells of nothing today.

My stop. I press the bell a long time before I really need to and I squeeze past the old lady and stagger down the bus, holding the bars as I go. When I look back, the old lady has moved into the window seat and is resting her large handbag on the space next to her. That's rich, I think. I'll tell Dr. Isherwood about her tomorrow.

When I step off the bus I have a moment of panic. Nothing looks as I remember it. I'm worried I'll get lost and be late. If I'm late they will change their minds about hiring me and if I don't have a job they'll send me back to secure care and— I take a breath. I look at the watch they gave me: I am forty minutes early. The walk there will take less than ten minutes. I want to be at least ten minutes early. Even if I am lost for twenty minutes, I will still be there on time.

This soothes me and when I look at the road ahead it looks just as it did before, the traffic lights and the railway bridge behind them. I walk slowly because I have time. Too much time, I realize, as I turn left. I'm glad I brought a book.

Inside the supermarket is a Costa coffee shop. When I arrive I have enough time to get a coffee but when I look at the menu behind the counter I can't believe how expensive it is. The man at the till asks me what I'd like and I pretend to look at my watch and tell him I'm just waiting for my friend. I walk away as if I'm looking around for someone and my cheeks burn. What if he sees me working later and he knows I was lying?

I wonder what it's like to meet a friend for coffee. I'm imagining the type of friend I might have, someone quiet, a woman—obviously—someone who wears glasses and puts her hair up in one of those claw clips. Someone who likes to read and hates loud places. I'm walking around in my own world, as Dr. Isherwood says I am prone to, when I see something that I can't ignore, even though I want to.

It is today's newspaper. A headline: Evil Duo Released from Prison.

For a second I think this can't be about me. The article says I've had cosmetic surgery, but I haven't had anything like that. So I unfold a copy from the shelf to see the rest of the article. As I read it I have to resist the urge to talk to it, to tell it it's lying. To shout that I'm not evil and to beg it to stop talking about it, that it doesn't understand and it just makes people mad.

Then I read a paragraph and I realize the worst part. The headline said "duo." Two. Not just me, but Sean is out, as well.